BACKLASH

ANTONY MELVILLE-ROSS comes of an adventurous breed. His grandfather, first cousin to the author of *Moby Dick*, was an explorer, and his father, among other things, was a test pilot. Antony Melville-Ross served in submarines where he won a DSC, before working in Intelligence after the war. He is now at work on his fourth novel.

Available in Fontana by the same author

BLINDFOLD
TIGHTROPE

ANTONY MELVILLE-ROSS

Backlash

FONTANA/Collins

First published by William Collins Sons & Co. Ltd 1979
First issued in Fontana Paperbacks 1981
Second impression May 1982

Made and printed in Great Britain by
William Collins Sons & Co. Ltd, Glasgow

PROLOGUE

For a moment the small man in the grey raincoat spun, capering jerkily, the briefcase at the end of his extended right arm tracing a swooping parabola as though he was practising for a hammer throw. Then, appearing suddenly tired, he collapsed to a sitting position on the wet road surface and keeled slowly over on to his side. His hat fell off and settled upside down beside him as if ready to receive coins.

A woman came out of the doorway of a house, turned and went quickly back inside as a plain green van rounded the corner at the cross-roads thirty yards away.

The wheels of the van bumped twice as it ran over the man lying in the road, then it slowed, made a U turn and ran over him again. It accelerated sharply away. The rider of the motorcycle which had first struck the man disentangled himself from his machine, kicked it into life and roared off after the van. He followed it to the left at the cross-roads where the early morning sun lit up a signpost reading Reichenbach 19 km – Plauen 40 km.

Nothing moved in the street they had just left, except the small man's hat rocking gently on its crown as the breeze played with it.

CHAPTER ONE

John Carr was five feet seven inches in height and disliked it. He disliked it so much that he never stood when he could sit and he was sitting now on a bar stool reading *The Times*, sipping occasionally at his drink. He read methodically and fast, missing out little and only that by choice. When he had finished, he turned the paper to the back page, folded it neatly, took a ballpoint pen from his pocket and started to work on the crossword puzzle. Seven minutes and four seconds later he replaced the pen in his pocket, the puzzle complete.

The barman said, 'You're slipping, sir. About twenty seconds longer than average.'

Carr smiled. 'Give me a break,' he said. 'Fourteen across was "Zoroastrian". It held me up for a bit.'

'Well, it would, wouldn't it, sir? Are you having another?'

'No,' Carr said. 'Good night.'

The barman watched him walk away across the room and turn left up the open staircase, moving with a peculiar effortlessness as though he weighed nothing. Carr intrigued him, although he didn't know him by that or any other name. Good looking, he thought, but it was always mildly surprising to see him get down from his stool. With those shoulders you expected him to tower over you. Might have been an athlete although the face evoked no memories and he'd be too old for that now. Forty-odd probably.

He shrugged and twisted Carr's abandoned paper round to face him. Fourteen across – 'Zoroastrian'. Perhaps the man was a school teacher doubling as games master. He decided to look the word up in the dictionary when he got home and slid the paper under the bar.

Carr went into a telephone booth in the foyer, dialled a number then swore softly as he pressed a two-penny coin into the slot. He waited a moment and said, 'Why do these bloody contraptions start bleeping at you before you can hear if you've got the right number?'

A female voice at his ear said, 'Erostyles. Can I help you?'

'Yes,' he told it. 'Explain to me why I have to risk one fiftieth of a pound sterling on the highly problematical   .'

'I'm sorry, sir, but I'm very busy. If you want to speak to someone here please say so, otherwise I shall have to disconnect you.'

Excitedly Carr said, 'Don't do that, darling. I wanted to place an order with your wholesale department, but I'd much rather talk to you. You have the most deliciously libidinous voice, or is it a bronchial infection?'

'What order do you wish to place?' the sharpness of the voice failed to conceal the agitation in it.

'I was thinking of a couple of gross of those teasing peephole bras that only you know you're wearing. Do you stock them in burnt umber?'

'We're closing for the night now. If you gave a genuine order to place perhaps you'll call again in the morning – when you're sober!'

'Then how about aubergine?'

'Oh, damn you!' the voice said. 'You'd better talk to wholesale.' It sounded close to tears.

Carr grinned and waited until a man's voice said, 'The articles you are enquiring about come in three styles. The one you want may be amongst them. I suggest you look in at our Berwick Street warehouse between five and seven. If you're near enough you might make it before they close tonight. If they haven't got the colour you want they'll probably have samples in red.'

'Thank you,' Carr said. 'I'll go and look.'

He walked along Piccadilly, crossed the Circus by the public subway and turned into Shaftesbury Avenue. He wasn't hurrying. Once through the litter of Berwick Market his pace quickened and after fifty yards he strode in through a shabby doorway. A peeling indicator board told him that the first two floors were occupied by photographic studios, but nothing about the remaining five. He went quickly up the stairs to the sixth floor. As with the others there was only one door on the landing. He pressed the bell push and turned his back to the door, the sight of the reflection of his feet in the top of the grimy window half-way down the last flight seeming to absorb him.

The sound of the door opening quietly came to his ears, but he stood without moving until he heard it close again just as softly and a voice say 'Yeah?' Another pair of shoes had joined his own in the mirror image reflected by the window glass.

He turned sharply then, his left elbow smashing into the side of the face of the man behind him, his right hand closing on cloth.

Carr decided that he had never seen the face before. It looked unnatural with the dislocated jaw displaced sideways, but he was satisfied that he was looking at a stranger. Three styles, Barnes had told him on the telephone, so there should be two other people inside the rooms beyond the door, provided that it was the right one and it should be. He was on the sixth floor where he had been told to go.

Irritation touched him briefly at the compulsive use of childish voice codes at unnecessary times, but he suppressed it. Barnes had only been with them for a month or so. He'd get over it, given time.

Red samples. He lowered the sagging body gently to the floor and turned it on its face. The fingers of the right hand were still clenched round the butt of the 'sample' in the hip pocket. He released them and drew the gun out. The man's keys were in a side pocket and he used them to open the door, then dragged him inside by his coat collar.

There was no one in the first room, but voices reached him through a door to his right. He opened it and said, 'Hello, Clancey.'

Two men stared at him from deep chairs placed to either side of an ornamental non-functioning fireplace. Neither spoke.

Carr looked down at the gun lying flat on the palm of his right hand.

He said, 'This is an FN 9 mm Army issue, Clancey. Have you been stealing government stores or playing footsy with the IRA?'

'What's it to you?'

The speaker was a small neatly dressed man with black hair brushed forward from the crown, his scalp showing pinkly through it. The second man was younger, wore skin-tight jeans, a suede jacket and shoulder-length brown hair. He was grinning.

'Nothing whatsoever,' Carr said. 'But I'd be grateful if you two would take your own out and drop them on the carpet.'

The younger man said, 'You got your lines wrong, mister.

You oughta had said "do it real slow and with the finger and thumb like. Likewise one at a time."' He was still grinning.

Carr said, 'Tell him, Clancey.'

'Do what the man says, youngster. I don't know his name, but I recognize bad news when I see it.' He looked up at Carr. 'What happened to Parkson?'

Carr's eyes were fixed on the ornamental fireplace between them. 'The guns,' he said. The one he had taken from the man outside still lay flat on the palm of his hand. He watched Clancey reach slowly under his left armpit, the movement at the very edge of his field of vision.

'Whatever it is, take it out and drop it, Clancey,' he said. 'Then the gun. You're left-handed. Remember?'

'Nothing there,' Clancey said dully. 'I was trying to . . .'

'Mask the movement of your left arm?'

'Yes.'

'Nice try.'

Clancey's gun thudded on the carpet. Carr remained motionless and a long fifteen seconds dragged by before the younger man's followed it. The grin had left his face.

Carr said, 'If Parkson is the man who let me in, he's lying down next door, but I'm more interested in Ludwig Keller. Don't say you've never heard of him. The prison break is on every placard in town. You organized it very well, but made the mistake of letting yourself be recognized. Your second mistake was in coming back to Soho. You are known to use a flat in this building and another in Dean Street, neither registered in your name. You didn't make it very difficult for us. Now make it easy for yourself and tell me where Keller is.'

Clancey sat up very straight in his chair and ran his fingers nervously through his hair from front to back. It stood ridiculously upright like the crest of some improbable bird, beads of sweat forming on the baldness beneath.

He said, 'I can't. It's as simple as that. I just can't do it. I wouldn't live a day.'

'Don't be banal, Clancey.'

'I tell you it's the truth, man.'

Carr sighed. 'Ah, don't give me a hard time,' he said. 'I've only just bought this suit. Let's hear from you or your "wife" here. Where's Keller?'

The long-haired youth snarled and lunged for the gun at his

feet. Almost absent-mindedly Carr kicked him below the ear.

The barman said, 'Back again, sir?'

Carr nodded. 'I thought I'd have a nightcap on the way home.'

Idly he watched the single measure of whisky drain from the 'optic' into a glass, then his glance shifted to the mirror behind the bar. The room was sparsely occupied and nobody was paying him any attention except a pretty girl sitting alone at a table. Their eyes met and Carr was the first to look away.

Soda water hissed into the glass and the barman asked, 'What's that "Zoro" something or other word mean, sir?'

He reached under the bar for the newspaper and Carr said, 'A Zoroastrian is a follower of Zoroaster's religious teaching to the Zend-Avesta. It's based on the struggle between Ormuzd, god of light and . . . listen, tell one of your acolytes to ask the red-head in the green dress if she'll join me for a drink.'

The man looked across the bar and frowned.

'But that's Melissa Page, the actress, sir. Lord Drew's wife.'

For the first time he noticed the coldness in his customer's grey eyes. Suppressing a shrug, he turned and spoke to one of his assistant barmen.

Twenty minutes later he watched the pair walking up the open staircase together and decided that he had changed his mind about the man being a school master. Irritably he wrote 'Zendavister or something' beside the crossword puzzle, tried to remember the name of the god, but could not. He hoped there wouldn't be any unpleasantness when His Lordship arrived.

CHAPTER TWO

The club servant said, 'There's a Mr Havelock-Templeton downstairs asking for you, sir.'

Colonel Barry looked up from the copy of the *Evening Standard* he was reading and smiled at the old man standing beside his chair.

'Thank you, Henry. Ask them to show him the way up, would you? He's dining with me.'

When Havelock-Templeton came into the room Barry tossed the paper aside, got to his feet and said, 'Hello, Julian. Let's go straight in. There's never anybody in the dining room at this time of night. We'll be able to talk.'

'Suits me, Charles,' his guest told him and followed the big, hairy man through the doorway. When the waiter had taken their order he said, 'I gather your scheme worked.'

'Do you? Why?' Barry asked him.

'Well, I know that he was never out of it but, according to the radio, Keller is back in prison. That's pretty quick work, so I assume that Carr did his stuff. If he hadn't, you would have given him longer before authorizing the news release.'

Barry nodded. 'Carr did his stuff all right. He got the address of Keller's supposed hide-out from Clancey, telephoned it straight in and asked for an ambulance to be sent to Berwick Street.'

'So somebody got hurt.'

'Parkson has a dislocated and broken jaw. Young Mellor is still unconscious, but they aren't too worried about him. I'm sorry, Julian, but . . .'

'Don't worry, Charles. These things happen.'

'I hadn't quite finished.' Barry's voice was without inflection. 'Clancey died on the way to hospital or, if you prefer the official terminology, he was found to be dead on arrival.'

Neither man spoke for a time, then Barry went on, 'I gather it wasn't altogether Carr's doing. No, that's stupid. I mean I don't think it was intentional. Clancey had very severe bruising around the abdomen, but wasn't marked anywhere else. I'm told his heart gave out.'

'I see.'

'Yes,' Barry said. 'As I was saying, I'm sorry, for what that's worth. My scheme worked at inordinate cost to Clancey – and you.'

Each watched as an avocado pear was placed in front of him. Neither made a move to eat it, but Barry cut his into small hemispheres with a spoon. Havelock-Templeton broke the silence.

'Does Carr know about Clancey?'

'Yes.'

'What did he say?'

' "Send his widow some aubergines from me and tell him to get his hair cut." '

'Is that supposed to mean something? It sounds in poor taste.'

'It was a reference to Mellor's long hair. Carr has never got used to the fashion. He probably baited them about homo-sexuality.'

'And the aubergines?'

'Carr's identification word for the day. In the colour sense, not the fruit. He hates codes and drives my switchboard girls out of their minds by fooling around with them.'

'The girls?'

'No, Julian. The codes. Eat your pear.'

For a moment they ate in silence, then Barry said, 'You know, you mustn't blame Carr. He genuinely believed that Keller had escaped, knew the opposition would give a lot to have him back and thought that Clancey and your other two chaps were adverse parties. I told him so myself, so I'm the one to blame.'

'So am I, for that matter. I agreed to lend you Clancey and that's that. On the credit side you now know that Carr is in the clear. How about the others?'

Barry stabbed his spoon into his mutilated avocado, pushed the plate away and stared at it. His guest thought he had never seen him looking so old.

It was thirty seconds before Barry answered.

'I shall be sending Trelawney – you know Trelawney, don't you?'

'No, but I think I've seen him. High-rise block of a man with a broken nose?'

'That's him,' Barry said. 'Well, I'll be sending him around Europe on a non-existent job which should tell me something within a few weeks. Then there's Foster, my number two. I set something up in that direction some time ago and I have a meeting at eleven tonight to discuss . . .'

He stopped talking, tugged irritably at his beard, then went on. 'This is pointless. I can't give you details about hypo-thetical situations involving I don't know how many people. There are quite a few with potential access to sensitive information.' Another slight pause, then, 'Listen, Julian, I want you to do something else for me and before you say "no" I promise you that there'll be no question of putting any more of your people at risk. All I want is a photographer my lot won't recognize. Someone else too, but I know where to find him myself.'

'What sort of someone else?'

'A lip-reader. There's a Dr Gowan . . .' Barry let the sentence trail away into silence.

'I see, but wouldn't a directional microphone do?'

Barry shook his head. 'It'll be on a golf course. Distances too great and too much aircraft noise out of Heathrow.'

'Okay, Charles. A cameraman with telescopic equipment. I'll lay that on. Now tell me something about Carr. I'm not being inquisitive. It's important for me to know what sort of man can mangle one of my operational teams. I know Clancey had my instructions to talk under pressure, but the others knew nothing of that.'

'Let's wait for the *coq au vin*,' said Barry.

He began to think about Carr, wondering why he disliked him, could see nothing admirable in him at all, yet knew him to be virtually irreplaceable. Carr with his rapier-like mind and the sense of humour of a fourteen-year-old schoolboy. His twenty-five-year-old athlete's physique locked in a body twenty years older than that which he never bothered to exercise. Indolence coupled to wide-ranging knowledge. Disinterest in his fellow men, verging on disdain for the entire human race except that part of it which was female and good to look at. His indifference to pain and death, his own included.

The waiter brought the *coq au vin* and departed. Barry talked for a long time about Carr, trying to explain him. He made a poor job of it.

CHAPTER THREE

Down Gloucester Place and left into Blandford Street Colonel Barry moved at his usual deliberate pace, but as he neared the Thayer Street offices he slowed almost to a stop as if reluctant to start this particular day. The conversation of the night before had been long, the theory discussed plausible and the proposals put to him distasteful in the extreme. The fact that they had a greater chance of success than any plans of his own did nothing to make them more palatable and that, he supposed, was why his normal incisiveness had deserted him.

'I'll sleep on it,' he'd said.

He hadn't slept on it. The blank white ceiling of his bedroom had become a scratch-pad on which his eyes inscribed invisible columns of pros and cons. The pros were plentiful and explicit, but the space beside them carried only repetitive and irrelevant assertions of personal antipathy. It was close to dawn before he had fallen into a fitful doze and, three hours later, when he walked through the street doorway of the building which housed the Department his mood of disquiet was still on him.

Inside the doorway was a short passage designed to look as though it provided access to a medium priced apartment block, but there was no indicator board bearing fictitious names, no attempt either to reveal or to conceal. A Government Minister who had questioned Barry about this had been recommended to enquire at any of the major embassies if he ever forgot the whereabouts of an under-cover organization. 'It's even simpler in the States,' Barry had added. 'If you miss the signposts, just look them up in the 'phone book.'

He followed the passage to its end, turned left and presented an American Express card to a man sitting in a glass booth out of sight of the street door. The man read the serial number which only American Express would have known to be false, handed the card back and said ''Morning, sir. Nice day.'

''Morning, Sergeant. It is, isn't it?'

They had used the same greeting for nearly twenty years regardless of the weather, but never until Sergeant Cole had checked the card number.

'If anybody wants me I'll be down in Requirements.'

'Mr Young's not in yet, sir.'

'It doesn't matter,' Barry said. 'Open the door for me, would you?'

'Sir,' Sergeant Cole said and pressed a button beside his desk.

Barry took the stairs to the basement. The steel door at the bottom stood open and he smiled faintly at the sight of the big room beyond it. It was, as always, in a condition of chaotic untidiness, any flat surface, with the exception of a narrow path meandering across the concrete floor to the glassed-in office at the back, a resting place for apparently discarded, largely unidentifiable pieces of equipment.

Nobody, least of all himself, had ever objected because Young, the head of Requirements Section, liked it that way and Young was as near to being a genius in his field as made no difference. He made things, many things, almost any things. If any of them had failed to do what they were supposed to have done after receiving Young's seal of approval Barry had yet to hear of it.

Working his way through the shambles Barry found a crate with only a coil of heavy-duty electric cable on its top. He lifted the cable, propped it against the side of the crate, sat down and tried to decide whether or not there was any difference between a good and bad motive for employing an unhappy means to attain a justifiable end. A vague feeling of foolishness that he should be avoiding his staff, hiding from them really, while he tried to grapple with an amorphous moral problem grew in him. He shifted uncomfortably on the crate, but stayed where he was picturing himself as a Steinberg drawing of a man standing behind a spherical boulder balanced on a peak. A gentle push would convert the boulder's potential energy to kinetic. That it would crush people on its way down the slope he was well aware, but what distressed him more than that was the boulder's eagerness to be sent on its way.

He moved again restlessly and his foot touched some object on the littered floor. Idly he picked it up. It was about a foot long and cylindrical. There were three dials set in the wall of the cylinder, one end was blanked off except for two short lengths of wire protruding from it, the other held a concave lens. It meant nothing to him and he placed it on an oil-stained, splintered work-bench to his left.

'Careful, Colonel Barry, sir. Careful. That thing's highly unstable.'

The speaker was standing just inside the doorway removing his jacket, reaching for a dirty white overall hanging from a hook.

Barry shook his head resignedly. 'You're going to blow us all to blazes one of these days, Young.'

'Try not to do that, sir, but I was referring to the bench, not the gadget you was playing with. Great hopes of that gadget I have. Wouldn't like it to fall off.'

'Sorry,' Barry said and put the cylinder back on the floor where he had found it. Forgive the intrusion. I wanted a moment to decide if I was doing the right thing over a certain matter. Sometimes it's noisy upstairs.'

'Ah, yes, sir. Well my advice is "when in doubt – don't". There's a right way and a wrong way, and all of us knows in our hearts which is which.' The voice, heavy with understanding, went on, 'My gadgets taught me that and . . .'

Barry stood up hastily, said, 'Thanks very much. I must get on,' and walked out, wondering why someone as clever as Young had to resort to vapid remarks as a means of communication.

The lift carried him past the quiet first and second floors which housed the large and rarely used conference room, Records Section, Photographic Section and a tiny, well-equipped hospital. He got out at the third, walked once round the oblong formed by the passage separating the interior and exterior offices, meeting nobody, but hearing the clacking of typewriters and teleprinters, the buzz and click of cipher machines from behind closed doors. The circuit completed he stood quite motionless for a moment then, 'Christ!' he said to himself. 'Stop thinking like Young. You're not dealing with gadgets!' and went up the stairs towards his own room on the fourth floor two at a time. Most of the doors there were shut too, but Foster, his Deputy since Clayton had retired, had left his ajar and as he passed it he caught a brief glimpse of Foster's head bent over something he was writing.

At his own desk he lifted the receiver of the black telephone and dialled two digits. Then, his voice unnaturally clipped, 'We'll do it exactly as you suggested,' Barry said and replaced the receiver on its rest.

The boulder was rolling now.

CHAPTER FOUR

Trelawney circled the small Japanese with a cat-like grace which seemed to belie his two hundred pounds. With no warning at all his left leg jack-knifed and his foot drove towards his opponent's knee-cap, but before it reached its target he dropped it to the ground and stabbed at the slanting eyes in front of him with the spread first and second fingers of his left hand. Fractionally more than a second later his back hit the thick coir matting covering the floor.

He shook his head ruefully and said, 'What did I do wrong that time, Osaragi?'

'Nothing, Trelawney san,' the Japanese told him. 'It is just that I know you too well. That and your slowness.'

'My slowness? I thought I was at least medium fast.'

The Japanese smiled. 'For one so big you are very fast indeed. You were slow just now because you did not wish to blind me and that is kind but also ridiculous.'

Trelawney got to his feet, his six foot three inches placing his shoulder level with the top of the instructor's head.

'What's ridiculous about it?' he asked.

The Japanese's ready smile came again. 'For a long time you have done me the honour of being my friend. Do me a further honour. Refrain from pointing the finger at my advancing years. I am still able to look after myself.'

'All right, you old bastard. Let's try some more.'

'No,' Osaragi said. 'An hour is enough. We can start again after lunch.'

As they were walking towards the showers the door behind them opened. Trelawney turned and said, 'Oh. Hello, Jack. You want me?'

'No, sir,' the Royal Marine Commando who was Osaragi's assistant told him, 'but Thayer Street does. A bit sharpish.'

'What did they say?'

'For you to be there as soon as convenient, sir.'

'Okay. In that case there's time to eat. Eating's convenient. Mr Osaragi and I are going down to the pub for some beer and a sandwich. You coming?'

'Yes, sir,' Sergeant Pender said. 'I'd like that.'

Colonel Barry looked up from his desk and said, 'Ah, Trelawney. You made good time.' He gestured towards a chair, then asked, 'How was Hampshire?'

'Good as ever, sir, up to and including the unfortunate fact that Osaragi can still rub my nose in it whenever he's in the mood.'

'Nothing unfortunate about that. Do you good. Now listen. I've got a job for you. How's your Polish?'

Before replying, Trelawney looked at the burly figure of the man he had once completely distrusted and come close to despising. His glance took in the hair, beard and eyebrows, all of them grey with touches of white, all of them shaggy, and he recognized two things. The first was that for some time past he had liked him very much, the second that Barry's facial resemblance to a colonel and an Old English Sheep-dog was about equal.

'*Czarny kot bardzo lubi biale mleko,*' he said.

'Meaning what?'

'The black cat is very fond of white milk, sir.'

'That bad, eh?'

Trelawney shrugged. 'I can produce a couple of dozen similar gems, but if you want me to use the language I'll need a crash refresher course. It's been a long time.'

'All right, fix it with Foster's secretary. She knows the School of Eastern European and Slavonic Languages people. You've got three weeks. After that I want you to spend a few days in Sheffield.'

'Cover?'

'Yes. "Consolidated Non-ferrous Tubes" will have a stand at the Poznan Trade Fair. You'll be their interpreter so you'd better know what they manufacture. When you've been in Poznan for a couple of days go sick or something, then this is what I want you to do.'

Half an hour later the door closed behind Trelawney and Barry sat motionless for a minute staring at it. He was thinking about the remarkable change which had overtaken Trelawney, remembering the bull-headed, angry man with the chip on his shoulder he had first met, comparing him with the quiet, well-balanced agent he had just briefed. Remembering too, as clearly as if it had been days rather than years ago, the voice of his old friend and second-in-command Peter Clayton. 'He's already formed, if you take my meaning, and I don't think it likely that he can be forged into any other shape,' Clayton had said, and for once in his life had been wrong. But then Clayton had no way of foreseeing the relationship which was to develop out of Trelawney's first assignment for the Department.

The transformation had not begun immediately, but once started it had been rapid and Barry remarked on it to his secretary. Martha had found nothing surprising in it and Barry could remember saying that things like that didn't happen. 'They do with girls like Jane Trask,' she had told him.

He sighed, thinking about the beautiful woman Trelawney lived with, a woman who seemed to grow more beautiful with the years. It was all very satisfactory he supposed but, of course, he had never again allowed them to operate as a pair. That was right and proper, but it did nothing to relieve the anxiety he normally felt when he assigned either of them to anything.

He sighed again. The briefing he had just given had produced in him a brand of anxiety that was far from normal. It had also made him feel dirty.

'It's a combined gas-fired walking beam furnace and barrel type piercing mill,' the man in the white coat said and launched into a description of its function. He had done it so often before for the benefit of visitors that he did it by rote, his mind free to wonder about his present audience of one, a big man, blue eyed, black haired, with a broken nose and a small grouping of pockmarks on his right cheek which looked like the scars left by shrapnel. Formidable, the white-coated man thought, and not at all typical of the people he was required to show round the factory.

Trelawney kept an expression of what he hoped was intelligent interest on his face, but he wasn't listening. It was difficult to hear amidst the bedlam of fork-lift trucks dumping their reverberating loads of tubes, the hiss of high-speed circular saws slicing through copper and their piercing screams of outrage when they bit into cupro-nickel.

In his hotel room he already had enough pamphlets on the Company's end-products to keep him talking in Poznan for a year, let alone two days.

When the monologue ended Trelawney said, 'That's pretty clear. What was the name of the machine again?' The man told him and he wrote it down dutifully on the pad he was carrying.

Over a period of three days they showed him just about everything. He looked at long bays of annealing furnaces, with flat racks of tubes like multiple rocket launchers moving slowly, relentlessly into them through a screen of falling water which held a controlled atmosphere inside and kept out the corrosive air he breathed. He witnessed tubes, sometimes three at a time, squeal protestingly as a force too great to resist drew them through apertures too small to accommodate them. Furnace doors opened for him briefly and he glimpsed a seething cauldron like some maddened metallic sun before the heat tore at his face and he flinched away. A squatting, black iron brontosaurus the size of a small house groaned in labour and gave obscene birth to a glowing embryo of tube as big as himself.

After the man in the white coat had finished with him it was a relief to watch people doing quiet things with pipettes and beakers, carbon arcs and spectrographs. About the only thing they didn't show him was the Chairman of the Company and Trelawney knew that the Chairman would have made certain of that. Those of Barry's acquaintances of whom he asked a favour were always reluctant to acknowledge any connection with the granting of it.

Amongst the small crowd of people waiting outside the Customs barrier at Köln-Bonn airport were several holding oblongs of cardboard with names printed on them with magic marker. One of the cards bore the name Standish. Trelawney raised a hand to the man carrying it and moved towards the exit. The man fell into step beside him.

'I'm Standish,' Trelawney said.

'Diestel. I have a car outside.' The German accent was barely perceptible.

Trelawney nodded, walked two more paces and stopped. With his open wallet in his hand he turned and looked around the concourse.

'Where's the currency exchange bureau? I need some Deutsche Marks.'

Diestel glanced down at the American Express card which American Express had never issued and said, 'Don't bother. I have plenty.' He showed Trelawney his own wallet with a similar card in it.

Trelawney nodded again. 'My name's Trelawney.'

'I know,' the German told him. 'Mine's still Diestel.'

Neither spoke again until the BMW was gathering speed on the autobahn leading to Cologne then, 'How do you know?' Trelawney asked.

The German flicked his traffic indicator and pulled out into the fast lane before replying.

'I covered you here a long time ago. You had a pick-up to make and a "double" called Malling tried to interfere. You didn't need my help. I got rid of the body after you had gone.'

'Bullshit!' Trelawney said.

'You killed him with a middle-finger knuckle punch to the larynx. I was hiding behind the shower curtain in your room when you did it. The good Colonel Barry always looks after his trainees.'

They were approaching the city's outskirts before Trelawney spoke again.

'It took me the best part of two years to forgive the old devil for putting me on that spot for no real purpose.'

'Well, you'd hardly expect him to tell you that you were being nursed, would you?'

'Now that you mention it, no, I wouldn't,' Trelawney said.

He was alone for ten days in the flat Diestel took him to and didn't understand it. The Poznan Fair had been open for a week by then. He never went out because he had been told not to, ate regularly from the well-stocked store cupboards and the big refrigerator to give himself something to do and reference points to the blank days. Between meals he read for hours. Diestel had been thoughtful over the provision of books, but he couldn't read all the time and the German's taste in music was too classical for him. A tape of Mahler's Symphony No. 4 pleased him when played at protracted intervals, but Mozart and Beethoven were as far above his head as ever.

Jane was in his thoughts a lot as she always was, but it wasn't good to let his imagination stray too far when he didn't know where she might be or what Barry might have sent her to do. She had been at home when he had left. He had let himself into the studio apartment where they lived at 10 p.m. and, as was often the case, she had known that he was going away before he could tell her. 'Drink or hold?' she had asked. 'Hold,' he had replied and they had made gentle love far into the night. But that had been ten days ago and she could be anywhere now. It was a relief at noon on the tenth day to answer the door bell and find Diestel standing outside.

Trelawney motioned him in and read the message from Barry he was given.

'I've booked you on the two twenty-five Lufthansa flight to Copenhagen,' Diestel told him. 'You can take the hydrofoil on from there. Anything else you want?'

'No. No thanks,' Trelawney said.

He packed quickly, wondering why he was required to spend five nights at the Hotel St Jorgen in Malmo and to report only to Barry on his return to London. Report what?

By the time he had snapped shut the catches on his suitcase he had assumed that he was a passive element in a deception operation. Three floors down he stepped on to Maastrichter Strasse, turned right at the Ring and walked south. Before he reached Barbarossa Platz it occurred to him that someone else would be dealing with the Polish end whilst he led the watchers from Cologne to Malmo. Not realizing that he was right in fact, wrong only in interpretation, he abandoned conjecture as an unprofitable exercise and flagged down a cruising taxi. Throwing his bag into the back he got in beside the driver.

'*Flughafen, bitte*,' he said.

CHAPTER FIVE

The two men were opposites. One dark, slender, good-looking. The other, showing signs of incipient obesity, had faded red hair and the near-invisible eyebrows and lashes which go with that pigmentation. The dark one was talking softly, but there was anger in his words.

'Do you have to bring this junk with you every time? Why run the risk of carrying it around the building when you know the combination by heart?'

Patiently the other said, 'I know what the combination was four days ago. So does what you call this junk. It's built into its memory bank. You may remember my telling you that there's a triple-phase link between the combination and the key-operated lock. Get just one of the settings wrong and you set off the alarm, two, even if you've neutralized the alarm, and you activate the self-destruct unit.'

'So don't get them wrong!'

As though there had been no interruption the patient voice went on, 'If the settings have been changed during the last four days this *junk* will get incorrect responses from the combination and will not attempt to turn the key at whichever of the three phases it gets faulty reactions from. If, on the other hand, everything is as it was it will open the safe. Now, don't you think that's a lot easier than me having to go through an entire search sequence as I did the first time?'

'Nobody's changed anything since we've been doing this,' the dark-haired man said.

'Very well. You should know the combination by now. Go and open the bloody thing yourself, but give me five minutes to get out of here first and I'll pray for you that it's still the same.'

The threat was effective. 'Sorry, Jimmy. You're absolutely right. Let's get on with it.'

They moved quickly after that, hands gloved, faces distorted by the tension of the nylon stockings drawn over them. The door to Barry's room yielded almost instantly to the red-haired man's probe and they carried the piece of heavy equipment inside. In the light of the pencil-torch taped to its top it looked like a big camera with two short rods protruding from the front. One ended in a key, the other in a rubber cup. When they eased it towards the door of the safe the key entered the slot at the same time as the cup slipped over the combination dial.

The dark man glanced sideways at his companion, saw his nod in the dim backwash of light and pressed a button on the machine. It hummed softly and the dial rotated to the left, paused, turned left again, then right. Twice more, with variations, the process was repeated, the humming stopped and a pea-bulb glowed green. The action of withdrawing the machine was sufficient to swing the balanced door open.

Slightly less than four minutes later they were back in the lighted office where they had first spoken. Between leaving it and their return no word had been exchanged between them. Both pulled the stocking masks from their heads, smoothed their hair into place, then began to photograph the papers they had brought away with them.

'Important?'

'Very.'

The expression on the dark man's face was made up of equal parts of tension and elation. He was trembling visibly.

'You all right?'

'I am now. Sorry again about the nonsense I was talking earlier. I was a bit on edge.'

'Yes, and you still are,' the lock expert said. 'Take it easy while I put these folders back.'

The thought that an explosive device might be placed in his safe, designed to detonate when the door was opened, had worried Barry to begin with, mainly because it was almost invariably Martha, his secretary, who opened it first in the mornings. Then he had concluded that it would be stupid of them to do that as it came into the category of the goose and the golden eggs. There were many more certain ways of killing him at much less cost to themselves, so he stopped worrying.

He manipulated the dial-key interlock system and swung the door wide, grateful for the only breach of confidence of which Martha had ever been guilty. As a result of a lapse brought on by her exasperation his habit of using the safe as a depository for anything he didn't know what to do with at the end of the day was well known throughout the Department. Of all the objects she had correctly claimed to have taken out the following morning, a tin of live maggots in a fishing creel held pride of place in the retelling of the story.

On this occasion almost everything was exactly as he had left it the night before, even the half-empty packet of biscuits in the torn cellophane wrapper was correctly angled. Only the tennis ball with the tiny pin embedded in it, its head hidden by the nap, told him that the contents had been moved.

With a grunt of satisfaction Barry closed the safe, then left the building so that Martha would not know that he had been there before her.

CHAPTER SIX

Barry sat in the darkened room watching the image of Foster make a series of practice swings with a driver. He was talking to someone outside the field of vision of the camera lens. After the sixth swing he shouldered his club and stood, looking to his left, apparently listening. A man's back came into view on the right edge of the screen.

'Herrick,' a voice said and Barry grunted.

Foster turned and bent to tee up a ball. A moment later he swung at it and the ball vanished. Herrick walked on to the screen and both figures stood gazing down the fairway. Foster looked at Herrick, said something and grinned, then Herrick drove off. Again they watched the flight of the ball, then both men walked away, the three-quarter back view they presented to the camera becoming full back as the distance increased.

'Any more mouth shots?' Barry asked.

'Not really,' the voice told him.' There are several feet of them walking back to the club house, but they're only talking about the score card. There is another section showing them on the ninth green, which is the only one visible from the car park, but it's a long way off and I'm still trying to make something of it. I'll let you know if I have any luck.'

'All right,' Barry said. 'Stop the camera and let's hear the first bit.'

The picture faded from the screen and the lights came on. Barry began to fill a pipe, looking enquiringly at the short dapper man sitting beside him.

The man looked down at his notes and said, 'I've run it through several times and I'm pretty sure about it, but it doesn't seem to make much sense.' He took an immaculately folded handkerchief from his breast pocket, patted his moustache with it and rearranged it in his pocket.

'When the film starts, Foster is saying "important" or "import on each occasion." I'm not certain about the first word because his face is angled too far downwards. That and other head movements are the reason for subsequent gaps. Then he goes on, "quite definite about that and I think it makes everything much easier if we assume . . ." something. He turned his head away at that point and I don't see his mouth again until . . .'

Barry said, 'All right, all right. I've got the message. Just read me what you've got written down there and say "gap" where the sequence is broken.'

The lip-reader coughed. 'Very well,' he said. 'Foster says, "which is all you need to do, but leave it until tomorrow. It shouldn't be too difficult as long – gap – best we can hope for anyway. Some silly bastard will probably want to know why we haven't allowed for – gap – case tell him to get stuffed. I'm certain this is the best investment we can make." Foster stops talking and listens. That's all.'

'Not quite, Dr Gowan. Foster said something brief to Herrick after he had driven off. What was it?'

'Sorry, so he did. But it was only "Beat that".'

Barry grunted for the second time. 'I must say the gaps come up in damnably inconvenient places. Makes no sense at all.'

Asperity in his voice Gowan said, 'I'm not responsible for that, Colonel!'

Barry's shaggy head turned slowly towards the speaker, what was visible of his face registering surprise.

He said, 'My dear chap, don't pay any attention to me. I'm worried, that's all. Silly of me to have banked on this film and even if it hasn't given me what I wanted that's no excuse for barking at you. What you have got out of it is amazing.' He pulled at his beard then added, 'In fact, I should be most grateful if you would carry the thing a stage further.'

'Of course, Colonel. What would you like me to do?' Gowan sounded mollified.

'Run the thing through again, time the gaps and see if you can give me an estimate of the number of words or syllables in them based on his rate of speaking, assuming that he is talking all the time. If you can see that he is silent, then amend the duration of the gap accordingly. It's a pretty long shot, but we might just be able to guess some meaning into it. Any additional words you may be able to isolate would, of course, be invaluable.'

Gowan said, 'I'm afraid there isn't much hope of a positive identification of any more words, but I could give you a list of possible sounds relating to a particular word, or part of a word, if that would be any help to you.'

'Thank you. It certainly would.'

'Very well, Colonel. If you would have the projector and film sent back to my office I'll work on it this afternoon. I want to try the ninth green section again too.'

When Gowan had gone, Barry pushed himself out of his chair and looked at the silent man sitting beside the camera.

'Busted flush I'm afraid, Julian. Thanks for playing projector operator.'

Havelock-Templeton said, 'Any time.' He was looking at Barry thoughtfully.

'Are you in a hurry, Charles?'

'Why?'

'Foster can't play golf. I don't mean he isn't very good at it

Apart from driving the ball off the tee in roughly the right direction, he can't play golf at all.'

Barry sat down slowly. 'Go on,' he said.

'Later on there are some shots with the flight of the ball in line with the camera. Foster seems to be equally allergic to the fairway and the greens. Just about everything he hits, when he hits it at all, goes into the rough or a bunker.'

'So what? You might be describing my play.'

'Possibly, Charles. But I expect you go and look for your ball which is something Foster doesn't do. Herrick drops another for him on a fair lie. In one scene, where there are people not very far away, I'm pretty sure that Herrick drops a ball down inside his trouser leg. The angle isn't perfect, but I think that is what he's doing.'

Barry's eyebrows shot up. He looked like an instructor regarding a pet pupil with undisguised approval.

'Well done, young fellow,' he said. 'It's the oldest cheating trick in the book, but it's the first time I've heard of your opponent doing it for you. You're telling me that Herrick helps Foster to keep ahead of whoever is coming up behind so there is no risk of their being overheard or "read" by someone like Dr Gowan.'

'I'm suggesting it.'

'Let's see the whole film,' said Barry.

At home that night Barry received a telephone call from Dr Gowan.

'I have some notes for you here, Colonel. Will you have them picked up?'

'Right away and thank you very much,'

'They aren't very encouraging I'm afraid, but there is one thing of interest.'

'Yes?'

'You remember my referring to the ninth green?'

'I do.'

'Well, I seem to have come up with a piece of evidence indicating fear of being observed. Both parties have worried expressions on their faces and the second, alphabetically, makes two references to a lip man. The first is "if lip man gets" and the second "when lip man starts to". I'm only surprised as they had thought that far, they didn't think a little further and anticipate the possibilities of a camera with a telescopic lens.'

'Careless of them,' Barry said. 'I'm very much obliged to you, Dr Gowan. You've just fitted another piece of the jig-saw in place.'

He put down the receiver and sat staring at it for a moment, then he said, 'In fact you may have completed the whole damn puzzle, Dr Gowan. Let's hope so anyway.'

Barry called the night duty officer at Thayer Street and asked him to send a car for Gowan's notes then sat motionless by the telephone. He was thinking that specialists were very strange people. Young who could build a book-sized box of tricks which listened through walls or blew them to pieces depending on which face was outward, but talked like an old-fashioned nanny. Gowan who could read words from slight movements of mouth and jaw, but saw no significance in the omission of the indefinite article from what he had read.

He moved to an armchair to wait for the report from Gowan which he no longer needed.

CHAPTER SEVEN

The stridency of the bell jerked Foster out of sleep with a violent start. He cursed his nerves and took it out on the alarm clock with a downward sweep of his palm. The clock fell to the floor and he groped for it in the darkness, the upper part of his body hanging over the side of the bed. The bell was still ringing.

'It's the telephone, you ass. You know – Burr Burr, not Brrrrrring.'

'Hell. So it is. I'm half asleep,' said Foster and was still fumbling for the receiver when the light on the other side of the bed came on.

'Thanks,' he said. 'Hello, Foster here.' He listened for a moment while the ear-piece muttered at him. 'I see . . . Yes. Yes, of course. I'll be there in half an hour.'

He replaced the receiver and turned to the girl beside him. She was sliding the shoulder straps of her nightdress up her arms, her brown eyes wide and clear as though she had been awake for an hour.

'You're beautiful,' he said.

'I wish I were. I very nearly was, then I turned out funny.

Who was that, Nigel?'

'Barry. He's at the office now. He wants me. There's some flap on What's the time?'

'Twenty past four.'

'Christ! Wouldn't you know it? Make some coffee while I shave, will you, darling?'

She flung the sheet aside and swung off the bed, her legs as long as the nightdress was short. Appreciatively he watched her walk towards the kitchen, her hips flexing slightly. She *was* beautiful, but he knew what she meant. There was something odd about her face, as though it rightly belonged to somebody else, but he found the oddity devastating.

He drank his coffee sitting on the side of the bed, then lit a cigarette, felt the collar of his pyjamas grasped and was pulled backwards across her legs. The girl took the cigarette from his fingers and stubbed it out.

'You really can't start that at this time of day and it's impolite to make love to a lady with a cigarette in your hand.'

'Fiona! Not now, for God's sake. You know it makes me shaky, particularly whan I have to go out.'

'The shakes will remind you of me and it's better for you than smoking.'

He surrendered to her weakly.

Foster let himself out of the flat and on to North Audley Street fifteen minutes later. He began to walk towards Manchester Square, his feelings a mixture of happiness and jumping nerves. As he crossed an almost deserted Oxford Street, he tried to compose himself for his meeting with Barry, wondering what it could be about, what it was that couldn't have waited for another four hours.

Ninety minutes later he left the offices on Thayer Street and walked through Manchester Square again on the way back to his flat. He was steady, but still nervous.

Fiona Langley, dressed in street clothes, was frying bacon and eggs.

'They've got Lippmann,' he said.

She scooped the eggs out of the pan on to two plates, turned the bacon over and then stood looking thoughtfully at him.

'I wonder how,' she said.

'Knocked down by a truck in some place called Zwickau, between Leipzig and Plauen. It wasn't an accident.'

She took the bacon out of the pan and arranged it beside the eggs, then carried the plates into the living room.

'I didn't mean that. I was wondering how they got on to him. He had the best cover any of our people ever had.'

'The old man thinks there has been a leak from the office. A deliberate leak.'

'Does he now? Any idea from which direction?' The question was asked lightly.

Foster sat down slowly at the breakfast table, unnoticing for once the flowers and pretty feminine touches to the table setting he had never known until his secretary had moved into the flat with him a few weeks before. He was looking at her face. She was right, he decided. She wasn't actually beautiful at all. More bizarrely attractive, but bizarrely very attractive, particularly now with concern for him so clear in her expression. That she realized that she was as deeply implicated as he, he didn't doubt for a moment, but her concern was for him alone. It came to him that he wanted to marry her.

He said, 'How did you manage to have the eggs on the minute I walked through the door? Are you psychic?'

'No, Nigel. I am not psychic. I watched you coming up the street and will you please answer my question?'

'I haven't worked it out yet,' he said. 'Obviously I'm the prime suspect. I have to be as the only one Barry told about the Lippmann assignment, but when I said as much to him he gave me that "up through the eyebrows" look of his and asked if I wasn't forgetting himself and our two secretaries.

'While I was telling him, in effect, not to be stupid, he just sat and grinned at me then said, "Relax, Nigel. I know who it is."'

He began to eat his eggs and bacon.

Quietly Fiona said, 'Nigel Foster, if you don't get to the point I'll start throwing things.'

'Herrick.'

The single word seemed to Foster to hang in the air between them like a sky sign drawn by some Lilliputian aircraft and that by looking at it he could reproduce the exact voice intonation he had used.

'Nigel, it's impossible to believe! Is Barry sure of this?'

'No,' Foster told her. 'He isn't, but he's got some rather convincing evidence that Herrick is involved in something. I don't like the look of any of it.'

'What happens now? Is he pulling Herrick in?'

'Not yet. He's placed him under twenty-four-hour surveillance.'

'Which Herrick will notice at once. You can't put tails on people like him or tap their telephones, so it's a flushing operation.'

'That's a clever girl. If he tries to run, we take him in.'

'Then narco-analysis, I suppose.'

Foster breathed in slowly and very deeply. 'I imagine so,' he said.

After that they ate their breakfast in silence. She had filled his cup to the brim with coffee. Some of it slopped on to the tablecloth when he drank and she stretched an arm towards him, encircling his free wrist with her fingers, exerting gentle pressure. He looked up gratefully at the wise, candid eyes watching him.

A little before half past eight, he said he had to get back to the office.

'All right. I'm ready.'

'There's no need for you to turn up for another hour yet.'

'Never mind,' she said. 'I'll be around in case you need me. This could be a bad day, darling.'

She had been quite right. The day had been a bad one. Foster sat tiredly, shoulders hunched, on a straight-backed chair in his flat staring at the drink she had placed in his hand.

'I'll get us something to eat,' she said.

He looked listlessly at his watch. It was ten minutes short of midnight and they had eaten practically nothing since the bacon and eggs that morning. There hadn't been time. Herrick's disappearance had seen to that.

'No you won't. I'll do that. Take your shoes off and flake out on the sofa.'

Without looking at her he walked into the kitchen, his glass trailing from a lax arm as though he had forgotten it was there. Fiona Langley caught glimpses of him as he moved between store cupboard and cooker. She thought that his casual, fluid movements suited his slim build and saturnine good looks, but they did not deceive her. The pose he adopted when he was under strain had become increasingly familiar to her over recent days. Now she knew that his nerves were stretched taut and wondered how close to breaking point he was. Close, she thought. The pose was usually for others, not her.

'Nigel?'

The sound of the refrigerator door closing reached her ears, then his voice.

'Yes?'

'Switch off now. There isn't anything more that you can do tonight. Herrick has gone, he'll be found when he's found and your worrying isn't going to make that happen any sooner. You said yourself that Barry doesn't seem to be worrying.'

She heard Foster growl then say, 'The old fool is so pleased with himself for having been proved right he isn't even thinking. What I fail to understand is how Herrick got away so easily. According to Barry he had four tails on him, none of them our people, and he had shaken the lot in two and a half hours. That must have taken some doing. What . . .'

Sharply she said, 'Stop it, Nigel! You can't be thinking either. You've told me that three times today already, plus the fact that Barry is certain Herrick can't get out of the country. There isn't any need to go over it all again. Think about something else.'

'Like what?' His voice was harsh.

'You could start with me.'

Something she had said before she had taken him so easily that morning came to his mind and rage shook him. He found himself standing in the kitchen doorway staring at her, a saucepan in his hand.

'I know,' he said. 'It's better for me than smoking!' The blood had drained from his face and he was trembling in a ridiculous, jerky fashion. 'You simply don't understand!'

'But I do, darling. I understand perfectly well. Jimmy Herrick was your friend. It's so awful when someone close to you does something like he has done.' There was no sharpness in her voice now, only a melting pity.

Foster shook his head dazedly, closed and opened his eyes as though he was having trouble focusing them. 'Yes.' He said it as if he were puzzled. 'Yes, that's right.'

'Come here, Nigel.'

He crossed the room towards her obediently. Then he was kneeling beside the sofa, head softly cushioned, long fingers kneading the nape of his neck.

He was still holding the saucepan.

CHAPTER EIGHT

'You say it was full daylight? . . . Well, that's light enough and she was close enough to see clearly. Anyway, she'd have no reason for inventing details of that sort. What? . . . Oh, of course she couldn't and it doesn't matter. I'm not interested in the van, just the motor-cyclist. Thank God for an observant woman and thank you too. Goodbye.'

Barry put the green 'scrambler' telephone in the top right-hand drawer of his desk, closed it and sat back in his chair, his eyes turning to the black 'phone on the table beside him. For nearly two minutes he stayed like that, just staring at it then reached out and lifted the receiver. He dialled the same two digits he had used when he had thought of himself as the Steinberg man setting the boulder in motion.

'I shall need to see you tonight,' he said. 'We have another problem.'

He listened for a moment before saying in a dull, flat voice, 'I see. Naturally you must. I'll talk to you tomorrow.'

Leaning forward on his desk, his face buried in his hands, he saw and heard nothing until a voice said, 'Charles!' The name was spoken sharply.

He looked up at the speaker and managed a tired smile.

'Now don't you start. Whenever you call me "Charles" I know I'm in the dog house.'

'I can't think of a more appropriate place for you in this mood,' Martha told him. 'If you're not careful you'll be sobbing into your beard next!'

His nod seemed to concede the possibility, then he said, 'Do sit down, Martha.' Long ago he had resigned himself to the necessity for issuing this gentle instruction without which, despite his early protests, she would continue to stand stiff-backed before him. For a moment he thought that this time she was going to refuse, then watched the little old lady settle herself awkwardly on the upright chair at the corner of his desk. She was frowning at him.

'You heard that "scrambler" conversation?'

'I'd just played the tape back and looked in here to find you moping. It's only another problem, Charles.'

'Yes. Only another problem and I don't know which disgusts me more, the problem or the solution.'

The frown had gone and her voice was gentler when she said, 'I know, Colonel.'

He looked at her thinning white hair combed straight back and secured in a bun high up on the back of the small skull, at the deep clefts gouged by pain on the forehead and around the mouth, at the intelligent eyes masking their back-drop of pain. How long had it been now? Thirty – thirty-one years. So the little old lady was about forty-eight.

Suddenly he was back in Buckingham Palace, sensing the row upon row of faceless people in the vast room, seeing the solitary figure with a face, the King's face, step down from the dais to hang the George Cross from the hook attached to the shoulder of the dress the nurses had made for her. Stooping over her wheel-chair the King had talked to her for much longer than he did to others receiving decorations and Barry thought that for part of the time he had been crying, but had never been sure. It had been difficult to see with his own eyes misting over.

He supposed she had lied about her age and supported the lie with a false birth certificate; a small matter for someone as talented as she. But in whatever manner it had been achieved the eighteen-year-old, bi-lingual child parachuted into France had become a five-month wonder, almost a legend, before the Gestapo took her.

They'd used an ordinary hammer on her toes, pulping them one at a time. She hadn't answered their questions, so they whipped her naked round and round the prison yard, forcing her to run on her ruined feet. Once she completed nearly a whole circuit without their having to revive her. She had told them nothing. When she could no longer stand they had spreadeagled her on a table, forced some form of heating element into the vagina and switched on the current. She may have talked then, but no one would ever know. Her memories were of terrible pain and of voices saying things she didn't understand. Not even individual words. Whether or not she had broken hadn't mattered. A marauding RAF 'Typhoon', running short of fuel and looking for something to fire at, had released its full salvo of rockets at the block she was in. A day later, when the Army reached the place, only she was alive. Admittedly, falling masonry had fractured her spine, but she was alive and that, Barry thought, was the finest example of double-edged irony he had ever encountered.

It had been two years before she was finally discharged from hospital and another five before she rated herself as stable enough to accept Barry's offer of a job as his secretary. When she did she also accepted the onerous conditions of service without hesitation, but imposed two of her own. Nobody but Barry was to know about her decoration, or the cause of what she described as a 'touch of polio as a child followed by this wretched arthritis'.

'Then you'll have to change your name,' he had told her and been told in return that her lawyers were even then drawing up a deed-poll application.

After all the years between, he could still hear himself saying, 'That wasn't what I meant,' and her soft voice replying, 'I know.' It had been the fourth time she had refused him. Since then he had asked her to marry him at approximately yearly intervals with no greater success.

Well, it was nearly over now and he could be thankful for that, but sad that it had to end on this note. Only a little more than a year to serve then he could sell the lease on the flat and settle down at the cottage in Dorset. Really do something about the garden if Dropitsir, his Airedale, could be weaned from his excavation proclivities. Dropitsir accepted the flat as a *pied à terre*, but his heart was in gardening. And Martha? Would she follow him into retirement and to Dorset? He hoped so very much. It was hard to imagine life without her after all this time.

'Colonel?'

Barry came back to himself. 'Yes, my dear?'

'Don't brood about it. We both know what you have to do next.'

'I wasn't actually,' he said. 'Only indirectly anyway. I was thinking about something else, but you're quite right. Ask Mr Foster to come and see me, would you?'

He watched her limp towards her room, wondering how he dared think that *he* had troubles.

'Martha.'

She turned. 'Yes, Colonel?'

'Thank you.'

She frowned at him again, but there was no anger in it. Only mockery.

He sat waiting for Foster, half his mind on what he was going to say to him, half on his dog's ridiculous name. A year earlier Martha had christened the fiercely determined stiff-legged puppy with its rolling eyes and ferocious growl denying Barry the possession of his practice putter. Barry's commands had been both repetitive and ineffectual.

Foster came into the room quietly, closed the door and stood leaning his back against it. Barry thought that the casualness of his stance was studied, more studied than usual.

'Sit down, Nigel.'

Foster moved across the room and sat. He took a nail file from his pocket and began working on a chipped nail. He didn't speak.

Barry said, 'I wish you wouldn't do that.'

Foster put the file away. 'Sorry,' he said. 'You wanted to see me.'

'Yes. How, I don't know, but Herrick got clear away and if I detect an "I told you so" expression on your face I have to confess that it is justified.'

Foster shrugged and said nothing.

'He's calling himself Hendrix now, by the way. Odd how they like to stick close to their real names. Some personal identity thing I suppose.'

'Odd, yes,' Foster said. He sounded bored. 'How do you know?'

'How do I know what? That he is calling himself Hendrix, or that he has got himself out of the country?'

'Either,' Foster said. 'There's likely to be a connection.'

'Yes.' The word came out vaguely as though Barry had little interest in the conversation. He answered neither question, looked idly at the objects lying on his desk, then picked up a prism paper-weight and placed it in the middle of his scribbling pad. For a moment he angled it back and forth until it caught the light from the window, digested it and spewed it out again in a fan of faint rainbow colours on the paper. The click of a lighter seemed to remind him that Foster was still there.

'Herrick reached Hong Kong yesterday,' Barry said. He paused, then added, 'Richard of York gave battle in vain.' It was silly of Foster, he thought, to light a cigarette when his hands were unsteady.

Foster was looking at him through narrowed eyes. Apart from that and the faint tremor of the cigarette he still looked relaxed.

'Are you trying to tell me something?' Foster asked.

'Trying, my dear boy? I thought I was succeeding. It really isn't all that difficult to understand. Herrick is now in Hong Kong. He flew in yesterday. In what way is that obscure?'

There was a distinct edge to Foster's voice when he said, 'I wasn't talking about that. You said something about Richard of York.'

'Did I, Nigel? Thinking aloud. Sign of incipient senility probably. It's a mnemonic. Helpful if you want to remember the colours of the spectrum. Just take the initial letters and you have them in their correct order. Red – orange – yellow – green – blue – indigo – violet. See? They're on the paper here.'

'Fascinating,' Foster said.

'It is, isn't it? Do you have a favourite colour, Nigel?'

'No.'

'Really? Not even the colour of Miss Langley's lipstick? You do surprise me!'

Foster ground out his half-smoked cigarette. 'Do you want me to arrange a date for you with her, or can we get back to Herrick?'

Barry said, 'Ah yes. Herrick. As far as I have been able to establish, Hong Kong is a blind. In all probability he thinks he is clear of us already, but isn't taking any chances, so he's doing a little ducking and swerving. His next destination is the States, but I doubt he'll stay long there. Nevertheless, it's the obvious place to intercept him.'

Questions swirled in Foster's mind like dry leaves in an autumn gale, but he sat silently, voicing none of them.

Eventually Barry said, 'I want Carr to handle it,' and watched the merest hint of animation touch the impassive face of the younger man. He wondered if there wasn't a trace of relief written there too.

Foster said, 'So it's like that.'

Barry nodded 'Can you see an alternative?'

'I wish I could It's just that I don't like having to resort to hatchet men. It's a sort of defeat. Additionally, I don't like Carr

Foster smiled faintly, without humour, and added, 'All of which is irrelevant.'

Barry nodded again. 'I know how you feel,' he said. 'You wouldn't like to be hunted down by Carr any more than I.'

Foster lit another cigarette.

'When?' he asked.

'At once. I want Carr in New York by tonight. That should give him time to get his bearings before Herrick arrives in the country. Call Carr in this morning and brief him. Not that there is much to say. Tell him who, as much of why as you think necessary and point him in the right direction. When, where and how is his business. He'll have his own ideas on that.'

'Very well. I take it that the schedule is tight enough for me to get Humphreys to turn someone off a plane at Heathrow if necessary. It's the height of the season.'

Irritably Barry said, 'We don't appear to be communicating too well today, Nigel. Is anything worrying you?' Without waiting for a reply he want on, 'I said I wanted Carr in New York tonight. If you have to commandeer an RAF Strike Command "Vulcan" it'll make a mess of our budget, so I suggest you get him on a scheduled flight.'

Foster got languidly to his feet and walked to the door. When he reached it, he stopped and looked at Barry.

'You wanted Herrick out of the country, didn't you? You let him get away deliberately.'

'That's right,' Barry told him. 'We'll take care of our own now. Treason trials don't help the national image.'

'You could have lost him behind the "curtain" like Philby and the rest. You still may.'

Barry shook his head. 'I doubt it. The workers' paradise has lost a lot of its allure. Herrick was out for money. He'll go somewhere he can spend it.'

Foster opened his mouth to say something, shut it again and let himself out of the room. Some, at least, of the leaves fluttering inside his skull had settled.

His morning tea was waiting for him in his office, the saucer covering the cup. He drank the tea quickly, depressed to find that his hands were still shaking, then lit a cigarette. As an after-thought he flicked down the switch which turned on the 'Do not disturb' sign outside his door. Thoughts rushed in on him, clamouring for attention, but he forced them aside and began making telephone calls. When he had spoken to Carr and made arrangements for his trans-Atlantic flight, he lay back in his chair and let the thoughts have their way with him.

The sooner Herrick was permanently silenced the better and it was best that Carr should handle that aspect of the matter. Carr would make no mistake. The conceited bastard was incapable of making one.

So far, so good, but the rest wasn't good at all. Well, some of it was. They had fed Barry's embryo network in the Gdansk area, which Trelawney had been sent into Poland to activate, to the Polish Security Police before it had even got off the ground. Barry had been close about that one, but Trelawney's asking Fiona to arrange a refresher course in Polish for him had been warning enough. The rest had been easy. The UB had acted with precision. At 2.00 a.m. on 19 June the network existed. At 11.00 p.m. on the same day all seventeen of its members, fourteen men and three women, were arrested simultaneously. The only disappointment had been that Trelawney had somehow evaded capture. The attempt on Rafferty had been botched, but Chandler had been disposed of and the Lippmann operation wrecked.

But now the small organization with its external links so carefully forged over two years had received a set-back which, if not fatal, could be described as nothing less than major. If there were as many as five men in the British Isles, even in the whole of Europe, who could be considered Herrick's peers in breaking and entering Foster knew he would be surprised. Ten or more times he had watched Herrick open Barry's safe and been astonished at his expertise. The sophisticated equipment Herrick had handled so deftly had been beyond him, but the information the open safe provided had not.

Foster sighed and lit another cigarette from the stub of the old one, wondering who Barry would employ to replace Herrick and his lost speciality. Not that it mattered, he decided. It would be nobody he could risk trying to get close to.

He began to think about his own position, of anything that could connect him with Herrick, as if unaware that he had thought of little else since they had begun to work together. They had played golf as a perfectly open and secure method of communication away from the office but, that apart, had never deliberately sought each other out. When the safe had been opened it was done when he had been night duty officer, with nobody but the two of them on the fourth floor. They had made very sure that there was no concealed electronic detection equipment in Barry's room, then worked in silence, gloves and stocking masks in case that wasn't sure enough. No alarm had ever been raised.

So that was all right. Herrick was abroad now and would die there with his secrets when Carr, with casual insolence, struck him down. That that would happen when and where Carr decided, he had no doubt at all.

Why, then, this tenseness?

Had he a favourite colour? Fiona's lipstick perhaps? A sexual or political innuendo? Stupid! The old goat was jealous. It could be nothing more. Foster almost smiled at the thought of Barry attempting to satisfy her demands, then frowned quickly instead, conscious of the exhaustion she induced in him. The smile came then, there *were* worse forms of suffering, but it didn't stay with him.

What else had Barry said? Some question about anything worrying him and that bit about not wanting to be hunted down by Carr.

Then there had been the searching of his flat. He'd reported it to Barry who had sent along a fingerprints man and Young to look for 'bugs'. Barry hadn't been particularly concerned when they found nothing, certainly not as concerned as Foster himself who felt that the search had been cleverly careless without being obvious, as though he was supposed to discover that it had taken place. He didn't like that idea.

Probably his worst jolt had been Fiona's mention of narco-analysis. That had frightened him, not because the possibility hadn't occurred to him, but because it had to her or, more precisely, because she had voiced it. And that futile re-action, he knew, only served to show the state his nerves were in.

It was as though thinking of his nerves had brought about a change in his body chemistry, as though they had intercepted his admission and resented it. Their endings seemed to be suck-ing the warmth from his skin, forcing a film of cold moisture into his arm-pits until it coalesced and trickled down his sides like melting snow in a late spring thaw. He shivered, then shook himself in angry desperation. Carr would be arriving in less than an hour. It was vital to be in control of himself before then.

The realization brought on an urgent desire for Fiona. It was only her presence he wanted, so that he could look at her and all he had to do to achieve that was press a bellpush, but there had to be a reason. Why there had to be a reason he was unsure, but his brain sought tiredly for one anyway.

Twenty-five minutes later he looked gloomily at the messy pile of ash and half-smoked cigarette ends in the saucer which had covered his morning cup of tea. The cup itself had made a sticky ring on the leather top of his desk. He carried the saucer into the small wash place next to his office, tipped the butts into the lavatory pan and flushed it. Then he washed the saucer in the hand basin and dried it with a paper towel. Back at his desk, he poured a few drops of cold tea from the cup on to the saucer for realism and replaced the cup on it. The stain on the desk transferred itself to his handkerchief.

Satisfied, he switched off the sign outside the door. The action seemed to trigger off the memory of some notes he had typed out in rough the day before. He preferred typing his memoranda, messy as the result invariably was, to giving dictation. It was easier to think with two fingers poised over the keyboard and nothing to distract him. He found the notes in his drawer and pressed the button marked 'Secretary'. The door opened almost at once and Fiona Langley came in wearing the enormous black-tinted sun-glasses she liked to affect when she was on duty.

Foster looked at her, liking what he saw, well aware that he always liked what he saw when he looked at her and felt better when she was in the same room with him. She invariably knew, he thought, when he wanted her and what he wanted her for before he himself did. Things like coming to the office early with him the other morning. What day had that been? It didn't matter. And the time . . .

'Nigel.'

Her face came back into focus and there was a small compassionate smile on her lips.

'Yes?'

'It's office hours and you rang for me.'

'So it is, and I did. Type this lot in fair for me would you and consign my efforts to the shredder? No hurry. It's only background stuff on Schaeffer for Records.'

She walked to his desk, took the papers from him with one hand and picked up his cup and saucer with the other.

'How many?'

'Original only, of course. Funny question from you.'

'Cigarettes.'

'Oh,' Foster said. 'Several I suppose.' He looked up into her eyes encircled by their arresting frames. They were mocking. 'Where did I go wrong?'

'A stub or two and I might have been led to believe that you were improving, but the simpering virginity of this saucer is too much to swallow. Anyway, the place stinks of smoke. How you made such a great agent I shall never understand. As a penalty for ineptitude you will take me out to dinner tonight.' She paused, then added, 'Somewhere expensive.'

'Will I be allowed to smoke?'

'That depends on how awful this typing is. I wonder when you will pluck up the courage to dictate to me.'

He watched her walk towards the door, wondering how much, if any, of her last sentence referred to shorthand.

'Fiona.'

She turned and regarded him gravely.

'Yes, Nigel?'

'Will you marry me?'

For a moment she continued to look at him, then, 'Not in office hours, Nigel.'

She had spoken lightly and he smiled, not dissatisfied, but the smile faded quickly as some compulsion, perhaps the necessity to confide, perhaps the need to keep her there a little longer, made him say, 'I've had to send for Carr.'

'Herrick?'

'Yes. But he's changed it to Hendrix now, as if that made any difference. Some personal identity thing according to our esteemed Director.'

'Did you expect anything less?'

'Less? Oh, I see. You mean than using Carr, not the change of name.' He shook his head.

Her sigh was a barely detectable exhalation of air. 'You hate it so, don't you, darling? All of it, despite the blasé façade.'

There was no mockery in her eyes now and he thought that

looking into them must be a little like drowning. He didn't reply.

'I'll let you have your ash-tray back,' she said.

When the door closed behind her he began picking away at his uncertainties again. Barry had been very quick to put the finger on Herrick. Why just Herrick? A man with Lippmann's record would be a magnet, or a target, for half the world's intelligence organizations, yet without hesitation Barry . . .

'Stop it!' he ordered and half his mind obeyed.

CHAPTER NINE

Carr walked into Foster's office without knocking, strode to the armchair in the corner and sat down, crossing one leg over the other. His movements were controlled, economical. Once in the chair nothing moved except his eyes.

Foster looked at him, 'Do have a chair, Carr,' he said.

Carr yawned. 'No thanks,' he replied, 'I prefer to stand.'

He rested his head on the chair back and his eyelids drooped, closed.

'Are you tired, Carr?'

'Mmm. Your telephone call released me from the coils of a female python called Melissa. Can't remember when I fell into them. Last Friday I think, or was it Tuesday? I must introduce you to her some time. She's the bedroom decathlon champion of SW1 and I don't rate the chances of the other postal districts very highly when it comes to the finals.'

'Getting old, Carr?'

'That's right, but there's also this business of my IQ. It's 159. Takes it out of you you know. Did you ever try to live with an IQ of 159?' his eyes opened, fixed themselves on Foster and closed again.

'Don't bother to answer that,' he said. 'And stop calling me Carr. I know my name.'

Foster contemplated the recumbent figure in the white canvas slacks and black shirt knotted at the waist with distaste. The meaningless medallion on the bare chest, supported by a silver chain, annoyed him particularly and he wondered when this image had occurred to Carr who normally dressed rather conservatively. Pettishly, he concluded that Carr had adopted it that morning simply to irritate him. Everything about Carr annoyed him. The annoyance, he knew, was born of envy and that knowledge annoyed him the more.

Carr was everything that Foster would have liked to have been; of exceptional physique, highly intelligent, dangerous. He appeared to have no nerves at all and, consequently, no need of the façade Fiona had spoken about behind which Foster spent his life.

Foster narrowed his lips and swallowed, trying to force down hate which had formed like a bubble in his throat.

With total lack of interest Carr said, 'As you don't seem to have called me in for anything specific, tell me about this bird you're shacked up with. One of the ugly sexy type, they tell me. They're often the best.' He opened one eye and closed it again. 'Works for you, doesn't she? I'd like to meet her some time.'

The bubble in Foster's throat expanded, burst and seemed to fill his system with flaring gas. He fought the blaze down. It was essential that they should work together in harmony, now of all times. There must be no mistake over Herrick.

He was surprised and pleased at the levelness of his voice when he said, 'We don't need Herrick any more.'

Carr said, 'Is that right?'

'Yes,' Foster told him, 'that *is* right.'

'Surprise, surprise. Where is he?'

'Hong Kong, using the name Hendrix.'

'Then you can count me out. I'm so well known there that the tri-shaw boys ask me for my autograph. Send Trelawney.'

'Trelawney's on a job.'

'Chandler then.'

'Chandler was killed in Bucharest. Didn't you know?'

'So you'll have to flush him.'

'What?' said Foster.

'Herrick, Hendrix, whatever he's calling himself. You'll have to get the local boys to flush him out of Hong Kong. I can't operate there.'

'You don't sound particularly concerned about Chandler, Carr.'

'I told you you shouldn't use him in Rumania. You need a

different technique there. It's the least predictable of the satellites.'

Foster stared moodily at the man in the armchair, then said, 'I wonder how you would react if you lost a friend. The question is academic, of course. I don't suppose you ever had one.'

'I didn't hear you ask a question. You were wondering and supposing.'

'All right, Carr. Did you ever have a friend?'

'Yes.'

'Like who?'

'Chandler. Now can we get back to Herrick?'

Foster let his breath out slowly. Stiffly, he said, 'You have a remarkable aptitude for putting people in the wrong. I apologize.'

Carr grinned. 'Oh, don't worry,' he said. 'My aptitudes should only concern you professionally. There's no need for you to apologize for my personal idiosyncrasies.'

Anger took hold of Foster again and he had to struggle to remind himself that the tape recording of this conversation was worth any amount of Carr's sarcasm and that, in any event, the tenor of the exchange had been of his own setting. He shook his head angrily in an attempt to clear his brains, which the tautness of his nerves seemed to have scrambled, but even so the conviction remained with him that Carr devoted much of his time to devising means of making him appear foolish. It never occurred to him tnat, except when a job required it, Carr rarely spared him a thought.

For it to have done so, he would have needed to know a great deal more about Carr; to have known that for Carr there were only two categories of people; those to whom he was utterly indifferent such as Foster and Chandler, and those he disliked. The latter group consisted of those he had to kill and if the dislike did not exist naturally, he engendered it. When he did that, a fused bomb inside him armed itself.

Carr was consistent in his private brand of nihilism. In the former category he included himself and there was no inconsistency in his love of attractive women. They were not people. They were music and light and warmth and a wise insanity which, even if he did not understand, he accepted as a natural state. Barry knew, and could have explained it as badly as he had done to Havelock-Templeton, but then Barry was a great deal cleverer than Foster and his perception was not blunted by fear.

Pulling the frayed ends of the dialogue together, Foster said, 'As it happens, you won't be required to go to Hong Kong. Herrick is heading for the States.'

Carr stretched, opened his eyes and stood up. Half-way to the door he said, 'When you've made up your mind where you want me to go, send me a postcard.'

'I want you in New York by tonight, Carr.'

Carr turned and looked at him. 'Thanks for working up to it gradually, Foster. The shock would have been unbearable if you'd told me that a quarter of an hour ago.'

Coldly Foster said, 'What support do you want?'

'One – FBI contacts in New York, an "in" to the CIA wherever I need it and carte blanche to call on them for whatever services I need.'

'Why the CIA?'

Carr said, 'Jesus, you don't suppose he's going to stay in the States do you? He's running a risk going near the place at all. Probably has no choice. Money or something cached away there he has to collect. I imagine he'll make for Mexico or South America. What the hell do you think I want CIA assistance for?'

Foster grunted and Carr went on, 'Two – All points of entry to the States covered as of now and a tail on him when he arrives. Three – His file and my own.'

'You're not serious,' said Foster. 'About the files, I mean.'

Carr walked over to the desk and rested his fists on it.

'Pull yourself together, Foster,' he said. 'I'm not going to gun Herrick down on the Staten Island ferry. I've got to get close to the man, preferably at some place a long way from anywhere. To do that I've got to make him think he'a got some hold over me, like possession of my file. I'll probably give him his own too, so he doesn't feel threatened, but I'll decide that when the time comes. He must be given no reason to suppose that I'm other than genuinely on the run like him.'

'I'll have to ask the Director.'

'Then ask him.'

'It's unheard of, you know, Carr.'

'What is? Asking Barry something?'

'No,' Foster said with heavy patience. 'It's against all the precepts of intelligence to allow an agent access to his own personal security file.'

Mimicking Foster's tone, 'I am not interested in security files,' Carr told him. 'Herrick is not interested in security files. The reason that neither Herrick nor I is interested in security files, Foster, is that neither we nor anyone else outside the Department gives a solitary goddam how our security classification is arrived at. What I'm asking you for are the master files with all the "action man" crap in them so that good old Herrick has something to incriminate me with. If they're too bulky, extract the mission summaries and let me have them. If they contain material still of interest to the senior opposition, change it around enough to confuse them. You can give your imagination an airing on that, but do be careful with Herrick's, won't you? He might remember what he actually did.'

For a moment he stared down at Foster's angry face before adding in his normal voice, 'Just stop quoting maxims at me. If you want me on a plane today you'd better get your skates on.'

Woodenly, Foster asked, 'Don't you even want to know why you're being given this assignment? What the Herrick set-up is?'

Carr glanced back at him from the door.

'What's it to me?' he said.

Barry switched off the tape recorder, sat quietly for a time gazing in front of him, then looked up at Foster.

'It's highly irregular, but do as he says.'

'Very well.'

Fingering his beard Barry said, 'I hope the degree of antagonism between you and Carr indicated by that little exchange doesn't exist between you and any other member of the staff.'

'It doesn't,' said Foster. 'As I told you, I just don't like Carr. He's a smart-arsed bastard.'

'Yes,' Barry agreed. 'He's all of that.'

Foster took the two files Barry had given him back to his office and began to work on them. He made handwritten amendments to fourteen pages of Carr's file and two of Herrick's then took the results to Barry's secretary for reproduction in the original type. Sitting in a chair near her desk he watched the small white-haired figure as, uncomplainingly, she changed the ribbon five times before she achieved a matching depth of colour which satisfied her for the first of the sixteen pages. After that, he left her to it.

At lunchtime he found that his nerves were jumping again. He drank too much, ate nothing and was still a long way from sober when Fiona made cocktails for them both before they left to dine at Claridges.

CHAPTER TEN

Fiona Langley put her bag on the desk and hung her light summer coat in the small alcove where the xerox and teleprinter machines stood. The clock on the wall told her it was 9.07 and the mirror that she was looking severely pretty with her big glasses and her dark brown hair drawn back into a soft knot at the nape of her neck. Businesslike but decorative she thought, with only her mouth preventing her from being lovely. She hated her mouth. Closed it was passable, although set in a permanent pout, but open the lips stood away from the teeth as if in grotesque preparation for kissing. Men didn't seem to mind, but she felt that it made her look moronic. She closed her lips firmly over even but slightly discoloured teeth and walked along to Foster's room.

She emptied and cleaned his ash-tray, then began to dust the desk, humming quietly to herself. No cleaning women were admitted to this part of the building.

Somebody tapped softly on the door. She called, 'Come in' without looking round or stopping what she was doing and heard the door open and close again. When she looked up, Colonel Barry and a man she didn't know were standing near the door watching her.

She said, 'Good morning, sir. Mr Foster hasn't arrived yet.'

Barry nodded abruptly. 'I know,' he said.

Fiona looked at him questioningly and as the silence stretched one of her eyebrows rose as though in encouragement, but ten seconds or so went by before he spoke again.

'Miss Langley,' he cleared his throat. 'Miss Langley, I'm afraid I have some very bad news. Mr Foster is dead.'

Fiona's chin seemed to retract and her teeth closed on her

lower lip. She stared at him, eyes wide, and his own dropped momentarily in embarrassment, then lifted to meet hers again.

A smear of blood appeared on her front teeth and a tiny rivulet ran over her lower lip and on to her chin. She tasted it and put the duster to her mouth.

Barry said, 'Here. Steady now,' and stepped towards her holding out the handkerchief from his breast pocket. She stared at it blankly, not moving.

'I'm terribly sorry, Fiona,.' Barry said.

With a slash of her hand so sudden and so violent that he dropped the handkerchief, she knocked his extended arm aside.

Her voice a grating whisper she said, 'Get out of here, you whiskery old bastard. Get to hell and damnation out of here!' Then she ran past the two men, yanked the door open and slammed it behind her.

Colonel Barry sighed, picked up his handkerchief and looked at the other man. They raised their eyebrows at each other.

'I'm afraid I didn't handle that very well,' Barry said.

'Not your fault,' the man told him and they left the room, treading softly as though Foster's body was lying in state in it. Neither spoke as they walked along the corridor to Barry's office. A third man got to his feet when they went in.

'How did she take it, sir?' he asked.

Barry sank into the chair behind his desk.

'Not very well, I'm afraid, Superintendent.' He was conscious of having said 'I'm afraid' three times in three minutes and felt mildly irritated about it. 'Now I know what it must have been like to be the bearer of ill tidings to some old-time monarch. The poor kid would have happily had me strangled. Don't you agree, Sergeant?'

'I do, sir.'

'She was pretty gone on him then, was she, sir?' the superintendent asked.

'Oh, yes. Very. They were having an affaire.'

'Is that sort of thing tolerated in an organization of this kind, sir?'

Barry said, 'What? Good God, man, yes. We would rather have our senior people sleeping with their confidential secretaries than with their wives. The secretaries have high security clearance.'

The superintendent said, 'I hadn't thought of that,' and the sergeant smiled as though he had.

'I think,' Barry went on, 'we had better give the young lady time to calm down before you two gentlemen . . .' He stopped talking as a buzzer sounded and flicked down a switch on his desk speaker.

'Barry.'

The voice from the speaker was clipped, brittle but controlled.

'This is Fiona Langley, sir. That was indefensible behaviour on my part. I should like to apologize most sincerely and I will, of course, tender my resignation to you formally this morning.'

Barry glanced from one to the other of the two men, then back at the desk speaker.

'No you won't, Fiona, and I won't consider any apology to be called for under the circumstances.' He paused, then asked, 'Look, how are you feeling?'

The box on the desk was silent.

'Fiona?'

'I'm all right, sir,' the box said quietly.

'Could you face talking to a couple of police officers? They're with me now.'

The box emitted a small choking sound and Barry asked, 'Would you like me to send out for some brandy first?'

'No thank you, sir. I'll come right away.'

'Good girl,' said Barry.

She arrived almost at once and Barry said, 'Superintendent Spence, Sergeant Kepple, Miss Langley. You saw Sergeant Kepple with me – er – earlier on. Sit down, Fiona. These gentlemen are making enquiries into this tragic business. Unpleasant as it may be for you, they have to ask you some questions. Do the best you can. If they touch on anything of a confidential nature affecting this organization I shall tell you not to answer. Okay?'

'I understand, sir.'

'Right. Fire away, Superintendent.'

Spence said, 'Miss Langley, we'll keep this as short as possible. You knew Mr Foster well, I believe.'

Fiona was sitting with closed eyes, her hands lying on her lap.

'Intimately,' she said.

'Do I take it from that that there was some emotional attachment between you?'

She opened her eyes and looked at the policeman 'I have already said that I knew Mr Foster intimately.'

'In other words you were his mistress.'

Colonel Barry grunted in irritation. 'Is this really necessary, Superintendent? Miss Langley has given you her answer and I see no reason for causing her further pain by crossing t's and dotting i's.'

'I'm sorry sir and Miss Langley, but I have reason to believe that Miss Langley may have been the last person to see Mr Foster alive. She is, for example, known to have dined with him at Claridges last night. He had the bill in his pocket.'

Fiona Langley turned her regard from the superintendent to the Colonel. 'It's all right, sir,' she said. 'Then I went to his flat with him. They'll have found out from the doorman who got us our taxi. It doesn't matter any more. You see, I killed him.'

Barry jerked forward across the desk as though he had been struck in the stomach, his 'You did what? Do you realize what you are saying, girl?' a counterpoint to Spence's 'Miss Langley, it is my duty to warn you that anything . . .', but she ignored them, speaking as they spoke, over-riding the official caution.

'I killed him,' she said in a drearily hopeless tone, 'as surely as if I had shot him myself.'

Sharply the superintendent said, 'What gives you the idea that shooting was involved?'

'I just assumed it was. It's the way officers usually commit suicide. Nigel Foster was an ex-Captain of Royal Artillery.'

Sergeant Kepple spoke to her for the first time. 'And who, Miss Langley, said anything about suicide?'

She closed her eyes again and her head sank forward. In little more than a whisper she said, 'If it had been an accident or illness you wouldn't be here asking me questions. It isn't beyond the bounds of possibility that somebody killed him, I suppose, considering . . ' She stopped talking and looked quickly up at Barry, her expression mortified.

'It's all right,' he said. 'Everybody knows that much.'

She nodded vaguely and let her head droop again. 'But it's much more likely that he . . . that he . . .' The soft voice faded and the three men waited quietly.

Quite suddenly and much more loudly she said, 'May I change my mind about that brandy, sir?' She didn't raise her head and her eyes stayed closed.

Barry depressed a switch on his speaker, gave an order, then sat back fiddling with his pipe. No one else moved.

When the brandy came, Fiona gulped half of it down, choked, swallowed the rest, choked again and handed the glass to a concerned-looking clerk. As the door closed behind him she began to speak again as though there had been no interruption.

'It's much more likely that he killed himself. He proposed to me during dinner and . . .'

She hesitated and Spence said, 'You turned him down.' He might not have spoken.

'I asked him what was the matter with our present arrangement. It didn't seem to be such an awful thing to say and I really wanted to know, but it upset him and when we got back to his flat we had rather a lot to drink and there was an awful quarrel and I told him I was going to leave him.

'We almost made it up after that and had some more to drink and then he started asking me to marry him as though the subject hadn't been mentioned before and I said why and he got angry and I got angry and he said he would kill himself if I didn't and I told him not to talk like a fool and he said I will you know and I said . . .'

It was the sergeant who said, 'Take it easy, Miss Langley.'

She raised her head and looked at him gratefully, nodded and went on, 'I said the most terrible thing. People always say it and I said it.' Her words began to come singly or in pairs with an upward inflection before the pause. 'I said . . . that . . . people who . . . threaten to . . . commit suicide . . . never . . . do and . . . then . . . I went home.' She didn't cry, but her eyes were stretched wide, the moisture in them making the pupils indistinguishable from the dark brown irises.

Barry sighed softly and said, 'All right, Fiona. I don't think Superintendent Spence needs you any longer. Is that correct, Superintendent?'

'It is, sir. We needn't detain you further, Miss Langley. Thank you for your help. I'm sure I'm speaking for the three of us when I say that you have all our sympathy.'

Fiona said, 'Thank you,' walked to the door and turned to look at the Colonel.

'How . . . How . . . ?'

'Gas.'

A small, perplexed frown touched her forehead.

'I . . . I thought North Sea gas wasn't poisonous.'

'It's no asset to a life-support system, Fiona. Not with your head in an oven and an overdose of barbiturates in your stomach.'

She looked at him expressionlessly for a long time, then the tears came silently and she went out.

Spence said, 'You're going to have to watch her, sir. She's been hard hit.'

'I know,' said Barry.

Fiona Langley began to cry in earnest two hours later and no one could stop her. She was taken to her flat and the woman staff member who had offered to stay with her reported by telephone the next morning that the crying had gone on virtually without a break throughout the night. She recommemded hospital and sedation.

'Arrange it,' Barry told her. 'I can't have this place thrown into turmoil by a bawling woman.' His voice was harsh and she wondered what had become of the concerned, avuncular man of the day before.

CHAPTER ELEVEN

'Lexington and 58th, bridge route,' Carr said and slammed the door of the cab. He sedulously avoided the use of the word 'please' in New York when talking to cab drivers and shop assistants. It seemed to embarrass them.

'Lex and 58th it is, mister.'

Carr liked the Triboro Bridge route from Kennedy Airport. However often he took it, he never tired of the view of Manhattan it gave. Even the dull slab of the United Nations building looked dramatic against the back-drop of pinnacles, pinnacles which turned grey-pink in colour when the light was right. He liked it best then. It gave the city an air of mystical, almost spiritual, delicacy and that, he thought, was very funny. It was dark now, but he liked the lights almost as well.

'I like a guy who knows what he wants without me asking. You know that? Tells you something about him. Me, I'm interested in people. You know that? Take you, for example.

"Bridge route" you say. Right out. Not "how's the traffic?", or "take your pick", or like them out-of-towners with their "whatya mean, which route?" Tell an out-of-towner anywhere. You know that? Picked up a guy on Madison at 72nd yesterday . . .'

Carr settled himself comfortably and began to think about Herrick, wondering what he would do when he landed at Kennedy in the morning, always assuming that he didn't leave the North West Orient flight on the west coast. Not that it mattered if he did. The FBI would know and pass the information on. Barry had seen to all that. The same thing applied at Kennedy.

'. . . stopped at this Howard Johnson's and he says to come on in and grab a coffee with him and I tell him I have coffee right here in this flask and the meter is still ticking. The hell with that he says and . . .'

Carr decided that the best place to make initial contact with Herrick would be in the air. That would provide him with a captive audience and the time to put his deal across. What that deal would be depended entirely on whatever it was that Herrick planned to do or, more accurately, where he planned to do it, because his trade limited his choice of occupation.

'. . . just walked right in and told her that she wants to pull an act like that she gets to pull it all on her own because it's goodbye sweetheart and how did she dig that? She says she digs it just fine. You know that? Just fine she says, so I . . .'

It went without saying that Herrick would know that the longer he stayed in the States the greater his chances of being recognized. He would know too that Barry would have spread his net, hope that it had been spread in the wrong direction centred on Hong Kong, but not bank on it for long. What he could not know was that his course had been followed stage by stage and each leg of it reported to London. Had he done so, he would have attempted to go to ground before this.

'I tell you, mister, any high school football team could take them. You know that? Like I said to Ed, that's Ed Schenk my buddy I was telling you about, Ed I said, if those bums could . . .'

The glittering towers of Manhattan were in sight now and Carr watched their changing aspect pleasurably as the cab snaked its way through the heavy traffic towards the bridge, conscious that their magic would vanish like a dream as soon as he was amongst them. On the East River Drive he put Herrick out of his mind. He would be told as soon as he passed through Immigration and take it from there. Too many quantities were unknown to enable him to plan ahead. The only certainty was that Herrick was safe from him within the borders of the United States. With nothing left to think about he watched the street numbers idly until the cab made a right turn away from the river. A few minutes later the driver's monologue ended with a question.

'Which corner, mister?'

'Uptown.'

He got out of the cab, placed his suitcase on the sidewalk and handed dollar bills in through the window.

'Thanks, mister. Been a pleasure talking with you.'

Carr walked away in the opposite direction to his hotel until the cab was lost to sight. Then he retraced his steps. There was no particular reason for doing so. It was just habit. The hotel was small, little more than a boarding house with a grill-room and bar. It had external fire escapes. Carr stayed in similar hotels whenever he could. That was just habit too.

He stopped in the doorway of his room, watching the bell hop place his suitcase on the stand and fuss with the venetian blind, then he moved into the room, took off his coat and threw it on to the bed. The bell hop picked it up again and hung it on a hanger in the closet.

Carr gave him some coins and nodded his acknowledgement of the man's thanks. When the door closed he undressed, strewing the clothes haphazardly around the room, grinning at the thought of the bell hop's reaction. He showered quickly, located the ice-making machine set into the bathroom wall and scooped short cylinders of ice into a tumbler. The machine hummed, clicked once and rattled a cascade of ice over the small depression he had made in the ready-use tray.

Water dripping from his body, Carr carried the glass back into the bedroom, stood it on the television set at the foot of the bed and took a bottle of whisky from his suitcase. He filled the glass to the brim and wandered aimlessly around the room, sipping slowly at his drink.

There was a radio beside the bed. Carr walked across to it and switched it on. It told him the brand of beer he should be drinking, then started to play a number which made him wince.

He turned it off again and his eye was caught by a printed card scotch-taped to the top of the receiver. The tape was dry and cracked and the card looked old. It read 'CONELRAD – Two triangular Civil Defense insignia are marked on the dial at 640 kc and 1240 kc for the Federal Civil Defense Administration CONELRAD plan. If a national emergency should arise, all broadcasting stations may interrupt their programming and advise listeners to tune to either one of these two frequencies for emergency information and instruction.' He thought that was rather funny, picked up the telephone, asked who Conelrad was, told a puzzled voice to forget it and hung up.

For three minutes he played with the television set, tuning in to five different stations, paying no attention to the programmes, then clicked the switch to 'off'. His drink was finished, the glass still full of ice. He took it into the bathroom and the ice clattered into the hand basin. He filled the glass again from the machine thinking that its industry merited recognition.

With a fresh drink in his hand and dressed in his pyjamas he picked up the Gideon Bible lying beside the telephone. As he had expected there was a list of call-girl numbers inside the front cover. He put his drink down, found his pen and wrote 'Alice', 'Loraine', 'The Twins', one beneath the other at the end of the list and added telephone numbers. For a few seconds he admired his handiwork, wondering whose the numbers were, then put the book back where he had found it. He was, he knew, behaving eccentrically, childishly. The signs were familiar to him. He was keyed up, not nervous, he was never nervous, just keyed up waiting for the word go. His watch told him that it was only fifteen hours since he had walked into Foster's office. He had come a long way since then. Probably he was tired. Pouring his untouched drink into the hand basin he decided to spend what was left of the night in bed.

The telephone bell woke him at 6.19 and a voice told him that Hendrix had stayed on the North West Orient flight and would land at Kennedy in about four hours. Carr thanked the voice and went back to sleep.

At 10.45 the same voice said, 'He's booked in at the Americana. Room two two four five.'

'He would,' said Carr.

'You say something?'

'I said "that's good".'

'Oh. Want us to do anything?'

'No thanks. Just watch and report.'

'Okay,' said the voice.

Carr spent the day in his room, waiting patiently, the restlessness of the night before gone. Room service brought him his meals. After one more try at the television he wheeled it away from the foot of the bed and stood it with its screen to the wall. Nothing happened until five minutes to ten the following morning.

'Mr Carr?'

'Yes.'

'I'm afraid we've lost your boy.'

'The hell you have!'

'I'm sorry, Mr Carr. The word's gone out nationwide.'

'These things happen. Look, I'd like to come and see you.'

'Come right on over, Mr Carr. FBI Headquarters, Two hundred and one East Sixty-nine. Ask for Kendall.'

'On my way,' said Carr.

Kendall was about six foot six and looked like Anthony Quinn playing Anthony Quinn. He towered over Carr.

'I'm sorry about this, Mr Carr.'

'You didn't do it on purpose. How did he manage it?'

'Slugged a bell hop. Big guy. Walked out of the hotel wearing the man's uniform over his own clothes and carrying his own baggage. The doorman remembers seeing him load it into a cab, but thought nothing of it. No reason why he should. There are dozens of bell hops and this one wasn't doing anything unusual. The only reason he remembers it at all was that the bell hop went off in the cab. That's less usual, but not all that uncommon. Guests occasionally ask to have their baggage delivered someplace.'

'I see,' Carr said. 'Now there is only one reason for him to do a thing like that, isn't there?'

'I know it and I'm angry about it,' Kendall told him. 'He must've known he was under observation. I'll murder those guys when they come in.'

'I wouldn't be too hard on them. Herrick, Hendrix, whoever, is a professional.'

'What in hell do you think my boys are supposed to be, Mr Carr?'

Carr sighed. 'It's a matter of degree,' he said, 'and I wish you would stop calling me Mr Carr. The name's John.'

'Glad to know you, John. So's mine.'

They smiled at each other without friendliness.

'Look,' Carr said, 'Hendrix was trained in a very tough school indeed. He . . . oh, forget it.'

'Sure. Let's forget it. You were beginning to sound like those CIA heroes. They have the same line in their anthem. I sometimes ask myself what they think we do.'

Carr decided that it had been a mistake to try to protect Kendall's men from a dressing down by furnishing Herrick with attributes he did not possess and wondered why he had bothered. Concluding wryly that it was irritation at Kendall's vast size he walked past him and sat down on a straight-backed swivel chair.

'You don't mind, do you?' he said. 'I'm getting a crick in the neck talking to you.'

Some of the rigidity left the big man's shoulders and his face creased into a cross between a smile and a scowl. 'Lousing up this surveillance job made me forget my manners,' he told Carr, then asked, 'Who's this Hendrix working for anyway?'

'I don't know, but I'll tell you that at one stage we thought he was working for us.'

Kendall nodded, moved slowly round a grey metal desk and lowered himself into his own chair.

'And you aim to discourage him from taking up with anyone else.'

'I couldn't have put it better myself,' Carr said.

'Yeah? Well don't try pulling anything in the States, John. We wouldn't like that. We wouldn't like that at all.'

'You won't have to read me my rights,' Carr told him. 'Now, if it's okay with you, could we start looking for him?'

'Like I told you on the 'phone, we already are.'

'Yes, but I'd like to know when he's leaving the country, not when he's left it.'

Carr swivelled his chair towards the windows and stared at one of them unseeingly, his back to Kendall. He was silent for a long time and when he spoke it was as though he was talking to himself.

'I have just rendered an hotel employee unconscious for the purpose of purloining his uniform.'

'That makes two in one morning,' Kendall said. 'Maybe it's the latest thing with you Britishers.'

Carr ignored him. 'Rightly or wrongly I assume that these cases of assault, theft and leaving the hotel without reimbursing it for its hospitality do not add up to a Federal offence, but I am, nevertheless, desirous of placing myself beyond the reach of "New York's Finest". What do I do?' He swung his chair back to face the desk.

'You might start with giving the funny talk a rest, then you could win yourself a little time by heading for New Jersey or Connecticut. They're right next door.'

'There's a shuttle between La Guardia and Washington, isn't there?' Carr asked.

'Sure is. What about it?'

'I think that's where he's gone. It seems to me like the quickest method of getting a long way out of town.'

Kendall shook his head. 'Doesn't figure to me,' he said. 'There's a shuttle to Boston too. There are planes to all over. What's so special about Washington?'

'He's probably making for Central or South America and he'll be in a hurry now that he knows someone is watching him, plus that "Americana" thing. Washington is south, so let's assume that he shuttled there and will take the first available scheduled flight to – to where? Miami?'

'Could be. Could be LA, Houston, Phoenix. You name it. For all I know they could have a direct flight from Washington DC to Montevideo. So who cares? If your hunch is right, Washington is the key. Let's try turning it.'

The telephone rang four times during the hour after Kendall had spoken to Washington, but only at the fourth did his eyes flick round to meet Carr's.

'Right,' he said. 'Keep at it.' Then to Carr, 'Negative. Let's go eat. They'll transfer the call to the restaurant if anything comes through.'

No call reached them during the meal and they returned to Kendall's office, Carr suggesting without any particular conviction that it might be more convenient if he were to go back to his hotel.

'I really should get out of your hair now,' he said.

'It's not my hair I'm concerned about,' Kendall replied. 'I just want you and your friend the hell and gone out of the US as soon as possible. No offence intended.'

Carr's stomach was acid with too much coffee and his mouth

dry from too many cigarettes by the time Washington called with an affirmative on Hendrix. It was 8.17 p.m. and a messenger had only then brought them sandwiches and more coffee.

'Aren't you the clever boy,' Kendall said. 'He's booked himself through to Bogota – that's Colombia, South America – changing planes at Miami. The flight he gets there is Braniff originating from Kennedy tomorrow morning. You want to be on that?'

'Yes please.'

'Okay. I'll fix it in case you have trouble getting a seat. You can pay when you check in.'

'Two seats side by side in the back row.'

Kendall looked at him, frowning questioningly and Carr added, 'Don't get excited. I shan't start anything. I won't even hijack the blasted plane. All I want to do is make a deal with him and an aircraft is about the only thing he can't leave before he's heard me out. If all the seats are occupied we'd have to lock ourselves in the can together and that might cause comment.'

'You'd just better be levelling with me about this,' Kendall said and reached for the telephone.

Carr spent what was left of the evening in a bar, drinking sparingly and studying a Texaco map of Colombia and the street plans of its major cities. A man sitting next to him noticed the map and engaged him in conversation. Carr gathered that it was a great country, an opinion based almost exclusively on the beauty of its national airline hostesses.

Kendall himself picked him up at his hotel the next morning, drove him to Kennedy Airport and walked to the plane with him. They stopped at the foot of the aircraft steps and Carr told him that he was very grateful for all the help he had been given.

The big American looked down at him, said, 'Sure, sure,' paused, then went on, 'Do me a favour, will you, John?'

Carr raised his eyebrows and held them like that until Kendall spoke again.

'I'm a professional too, friend. I know your type like I know my own wife.'

'Congratulations. And the favour?'

'Don't come back here,' Kendall said, turned and walked away without offering to shake hands.

CHAPTER TWELVE

Barry finished reading aloud from the letter he was holding and put it down in front of him. It was signed by a retired Vice-Admiral, a full General still nominally on the active list and the Oxford don who had been Barry's predecessor. Underneath the signatures were the words. 'I agree' and the Minister's initials.

'Well, what do you say?' Barry asked.

'I say you've gone and turned over two pages or something, boss,' Rafferty told him. 'You know, like "Moses was sick . . . and the lot fell on Aaron".'

'I found that particular chestnut in doubtful taste when I first heard it at school,' Barry replied, 'and it hasn't improved with age. But let that pass. The *lot*, as it happens, has fallen on you. With Foster dead the Minister agrees that you are the most suitable person to take over as my Number Two here.'

He looked questioningly at the tall figure jack-knifed in its favourite position on the window-sill, hands clasping its knees. Rafferty had been his senior field operative for years now but, with his lanky frame and narrow shoulders, he still looked to Barry like an undergraduate who had outgrown his strength. Even the grey in the hair seemed as premature as it had once been and did little or nothing to dispel the illusion of irreverent immaturity which Rafferty wore like a cloak. There were many, Barry knew, who had died because of their failure to recognize the illusion for what it was; the last of them, on the north coast of France, only a few weeks earlier.

'Then the Minister must have perforated his Portfolio,' Rafferty said. 'I've warned you before about listening to party political broadcasts.' Then at the sound of Barry's irritated grunt he added, 'I'm not being much help, am I?'

'No, you're not.'

'I'm flattered, boss, really I am, but the job's not for me.'

'You realize that the post is a stepping-stone to this chair, don't you?'

Rafferty didn't bother to answer and Barry grunted again and said, 'I'd like to hear any recommendations you care to make.'

'We're quite sure that Chandler's dead, are we?'

'Positive,' Barry said.

'Then I'd opt for Trelawney.'

'Would you really? Would you take orders from him? He's only a Grade IV you know.'

'Hell,' Rafferty said. 'I hadn't thought of that.' For a moment he chewed his lip, scowling in concentration, then his expression cleared.

'Martha.'

From the adjoining room Martha said, 'Yes, Mr Rafferty?'

'Write this down, would you? "To Head of Personnel. Trelawney promoted to grade V with immediate effect." Sign the boss's name on it for him. You've been doing that for years and I'm the only one who can tell the difference. He's not feeling strong enough to . . .'

'Rafferty!'

'Boss?'

'Would it be too much to ask you to treat this matter seriously and to answer my questions?'

'I thought I just had,' Rafferty said.

Barry nodded his head slowly, pensively, before asking, 'Is it simply that you don't want the job, or do you think him the better man?'

'Both.' Rafferty swung his legs off the window-sill and stood leaning back against it. 'It isn't my kind of job and I've still got a year or so left in me to do what I've always done. Better man? Well, I could still kick the shoulder-blades off the big ape, but that's my speciality and it isn't exactly a prime requisite for the task we're talking about. Yes, he's the better of the two of us for what you want.' He levered himself away from the window, turned slowly and stared out of it. Barry waited, saying nothing. Half a minute later Rafferty turned towards him again.

'He's come a long way since you took him on, boss. Remember that nerve-gas thing back in the sixties? Real tearaway, wasn't he? That pouring paint over the face routine of his to persuade somebody to talk and bashing people about. I thought he'd revived some old naval traditions like if it's stationary paint it, if it moves hit it. You told me yourself you felt as though you'd wound up an alarm clock and couldn't stop it ringing.'

'Yes,' Barry said.

'Well, it's different now. He's a quietly forceful character with a first-class analytical brain. I imagine that that witch he lives with has had a lot to do with it.'

His voice gloomy, 'Yes,' Barry said again.

Rafferty looked at him hard before saying, 'It's an odd thing, boss, I usually enjoy listening to myself, but today's different. If you could feed me some line other than "yes" I might get my enthusiasm back. Audience reaction means a great deal to me.'

Barry said, 'Mmm,' paused, then went on, 'I'm obliged to you, Rafferty. I don't accept your view that Trelawney has any particular qualities that you lack, but he was to have been my nominee if you turned the offer down, as I thought you would. At least it's encouraging to me that you and I think along the same lines.'

'He was to have been? Are you telling me that *they* won't accept him?'

'I am. Too little known about him for him to carry weight outside the Department in my absence and too little experience. When I asked them how, if so little was known about him, they were in any position to pronounce on his experience I got the pained look treatment.'

'Any use taking it up with the PM, boss?'

Barry shook his head. 'No. They're right in a way, you see. I should have brought him in on some of those inter-organizational gatherings and let him carry my bag at liaison committees as I did in your case. I'll do that in future. His chance will come, but that doesn't help us now. Anyone else in mind?'

'Not in this shop.'

'Anywhere.'

Rafferty was silent for nearly a minute before he said, 'There's a chap with a fancy handle in charge of administration in Parminter's outfit I've always been rather impressed by. Name of Havelock-Templeton. He . . .'

As though the thought had not already occurred to him, Barry raised his eyebrows. 'Julian, eh? Now that's not a bad idea at all. You have your moments, Rafferty, but I wonder how I can entice him away from Parminter.'

'Show him a photograph of Jane Trask, boss. He'll come running.'

'You have your off moments too,' Barry said. 'I do not share your ability to deprive Trelawney of his shoulder-blades and that could prove a disadvantage to me if he discovered I had placed his wife on the transfer list.'

'His *wife*?'

The fingers of Barry's right hand began probing in his beard as though he had lodged something there and forgotten the precise place. He removed them and glowered at the tips as though disappointed that they held nothing.

'Yes,' he said, 'they were married about two years ago.'

He continued to stare at his fingers while he listened to Rafferty saying, 'Somebody's bent the bloody rules. Either that or I missed the amendment to the one which says marriages between field operatives, or between field operatives and members of the executive staff, will not be permitted without the resignation of one or other of the parties concerned.'

Barry looked up at Rafferty then and spoke slowly, measuring his words.

'When two people decide to live together, a state of affairs I am powerless to prevent, and continue to do so for a number of years, it doesn't seem to make much difference, except to them, if they want to make it official. Even I accept the fact that times have changed, Rafferty. That particular regulation doesn't mean anything nowadays. I doubt if it really ever did. An emotional entanglement is an emotional entanglement and always has been. You can't legislate against it.' He paused, then added, 'Trelawney wanted you to be his best man.'

'But you legislated against that.'

Keeping his face solemn, Barry said, 'Naturally. We have a rule stating that marriages between field operatives, or field operatives and members of the executive staff, will not be permitted without the resignation of one or other of the parties concerned. I didn't want to make you an accessory before the fact.'

'Very thoughtful of you, boss. I doubt if I could have lived with my conscience. I suppose you stood in for me.'

'Certainly not. I'm far too old to go through all that agonizing business of matching a nervous bridegroom drink for drink throughout the night before his wedding. I gave the bride away. Now let's change the subject. I . . .'

'Let's not,' Rafferty broke in. 'Let's stay with it a bit longer. He ignored Barry's quick frown and went on, 'You've sat on this bit of information for two years. Why tell me now?'

'Because they would rather you heard it from me than read about it in their files.'

Rafferty grinned, shook his head and said, 'Oh, no you don't, boss. I'm on to you. It could be weeks, possibly months, before you get anybody permanent sitting in Foster's room. If it's Havelock-Templeton, he can't just walk out on Parminter without a hand-over period. You want me to fill in, don't you? I'm sorry, but I don't buy it. One sight of a blue star file or above and you'll never let me operate outside the country again.'

The soft rattle of Martha's typewriter came to them through the open door of her room. For a long minute neither man spoke, then Barry said, 'Apart from a number of other places, Peter Clayton went into Russia four times while he was my Deputy.'

'Yes, but I'm not Clayton. If he'd run into trouble he'd have bitten into that trick denture of his. Exit Clayton. Fortunately I don't have a denture and before you suggest that I could have some toxic substance introduced into my upper left canine I'd better tell you that I've torn up the last five of my dentist's half-yearly reminders that I'm overdue for a check-up. Just the sight of his notepaper makes me come all over funny.'

Barry smiled tiredly and said, 'All right. I didn't want to tell you any of this yet, but you had better know that . . .'

'Just a moment, Colonel.'

Both their heads turned towards Martha's room and Barry asked, 'What is it, my dear?'

'I have something here which I think will meet the case.'

The typewriter rattled for a few seconds longer, then they heard the paper removed from the machine and Martha appeared in the doorway. She hobbled towards the window, held out a typed sheet to Rafferty and said, 'This is a list of the files it is essential that you read immediately in the event of the Colonel's death. Short of that, there's no need for you to be aware of their contents.'

The shake of Barry's head was emphatic. 'Not good enough. It'd take him days to read that lot.'

Martha's chin went up and there was a look of proprietary primness on her face. 'Mr Rafferty can absorb this amount of information in about ten hours, Colonel. I've known him to do it on a number of occasions.'

Barry made a non-committal sound and Rafferty said,

'Flattery will get you everywhere.' He took the paper, folded it and put it in his pocket without looking at it again before adding, 'Provided you conduct the boss to and from work, Martha. There's a filter system at the traffic lights just along the road. It's only been there for six or seven years and he hasn't figured it out yet. I don't want anything to happen to him before he gets his staff problem settled.'

Alone again with Martha Barry asked, 'How's his stomach wound?'

'Agony he says, Colonel. He told me he's going to sue the French Government for letting an ear, nose and throat specialist operate on him, so he's obviously perfectly all right.'

Barry nodded. 'Interesting his picking Trelawney and Julian H-T. Gratifying too. There'll be no axe grinding there.'

Back in his own room Rafferty stared thoughtfully at the paper Martha had given him. It was covered in a meaningless sequence of letters and symbols as though a touch-typist had started on a key to the right or left of the correct one and never looked down. Only the top line made sense. It read 'Please Please – Please'.

He tore the page into small pieces and dropped them into the waste-basket.

CHAPTER THIRTEEN

'There will be a forty-five-minute stop-over for refuelling at Miami,' one of the hostesses said over the public address system. Passengers continuing on to Bogota were requested to leave the plane for that time and take their hand baggage with them. She said it again in Spanish.

'Damnation,' Carr said quietly and unfastened his seat belt. The action triggered off a series of similar clicks around the cabin and the hostess's voice said, 'Please keep your safety belts fastened and remain in your seats until the plane has come to a complete stop.' He let his belt hang where it was, waiting for her to say that again in Spanish too. She did not and he pictured her watching an electronic scan which identified all the culprits as Anglo-American.

Outside the window beside him the sprawl of the terminal

buildings seemed to slide forward as though overtaking the aircraft when the pilot turned in towards them and Carr wondered where Herrick would have concealed himself so that he could watch the passengers disembark without being seen himself. Even Herrick of the brilliant hands but far from brilliant mind would have thought of that. Probably Herrick had himself covered too. It didn't matter. He had known from the beginning that he was bound to be spotted here whether the plane docked at an extendible loading bridge, or stopped on the apron. It was the forty-five minutes that had annoyed him. Forty-five minutes almost certainly meant sixty and that was twice the time he had reckoned on, time and enough to spare for someone to try to get in his way.

It was the apron they stopped on and light and heat struck at him fiercely as he moved out on to the platform of the aircraft steps. He put on sun-glasses as he went down them and surveyed the visitors' gallery carefully. He would be expected to do that. Just as carefully he checked all other potential points of observation while he walked, near the back of the group of passengers, towards the terminal. There was no sign of Herrick.

Inside the building he quickened his pace, striding towards a bar with glass doors at both ends. He went in, ordered a martini on the rocks, paid and took the drink to a table. Nobody came in and outside, through the glass, was only a drifting crowd of people, the same crowd, apart from its determinedly festive clothes, that migrated through any airport in the western hemisphere. Two minutes after entering it he left the bar through the door he had come in by, his drink untouched. He moved fast, but without hurrying, changing levels often and three times following the long walk-ways to different boarding gates before retracing his steps. At the end of ten minutes he knew only that if anyone was following him it wasn't Herrick, but then he hadn't expected Herrick to try to do that anyway. One more walk-way, he decided, then he'd try something else. He joined the queue at Gate 19, then returned to the main concourse. Nobody? Possibly, but he very much doubted it.

The washroom Carr turned into was empty, the cubicle doors open. He went into one, bolted the door and sat on the pedestal. The public address system talked to him quietly about flights departing for Denver, Panama and Oklahoma City.

He heard the main door open and swing shut again. Footsteps. So what?

' .   for New York and Boston now boarding at Gate Twenty-three,' the address system said.

'Is there a Mr Carr in here, please? A Mr John Carr?'

The voice was four feet away and Latin-American. Not Herrick. Definitely not Herrick.

'Yes,' Carr said. 'What do you want?'

'Western Union, sir. I have a cable for you.'

Carr smiled. 'Push it under the door.'

A pause, then, 'I can't do that, sir. I have to have your signature.'

'Oh, very well. Wait a minute.'

Carr made rustling noises with paper, climbed silently on to the seat and depressed the cistern lever with his heel. As the water gushed he grasped the tops of the partitions on either side of him and swung himself up. Crouching, he looked down at the man pointing a silenced gun at the door of the cubicle. He smiled again and dropped.

Face down on the tiled floor the man thrashed and squirmed like a speared fish under Carr's weight.

'When did Western Union start chasing people around lavatories instead of broadcasting for them?' Carr asked and clubbed the man under the ear with the side of his fist.

In the cubicle, with the door bolted behind him again, Carr tried to balance the unconscious body on the pedestal. For a moment it stayed upright, then toppled sideways like a rag doll. He sighed, knotted its tie to the cistern lever, pushed the gun into its belt with handkerchief-covered fingers and wiped his hand-prints from the tops of the metal walls.

There were still twenty minutes to wait. He lit a cigarette and stood, leaning against the partition, smoking, wishing that the paper was in a roll, not sheets. It would have been amusing, he thought, to have draped the figure with it.

When the voice of the girl on the public address system announced the Bogota flight the man was beginning to stir. Carr hit him again, walked quickly from the washroom, glanced at the 'out of order' sign the man had hung on the handle of the main door and made his way towards International Departures.

'Hope you enjoyed your visit to the States, Mr Carr,' the official who looked at his passport said. 'Come visit us again real soon.'

'I'll do that,' Carr told him. Herrick was only twelve paces ahead, but he didn't look back.

Aboard the plane Herrick seemed to be engrossed in the safety regulations. If he was aware of Carr passing him on his way to his seat near the tail he gave no sign of it.

CHAPTER FOURTEEN

Havelock-Templeton agreed with Barry that brandy and cigars would be acceptable.

'Good,' Barry said. 'We might as well have something where taste and description tally. I'm sorry about that dinner, Julian.'

'I thoroughly enjoyed it.'

'Did you? Then I can only recommend that you see your doctor. That jugged hare tasted offensive, looked offensive and its tactile effect on the tongue resembled that of rope. I can't comment on the smell because I've got a cold which is something to be thankful for, but I expect it followed the general pattern.'

Barry grasped his companion's elbow and guided him out of the club dining room.

'I hope your hearing is all right. It seems to be all you've got left and I want to talk to you. We'll sit over there.'

When they were seated Barry said, 'You're looking pensive, Julian. Anything wrong?'

'In a way.'

'Tell me.'

'I'm not sure I want to be talked to, Charles. Don't misunderstand me. I've valued our association, but I don't believe it should continue. Don't ask me if I'm still upset by Clancey's death. Of course I am, but it isn't that. It's my becoming involved too deeply in the affairs of another organization in which I have no executive powers, no powers of any sort. It's unfair to my own people and it's not the way, for my own peace of mind, that I care to operate. Big-headed of me, no doubt, but however eminent my master, I insist on the right to exercise my own judgement and express an opinion.'

He gave an apologetic shrug and added, 'That cannot be so between us for obvious reasons, so call on me any time you need some routine assistance, but give me no more details.'

Barry nodded agreeably and smoothed his beard to a point with a large hand. When he released it, it reverted immediately to the shape of a badly cut hedge.

'I went to see Parminter this afternoon,' he said.

'Oh?'

'Yes. He was a bit huffy at first, but eventually agreed that, as considerable promotion was involved, he could hardly stand in your way.'

'Are you offering me a job, Charles?'

'As my Deputy.'

'I'm very flattered. The post being vacant do I take it that Foster has followed Herrick?'

'I think the word should be "preceded". Rather fortuitously he committed suicide. His nerves were in a rotten state and I played on them. Early morning summonses, ambiguous remarks, having his place searched less carefully than the others so that he'd notice. That sort of stuff. Just trimmings really. He must have known it was over when I pointed at Herrick. Anyway, he got tight and proposed marriage to his secretary. More of a back to the womb thing than anything else I suppose. She turned him down and he loaded himself up with dope and stuck his head in the oven.'

'He guessed that you had let Herrick get away?'

'Yes,' said Barry. 'And I can only assume that he didn't fancy being hunted down by Carr or Rafferty if, as was likely, I gave him the same break.'

'How did you get on to them in the first instance, Charles?'

Barry smiled. 'Am I to understand that your reawakened interest indicates tacit acceptance of my offer?'

Havelock-Templeton stared at him. 'Lord, yes. Didn't I say so?'

'No. When can you start?'

'Four weeks – give or take. Largely depends on Parminter, but something like that.'

'All right,' Barry said, 'then this was how it was. Oh, I'm sorry. I forgot to order the brandy. Just let me . . .'

'We'll probably live without it, Charles. Let's have your story.'

'You speak for yourself,' Barry told him, walked out of the room and returned carrying two brandies. Settled in his chair again he asked, 'How much do you know about Communists in Parliament?'

'Not much more than that they exist. For years back any candidate standing as a Communist has invariably done so badly that he's lost his deposit. It's the ones who don't stand as Communists that get in. The crypto-Communists. Presumably they aren't confined to the left wing of the Labour Party, as one might expect, either. Or for that matter only to the Labour Party.'

'Quite right,' Barry said. 'Know any names?'

'Do you want me to guess?'

'No. I want you to know that we know them all. At least I hope to God we do. There are one or two junior Ministers we have been withholding sensitive material from and – well, never mind that now. The point is that I wrote a memorandum to the Prime Minister listing them and giving their case histories.' Barry raised his brandy glass and stared suspiciously at its contents as though it was some fine old wine he suspected of being corked, then he put it down again untasted. 'Two days later, Julian, we ran a house check on one of the junior Ministers and found a photo-copy of the memorandum.'

'Yes?'

'The leak hadn't come from the PM's office.'

'I see.'

'Do you? You've seen my safe, have you not?'

'I've seen it.'

'It's virtually impregnable, young man. It complains loudly if so much as touched in the wrong place and destroys its contents if it fears that it is about to be outwitted.' Barry leaned forward in his chair. 'Who can you say is capable of opening that thing without triggering something off, then closing it again to all intents and purposes undetectably?'

'Caley, Hollis, Pierre Tranigent, Klemski – ' Havelock-Templeton broke off and smiled. 'I know. Hollis is doing a stretch on the Moor, Klemski was deported in March and neither they nor the rest have a hope in hell of gaining access to your building. Herrick is the man you want me to name. That particular aptitude of his was one of the reasons you employed him. Perhaps the only one, was it?'

Ignoring the question Barry said, 'Presumably at the same time as that memorandum was copied, note was taken of two other pieces of information. Chandler's presence in Rumania and Rafferty's in France.'

Chandler's death in Bucharest had upset Barry badly. The mission had been low grade, the urgency minimal and the agent one of the most experienced in the organization. 'It's got to be done some time,' Chandler had said. 'I've been sitting on my backside for seven months and I'm running out of reasons for not painting the house.' Barry had acquiesced and Chandler had died, needlessly. He had also died inexplicably and that, for all his humanity, worried Barry the more. The crime, if it could be called that, bore no relation at all to the punishment meted out and such punishments were no longer the fashion since the killings and prompt counter-killings of the fifties had demonstrated their futility. To provide a reminder of this an assistant to the commercial Attaché at the Rumanian Embassy in London, whose true function was known to Barry, fell from the window of his fifth-floor apartment two days after the news arrived from Bucharest. Only then did Barry close Chandler's file.

Then Rafferty had been knifed in an alley in Deauville. Deauville of all places! The blade had entered his right side below the ribs and torn the outer wall of his stomach. Afraid to make any sudden movement which might add to whatever internal injuries he had, Rafferty had pretended to topple forward, taken his adversary by the throat and strangled him. He had managed to reach a telephone and call London, Barry had spoken at once to his opposite number in Paris and in less than thirty minutes Rafferty was on an operating table in a French hospital. Within about the same period of time he was out of danger.

Havelock-Templeton had listened to the recital interrupting only once with some commonplace remark when a late-dining member looked into the smoking room, nodded to them and left again.

Now he asked, 'Any trouble from the French?'

'Absolutely not,' Barry told him. 'They even flew Rafferty home in a "Mystère", or a "Mirage", or whatever the *Force de*

Frappe is using nowadays. I'll introduce you to Rambaud when you join us. He's a damned good man. Slapped the French equivalent of a "D" notice on the press, then let it be known that the dead man had been identified as Sicilian to give the newspapers a Mafia angle to chew on. Rafferty became an Australian tourist called Appleyard and a case of mistaken identity.'

'What was he doing there, Charles?'

'Waiting at the stage door of some cabaret for his girl to finish her act. He goes to see her whenever – whenever he's feeling lonely.'

'Couldn't it have been mistaken identity?'

Barry shook his head. 'The man came out of the stage door, addressed Rafferty by name and told him that the girl would be a few minutes late. He named her too. That was how he got close enough.' He sipped his brandy for the first time before adding, 'I keep a list of telephone contact numbers for my senior staff in case I want them when they're out on the town, in the country, whatever it is they like to do when they're off duty. Rafferty's list was the only one showing a foreign exchange number. I assume that, on the basis of "abroad" being a more suitable killing ground than "home", they traced the subscriber, set a watch on her place and waited for Rafferty to turn up.'

Havelock-Templeton frowned and said, 'I don't understand how it's possible to stab someone in the stomach and then allow your victim to strangle you.'

'Neither did Rafferty. In fact he was quite indignant about falling standards these days. Told me that his man clawed away at his hands, trying to dislodge them, when every kid over eight used to be taught how to break a frontal strangle-hold in the school swimming pool for his life-saver's badge.' Barry smiled at the memory of Rafferty's diatribe in the Department's tiny hospital section after an ambulance had brought him there from the French Air Force jet, his insistence that the French had linked Pasteur's stomach injections for hydrophobia with Noel Coward's 'Mad Dogs and Englishmen' and that he had been medically assaulted, his demands for an immediate audience with the French Ambassador. The Department's doctor had begun to suspect post-operative shock, but Barry had known that it was just Rafferty.

'What's funny, Charles?'

'Nothing,' Barry said.

'Then when are you going to explain how Foster fitted into this? You say he was nervous, but there has to be more to it than that.'

Barry sipped at his brandy again and nodded before saying, 'I made two assumptions. One, that a war of attrition against my senior staff had been started from within the Department. Foreign help appeared to be available to an unknown extent, but responsibility and initial action rested here. Two, that more than one person was likely to be involved. Herrick was very good at his job, but I couldn't see him as an instigator. Anyway, it's rare for traitors to operate singly. Look at most of the spy cases over the post-war years.' He drew a circle in the air with his cigar for Havelock-Templeton to look at. 'There have nearly always been colleagues, or wives, or whatever, involved, haven't there?'

'Yes.'

'Right. In the hope of confirming that my assumptions were correct I provided more sacrificial lambs for them to slaughter. I say "them" because I thought it probable that whoever else was involved would reveal himself in the process.'

'Are we coming up to that photographic session on the golf course by any chance?'

'Indeed we are,' Barry said. 'You see, I invented an agent or, more accurately, I selected an existing agent, a small time seller of information I've used occasionally and transformed him into someone very special. Very special to us.'

'Anyone I would know?'

'Shouldn't think so. Little Australian rat called Lippmann. Untrustworthy as they come. Unknown to him he acquired a personal security file – Directors' eyes only – a creditable service record and an assignment of quite exceptional importance and urgency. It's a saddening thought that he never knew of his heightened status.'

'So he was killed.'

'Yes. Murdered seven days after I briefed Foster on the mythical assignment and two before Lippmann was supposed to begin it.'

The younger man moved uncomfortably in his chair. 'Sorry, Charles, but I don't get it. Foster can't have been that stupid.'

'Oh, he wasn't,' Barry told him. 'I had placed this imaginary operation in East Germany and described it, together with

Lippmann and his supposed capabilities, to Foster in some detail. Among the points I omitted to provide him with were Lippmann's home base and the starting date, but they *were* in the action plan in my safe.'

'And you knew it wasn't just Herrick again, because the film told you so?' Havelock-Templeton broke in.

'That's right,' Barry said. 'The film and Dr Gowan.'

'And then?'

'And then what?'

'I think you said you provided more sacrificial lambs, not *a* sacrificial lamb. Or didn't I hear you correctly?'

'No, you're quite right. I expressed the hope after dinner that you had been left with one of your senses intact. Fortunately you have. I gave them another seventeen.'

'If this wasn't your club I'd buy you another brandy,' Havelock-Templeton said. 'It's obviously going to be a long night.'

Barry shook his head. 'If you'd start drinking yours I'll have told you the rest by the time you've finished it, but if you don't mind I'll smoke my pipe. I never really liked these things.' He pounded his half-smoked cigar into a shapeless mess in the ashtray, took his pipe from his pocket but didn't fill it. Then he said, 'They were all Poles in and around Gdansk on the Baltic coast. I've known that, helpful as they often are, we weren't getting all the information we might from the CIA – you'll be aware that they've been much thicker on the ground in Poland than our people for years back – so it seemed logical to set up a new network there.'

'Why you, Charles?' his guest asked. 'That's an SIS function.'

Wagging his pipe like a cautionary finger Barry said, 'You have to expand to survive these days, young fellow. Anyway, with CIA help I was able to select fourteen men and three women who seemed to be eminently suitable for what I had in mind, then I sent Trelawney off to link them up. You know the old routine. Each one is told the identity of the person to his right and to his left, but no more, which makes it really rather remarkable that the UB, or it may have been the KGB, was able to arrest the whole lot in one fell swoop at seventeen widely separated addresses. None of the tedious business of pulling in a suspect or two and persuading them to tell you the name of those next in line. They were so pleased with themselves that they authorized a press release. Seventeen dissident elements arrested for activities against the State. Trial pending. *Trybuna Ludu* and *Zycie Warszawy* both carried it using identical wording over one and a quarter columns.'

Havelock-Templeton looked down at the floor, then back at Barry. 'Either you're pulling my leg, or you're pretty free with the life and liberty of the people you employ. You'd made your case against Foster. Why the extravagant duplication?'

Barry grunted irritably before saying, 'Don't be silly. There was no duplication. That was Trelawney's test. I knew he had made contacts of his own he used for passing the usual mixture of real and misleading information in Bonn and Copenhagen and I sent him to stay near both those places. He didn't go to Poland at all, although I kept him away long enough for Foster to assume that he had been there and he didn't leak the information to his contacts either because, before you ask, the list of names I had him memorize bore no relation whatsoever to the people arrested in Poland. Their names were on the paper I left in my safe for Foster to find. Satisfied?'

Havelock-Templeton replied with another question. 'Who were these Poles you shopped?'

'Oh, don't lose any sleep over them,' Barry told him. 'They're all worthy card-carrying Communists. The Polish authorities will let them go when they've unravelled the tangle and realize they've been conned. There never was any network. As you say that's an SIS function, but the papers Foster read made it look like a joint endeavour.'

'So you're testing everyone in the Department.'

'Working from the top down.'

'And Carr and Trelawney both passed. What about Rafferty?'

'Shooting off a toe to avoid some unpleasant duty is something I've heard of,' Barry said. 'Committing nearly successful hara-kiri to demonstrate one's loyalty I have not. Rafferty is now my acting second-in-command. He is also extremely unhappy that this should be the case and wants to know nothing which might prejudice his chances of being employed abroad in future. That is why I have started the process of briefing you on current matters so that you can put him out of his misery at the earliest possible date. Now, if you aren't going to drink that brandy you can hand it over here.'

CHAPTER FIFTEEN

The deep blue of the Straits of Florida had given way to the jungle camouflage of Cuba beneath the plane before Carr got to his feet and, briefcase in hand, walked down the aisle towards Herrick's seat. His double reservation had been unnecessary. The plane had left New York half empty and after Miami there were even fewer passengers.

He sat down and said, 'Hello, Herrick.'

Herrick showed no surprise, no emotion of any sort.

'The name's Hendrix now, Carr.'

'I know. Let me be the first to congratulate you on a masterly piece of deception. How did you think of it?'

The merest flicker of annoyance brushed the face of the other and was gone.

'*How* did you know?'

'It's written on the label of that over-night bag beside you,' Carr said.

'Intensely amusing. If it isn't too much to ask, where did you pick up my trail?'

'It wasn't a question of picking it up,' Carr told him. 'Nobody dropped it. The reports of your progress out to Hong Kong were received with wonder and acclaim. Derek Spurling took over there and told London you were heading for the States. Then they sent for me. No problem really. Oh, I forgot. You did manage to lose yourself for a few hours after you took off from the Americana. I suppose you spotted the FBI lurking behind vodka martinis, or couldn't you afford the bill?'

Herrick snorted and turned his head towards the window, his long, narrow, rather beautiful hands resting motionless on the little folding table in front of him. Clever hands, Carr knew, and certainly the only beautiful thing about him. Carr looked at the thick, seamed neck pitted by some adolescent blood disorder, the sagging body and hair like pale rust. He thought about the averted face, pale too, with eyebrows and lashes so fair that it looked bald, unfinished. It was offensive, he decided, to look like Herrick and was amused at himself that the feeling this aroused in him was stronger than that of Herrick's proxy attempt on his life.

When Herrick spoke it was softly, slowly, as though he were rehearsing a speech he had been asked to deliver. His head was still turned away and Carr had to strain to hear the words.

'I can afford a lot of things now, John Carr. People don't keep only documents in safes, you know. As long as Foster got the papers he wanted I considered that whatever else I found was my affair. As a precautionary measure I have had this journey planned for a very long time and one of the things I have been able to afford is protection at every stopping place. At Bogota I have it in strength.'

Carr looked through the window beyond Herrick at the western coastline of Cuba fringed with white lace stitched invisibly to watered silk of palest green, darkening and merging into blue.

'I hope it's better than at Miami,' he said.

'Coming from you that's a strange hope.'

'Not in the least. Now that I've come to join you, a time may come when I shall be glad of a little fire-power myself.'

Herrick laughed humourlessly. 'Join me? Now I've heard it all. There's no question of your having been sent to write me off, of course. Barry's interested in my new career and asked you to come along and give me a helping hand. You make me laugh.'

'I know. I heard you do it, but before you go off into paroxysms of mirth let me make it clear to you that I'm absolutely serious. Things haven't been too good at home since you skipped. The whole damned Department is suspect and I, for one, am declaring myself redundant. I need a new job and I'm asking you for one because you've obviously worked out some set-up where you can avoid having me breathing down your neck. That suits me. I wouldn't like to have me breathing down my neck either.'

'Modest as ever, eh, Carr?'

'Of course. There's no need to brag when you're the best in the business.'

Herrick turned towards him then. His washed-out blue eyes met Carr's, held them.

'You know, John,' he said, 'this is all so childishly transparent that I'm tempted to use expressions like insulting my intelligence, but you're too smart to do that, so suppose you tell me what's on your mind. Suppose, also, that you do it now, before we reach Bogota. They hold life pretty cheap down there and they'll blast you at a gesture from me.'

'Nasty,' Carr said.

'Out with it, man!'

Carr yawned, pressed the call button for the air hostess and ordered whisky for both of them without asking Herrick what he wanted.

When she placed the plastic glasses and miniature bottles in front of them Carr said, 'My friend will pay. He's a successful safe breaker – er, I mean stockbroker.'

A minute later there was a distinct tremor in Herrick's voice when he whispered, 'If you want to die laughing we can arrange that, but with your puerile sense of humour you won't get a smile out of whoever does it.'

'Your nerves are bad, Herrick.'

'Hendrix, damn you!'

'All right, all right. Your nerves are bad, Hendrix. Now you listen to me. You're a breaking and entering man. A good one. That's what you're selling, because you don't have anything else to sell in this part of the world, or anywhere else for that matter. But it's this part of the world we're interested in, isn't it, Hendrix? Specifically Colombia. Now, somehow, I can't see you on any government payroll, not any more I can't, so perhaps it isn't such a great big coincidence that Colombia has more than its share of Communist orientated guerrillas. You're Communist orientated too and it's the guerrillas who are buying your particular talent. I imagine you'll be working on government offices, embassies, the army, the police and while you're tinkering with safes and strongrooms you'll need someone to guard your back.'

With a forefinger Carr tapped one of the elegant hands. 'Protection, Señor Hendrix. *That* word again. Not a hairy peasant with a big hat, a Che Guevara moustache and a collection of Castro firearms, clanking around after you like a bloody milk float. You wouldn't last a week. You need the best.'

'You, naturally.'

'Me, naturally.'

'I get a knife in me on my first job and the President hangs the Order of Simon Bolivar, second class, round your neck. Talk sense, Carr.'

'I brought your insurance policy with me,' Carr said and reached under his seat for his briefcase. He opened it and handed Herrick a thick, plastic-covered docket.

'Your service record, Señor Hendrix.'

Herrick ran a finger across the smooth surface, but made no move to look inside.

'So what?' he said.

'I thought you might like to have it.'

'Interesting bedside reading, but no practical use to me. They'll have a copy, or the original, in London.'

'Who cares?' Carr said and handed him the second docket. 'My service record, Señor Hendrix.'

Slowly and for the first time a definite expression formed on Herrick's face. He looked bemused.

'Is this genuine?' he asked, but Carr didn't reply.

Herrick turned the pages irregularly, reading a sentence here and there. When he was a third of the way through he turned to the last dozen pages and read them carefully.

'It's genuine,' he said, his voice as bemused as his face.

'It's genuine,' Carr agreed.

'Lunch, sir?'

Carr glanced up. It was the second air hostess, the prettier one with the champagne hair. She was smiling at him and he was aware that the smile was not entirely mechanical. Suddenly, the prospect of spending the evening looking at Herrick was very boring. He smiled back, took the two trays from her and passed one to Herrick.

'That would be nice,' he said and she flashed her teeth again.

They ate their meal in silence, then Herrick dabbed his near-colourless lips with a paper napkin and asked, 'How did you get hold of them?'

The public address system hummed experimentally, clicked, then a voice said, 'This is Captain Keir again, ladies and gentlemen. We crossed the – er – north coast of Colombia a quarter-hour back and are now about fifty minutes out of El Dorado, Bogota. It looks like we may have some heavy turbulence up ahead, so I'd be glad if any of you wandering about would go back to your seats and fasten your seat belts. Er – I'll steer around as much of this as possible so your lunch stays unshook. Thank you.'

Herrick breathed in, then exhaled noisily and Carr said, 'Your nerves really are bad, Hendrix.'

'If I were you I'd be more concerned about my suit than someone else's nerves,' Herrick told him. 'Why don't you save us both embarrassment and sit somewhere else?'

Carr grinned and moved to the empty row behind them, taking the window seat. At first there was nothing to see except some streaky cloud ten thousand feet below and the drab olive green of the ground twenty-five thousand feet below that. The hostesses moved quickly up and down the aisle collecting trays.

Five minutes later the first thunder-head was close, so close that it seemed almost to touch the starboard wingtip, a towering cliff of brilliant whiteness, marble smooth, motionless, holding secret the titanic power Carr knew it screened. He craned his neck, looking upwards to where the cliff curved inwards above the plane like a one-sided archway painted with purple shadows in its concavity. It was, he thought, one of the most impressive sights he had ever seen.

A second appeared to port and the 707 banked sharply, first one way then the other, following the twisting canyon of still air between the five-mile-thick trunks of the cloud forest. It lasted for several minutes, then the sky was an unblemished blue again. The plane had not bumped once.

'That's all, ladies and gentlemen. Clear air now,' said Captain Keir's voice and the 'Fasten seat belts' signs went blank.

Carr, who rarely gave anyone credit for anything, thought it had been a remarkable piece of flying. He moved back to the seat next to Herrick.

'I lifted them from Records' safe. It's not like that thing of Barry's. Didn't need your expertise.'

Herrick looked at him uncomprehendingly.

'Jesus! You're not still going to be sick, are you? You asked me how I got hold of these service records.'

'Oh,' Herrick said. 'Yes, those things can be cracked with a tooth-pick.'

The pressure from the let-down to Bogota had come to their ear-drums before Herrick spoke again.

'All right, you're on if I can clear it with Ratshelm.'

'I had a feeling there'd be a Kraut in this somewhere,' Carr told him.

Herrick didn't seem to hear. 'We should make quite a team,'

he mused aloud. 'And with this in some safe place,' he tapped Carr's file, 'I don't think you'll try stepping out of line.'

'By God you're quick,' Carr said mildly.

Herrick sat in a car parked at the roadside near the Tequendama Falls. The volume of water was little more than a trickle, but the drop prodigious. The falls must, he thought, be an awe-inspiring sight after the rains.

He turned his head to look at the driver.

'Shove him over there,' he said. 'They tell me it's a favourite place for suicides.'

The other spat through the car window, then jerked his head in an abrupt negative.

'Señor Ratshelm not like this. Near Bogota we do nothing. You bring to *tierra caliente*. We kill him quick.'

'Where's Tierracaliente?'

'Is all over. Means hot country. Is much rain forest. Soon we tell you which place.'

'How soon?'

'Maybe two-three days.'

'I'll probably be dead by then,' Herrick said. 'You'd better do the job bloody quickly. Like now!'

The driver spat again, started the engine and swung the car through a hundred and eighty degrees back towards Bogota. The tyres squealed thinly.

'Señor Ratshelm not like this,' he said. 'You wait two-three days.'

'Believe me? Of course he didn't believe me,' Carr said. 'But he thinks I think he did and that's the important thing.'

The man from the Embassy shifted his lanky frame uncomfortably in the cramped seat of the nearly deserted cinema. He didn't say anything.

Carr stared moodily at the moving figures on the screen, not seeing them. He was wondering why Purvis should be so interested in this Herrick thing, why he had pressed for details.

The screen went blank, a flickering oblong of whiteness, but the sound-track continued to shout at them in Spanish, then the figures materialized again.

Purvis laughed. 'Never less than five times a performance,' he said.

Carr turned his head and looked at the pleasant face next to him with the highlights on it shifting in unison with the flickering beam of the projector.

'Are you running me, Purvis?' he asked.

Purvis smiled faintly, still watching the film. 'Running you? Hell no. As far as I know you have no director. You're on your jack for this job. I have instructions to help – within reason.' He smiled again and added, 'But from your question I take it that I'm being over inquisitive. Sorry about that. Put it down to natural concern because if you are determined to get mixed up with ex-*Sturmbannführer* Hans Ratshelm and his pals you're entitled to it. Personally I think you're nuts.'

'I go where Herrick goes. Bogota's too public.'

Purvis squirmed in his seat again. 'That didn't seem to weigh very heavily with you at Miami,' he said. 'That's public too.'

'You've lost me,' Carr told him.

'Yes? Well, there's some FBI character called Kendall who's sorry *he's* lost you.'

'I know Kendall,' Carr said. 'What's eating him?'

'A case of assault on a man positively identified, oddly enough, as one of Ratshelm's storm troopers. He's not very well.'

'That *is* odd. When did it happen?' Carr asked and Purvis said, 'Skip it.'

'Okay. It was your digression and I don't see what a case of assault has to do with the FBI anyway. Tell me about Ratshelm.'

Purvis put a finger to the tip of his nose and pressed it as if to satisfy himself that it was stuck firmly in place.

'World War Two Russian front hero, Panzergrenadier-division "*Gotterdammerung*", or one of those fanciful names they went in for. *Ritterkreuz* with oak leaves, diamonds, banana skins, the whole bit. Shot more Russians personally than you could shake a stick at and now he's fighting for them or, at least, controlling a number of groups of Castro-trained guerrillas. He's in his fifties now, but don't let that mislead you. The Colombian army has been hammering away at him for ten years or more and they haven't dented him yet.'

'I see,' Carr said. 'Get the local CIA boy to contact me, would you?'

For the first time Purvis took his eyes from the screen and

looked directly at Carr.

'Very well, but I just hope you know what you're doing.'

'So do I,' said Carr and got to his feet. At the exit he glanced back. Purvis was engrossed in the film again.

CHAPTER SIXTEEN

'Are you busy, Colonel?' The voice betrayed tension.

'I'd have thought that was pretty obvious,' Barry said.

'What on *earth* are you doing?'

'Making a Mobius strip, my dear.'

Martha looked at the half-dozen ragged-edged strips of paper lying on the carpet around Barry's chair, watched him take a new sheet, fold it back an inch along one side and run his thumb-nail up and down the crease. When he tore the strip off it came away fairly neatly.

'It's easier with scissors,' he said.

'I'm sure it is, Colonel. Is my security clearance high enough to be told what it is?'

'What? Oh, I'm always forgetting that you were blowing up German troop trains on the Continent when you should have been in school. Do sit down. Now, if we join it into a circle like this, how many surfaces and edges are there?'

'Two of both.'

'Right, but suppose we give it a half-twist then join it like this, how many now?'

'The same.'

Triumph in his voice, 'Wrong!' Barry said. 'Only one of each. Ought to have some glue really, but I'll hold it while you draw a line right down the middle of the strip. When you get back to the starting point you'll have covered both sides of the paper, except that there is only one side now if you see what I mean.'

Martha made no move to take the pencil he was holding out to her. 'And they taught you that at school, Colonel?'

'No. Chap showed me at the club last night.'

'Well, it might interest you to know that that's the McAllister Report you're tearing up.'

'Damn. So it is,' Barry said. 'Never mind, it's a lot of

balderdash anyway. What have you got for me there, Martha?'

She glanced down at the papers on her lap. 'Mr Carr may have been active, Colonel. There's an FBI report here concerning an assault on a Colombian citizen at Miami airport at approximately the time Mr Carr passed through. The man died in hospital of brain haemorrhage. The FBI is annoyed.'

'There was a collision between a taxi and a removal van in Gloucester Place while I was walking to work this morning,' Barry said. 'It wasn't my fault.'

'Oh quite, Colonel. They're simply jumping to conclusions. They have no positive proof.'

'So you don't think Carr was involved?'

The small white head tilted in an oddly autocratic gesture. 'Really, Colonel. You've known me long enough to know not to put words in my mouth. If you juxtapose Mr Carr and a killing, the odds are likely to be better than even that he was responsible. I'm quite distressed to find that FBI perception is superior to your first-hand knowledge. One has to take into consideration . . .'

Martha hesitated, then went on, 'I'm sorry. I haven't told you that bit yet. It was all clear in my mind when I came in, then you muddled me with that piece of paper you're still playing with. What *is* it?'

'According to my fellow member it's a geometrical oddity of no known practical value,' Barry said, smiled, screwed the paper into a ball and flicked it away. 'If you cut along the pencil line you didn't draw and then halve the strip again you get the most surprising results, but forget it now. Go on about Carr.'

It would be all right now, he knew, until the next time, hours or months away. The fluttering of her left eyelid, which presaged the onset of pain and had been so apparent when he had arrived twenty minutes before, had stopped. He seemed able to do as much for her as anyone. Sometimes an engendered emotional outburst was necessary to break the spasm, at others it could be averted altogether, like today, with some idiotic distraction. Not knowing how or why it worked he was simply thankful that quite often it did. He liked to think, too, that the pain passed from her to him by some form of osmosis. It did not, but his knowledge of its existence became his resolution, made it easier for him to live with himself when, on the rare occasions when it was necessary, he had to order the ending of a life.

He had only to think of the victim as a survivor of the rocket attack from amongst the perverted group that had mutilated her.

'The point,' Martha said, 'is that the dead man at Miami was a known associate of a certain Hans Ratshelm who is the major guerrilla leader in Colombia. According to this signal from the Embassy at Bogota . . .'

'Purvis?'

'Yes, Colonel. He says that, according to Mr Carr, Mr Herrick is joining the guerrillas by some long-standing arrangement and that Mr Carr is going with him. Other than that Mr Carr has requested contact with the local CIA representative he has no hard information, but suspects that the Miami incident was an attempt on Mr Carr's life which backfired. I have prepared a note for you on Ratshelm. That's all at the moment.'

'So Herrick had himself covered at his stop-over points. Well, the final stages anyway.'

'It's a possibility,' Martha said, handed the papers across the desk, then added, 'Mr Rafferty would like to see you at your convenience.'

'Did he say what about?'

'Yes, Colonel. His sex life. Apparently you're ruining it.'

'Time somebody did.' Barry said. 'Give me ten minutes to read this stuff, then send him in.'

He read Purvis's signal and then Martha's lengthy note on Ratshelm. The latter made him frown as he tried to envisage what Carr intended to do. Not by a long way for the first time he wondered what thought processes went on in the mind of an agent assigned a human target for destruction. The report would be unlikely to tell him much, something dry and factual like 'At 15.37 on 28 July Subject was seen to enter the house he had been occupying for the past two weeks. An explosion occurred immediately and was followed by fire.' A clean kill, or so the report would have it, but sometimes, with some people, he doubted it was as straightforward as that.

'The enigma of the hunter as a human animal,' he said to himself, then moved his shoulders irritably. It had sounded silly, pseudo-psychological gobbledegook, but he knew what he had meant and wished that he did not. He knew too that ignorance of those thought processes and their outcome was a condition he was content to continue to live with.

He was aware of Rafferty coming in, crossing the room, and peripheral vision showed him settling himself, as always, on the window-sill. His own thoughts centred on him, then widened to encompass Carr as well, trying to form a comparison between these totally disparate individuals who yet had so many abilities in common. After a moment he cleared the unprofitable exercise from his mind.

'What's bugging you, Rafferty?'

Rafferty turned from his contemplation of a traffic warden circling a car as though it contained an explosive device before slipping a ticket under one of the windscreen wipers.

'Hello, boss,' he said. 'I thought you were off on some Yoga kick. Nice to have you back anyway.'

'Well?'

'No bugging. I made absolutely sure of that. Even probed my tooth-paste with a pin. Silly mistake. Fluoride-bearing peppermint-flavoured cream all over the place. If I'd had a knitting needle or something I could have prodded away through the nozzle and . . .'

Rafferty stopped talking when Barry spun his chair towards him, his expression furious.

'Just you listen to me,' Barry said. 'I don't want to hear about your tooth-paste. I don't want to hear any more of the fatuous remarks for which you are renowned. I particularly do not want to hear about your sex life, or in what fashion I am supposed to be ruining it. In fact, unless you have something sensible to say to me, I don't want to hear from you at all. Do I make myself absolutely clear?'

Startled and angry with himself at his totally uncharacteristic outburst Barry clamped his lips into a hard, straight line and glared at his temporary Deputy.

Quietly Rafferty said, 'Suppose you tell me what's bugging *you*, boss.'

Barry's face relaxed slowly. It would, he thought, be a relief to explain to someone that he was getting old, that he was old already, that Colonel Sir Charles Barry, a title he would inevitably receive and which, in his more light-hearted moments, he had thought sounded rather good, was something he no longer wanted. It went against the grain to accept the official seal of approval on a career which, to his mind, was ending in a sordid mess. Worst of all, he was afraid, that be it as Mrs or Lady Barry, Martha would decline to share his old age.

As quietly as Rafferty had spoken he said, 'I'm sorry, Patrick. I'm a little edgy over this tragic business of Nigel Foster, but that's no excuse for shouting at you. Stupid of me. You wanted to see me about something. What have you been up to?'

To Rafferty an apology from Barry was not common, neither was it unknown, but the use of his Christian name was an extreme rarity and it indicated distress. And that distress, Rafferty decided, indicated in its turn that his thinking over the past two or three days had been on the right lines.

He smiled and said, 'Tagging around after you and other people.'

'Me?'

'That's right, boss.'

'What the devil for?'

Rafferty swung his legs off the window-sill and began to walk up and down the room. There was nothing nervous about the change. He looked as though he had decided to go for a stroll to pass the time until luncheon. Barry followed him with his eyes.

'A little while ago,' Rafferty said, 'it came to my notice that I was attracting attention from strangers who seemed to be interested in my comings and goings. Now, I'm used to that with women, but . . .'

'How did it come to your notice?'

Rafferty stopped perambulating and looked at Barry curiously.

'Because I like staying alive, boss. It's practically an obsession with me. You might almost call me a life nut. In addition to that I'm not paid to get followed.'

Barry grunted and Rafferty went on, 'These weren't women, they were male, Caucasian and reasonably professional.' He took an envelope from his pocket and put it on the desk blotter in front of Barry. 'There are descriptions of eight men there, boss, with photographs of three of them. All I could get. They worked a rota system in tandem. I thought you might want to check that they *are* part of Parminter's crowd, or whoever you borrowed them from.'

'You seem to be jumping to . . .' Barry began, then stopped at Rafferty's interruption.

'Why don't you let me tell it my way? You'll be able to fire me sooner, or slam me in the cooler if that's what you have in mind.' He turned away then and resumed his stroll before saying, 'The first thing to do was lose my tails and find out if you were receiving the same treatment, so I did and you weren't, but certain others of the senior staff were. I reckoned that registered thirty per cent on my probability index that you'd set the bloodhounds on us. Subsequent actions of yours pushed the needle into the high nineties and this morning made it a certainty.'

For ten seconds, apart from the faint sounds of Rafferty's movements, there was silence in the room, until Barry asked, 'Is that all?'

'That's all.'

'Then you having told it your way as you put it, might I be permitted to ask a question or two? It's not all that clear to me.'

'Be my guest, boss.'

'Thank you. What subsequent actions of mine are you referring to?'

'Oh, those. Well, the night before last I was hanging around admiring your apartment block when Borthwick and his wife arrived. Twenty minutes later you took them out to dinner.'

'Really? What did we have to eat?'

'I wouldn't know, but when I got out to Coulsdon the Borthwicks' house was being worked over. Then last night you got all hospitable with Sheila and Ken Edwards and their place got done.'

'I see. So now we've attained a high probability factor. What was it about today that turned it into a certainty?'

'You haven't bothered to look in that envelope, boss.'

'All right, Rafferty,' Barry said. 'As somebody described someone else to me recently, you are a smart-arsed bastard.'

'Yes. Shall I collect my cards now?'

Barry seemed to switch off again and Rafferty watched him affectionately for a moment before moving to the window. For once he ignored the sill and stood looking down at the street. The traffic warden was a long way off, walking with controlled haste as though afraid of scaring off a potential victim before she could impose the statutory penalty on him.

Suddenly Barry asked, 'Got any idea what this is all about?'

'Some.'

'Tell me.'

'The Foster-Herrick business.'

Barry looked round at him sharply. 'What made you link the two of them?'

Rafferty said, 'Nothing made me, boss. I did it all by myself.' He took the seven paces separating the window from Barry's desk, placed his hands on the polished wood and looked down at the older man. 'Try this for size. Staff members being tagged and their homes being searched. Herrick under surveillance, for what reason I don't know, but he shrugs it aside and vanishes. Now that's not bad going for someone who couldn't shake off a head-cold, so I'm forced to the conclusion that you let him do it and when I ask Sergeant Cole for his "in and out" book I think I know why.'

He paused and Barry said, 'Go on.'

'Carr's name's in it on the appropriate day and now I *do* know why you let Herrick go, because Carr has disappeared too, which I see as being rather unfortunate for Herrick.'

'Disappeared?'

Almost plaintively Rafferty said, 'Oh, come on. He's elsewhere, not at home, absent and the mail's piling up inside the front door of his flat. I've been over the place three times. Methodical man, John Carr. Cancelled his newspapers and milk, switched off the power and emptied the refrigerator, so he expects to be away for some time. All right, so he could be fishing for haggis in Loch Lomond, but the fact that Herrick's pal Foster commits suicide immediately after Carr goes missing makes that as likely as those stories about Alice. Coincidence country and "Wonderland" are on a par in my book. Foster was afraid Herrick would talk before he died.'

He straightened, watched the imprint of his hands on the desk-top fade, then looked at Barry again.

'This organization's in trouble, isn't it, boss?'

Barry nodded and began to fill his pipe. When he had finished he put it down in front of him unlit. He didn't speak.

'Why put tags on me?' Rafferty asked.

'Because I knew you'd spot them and start nosing about. Better than briefing you because I didn't want you to have any preconceived notions. Dig up anything else out of the ordinary?'

'Nothing.'

'Thank God for that,' Barry said, picked up his pipe and lit it.

It went out almost at once, but he held it between his teeth, talking round it. 'You were right to bracket Herrick and Foster. They were just getting into their stride. The Deauville attack on you was organized by them.'

'Naughty. They might have done me an injury.'

'Chandler too.'

'Oh.'

'Yes, well Carr is in contact with Herrick, but I'm worried about his tactics. The information I have indicates that he has elected to take on something resembling an army. Okay, we all know about Carr and odds, but there are odds and odds.'

Barry took his pipe out of his mouth and pointed the stem at Rafferty.

'I want you to organize a one-man back-up operation in case Carr comes unstuck. Whoever you choose may have to wait some time for his chance and he'll be less conspicuous than a group which I can't afford to let you have anyway. Martha will give you the messages she showed me this morning which is all the information we have. All right?'

'Yes, boss.'

'Who will you send?'

'Any reason why I shouldn't go myself?'

'Several. You have an only partly healed hole in your stomach, I don't send operatives with a personal axe to grind on missions, from what you have just told me, and your complaints about your sex life, your time in bed over the last four days or so must have been short and, finally, I thought it was understood that you are acting as my second-in-command.'

Rafferty smiled. 'Then it'll have to be Trelawney.'

'That's what I thought,' Barry said.

CHAPTER SEVENTEEN

Carr's bedside 'phone buzzed quietly. He walked across to it and lifted the receiver.

'Yes?'

'Penultimate. Square root forty-nine. Now.'

The line went dead.

'Educated bastard,' Carr said and walked out of his room in the Tequendama Hotel. The lift took him to the top floor and he walked down one flight, then along the passage to Room 1507. When he pushed the door with his finger-tips it swung inwards and he followed it. A low-power lamp was burning on the writing desk against the far wall. The rest of the room was in shadow and the man lying on the bed with a newspaper held in front of him said, 'You Carr?'

'That's right,' Carr replied. 'Don't strain your eyes with the small print and put the gun down. I've seen that trick at the movies.'

The man lowered the paper. The gun in his right hand stayed pointing straight at Carr's chest.

'I could use some proof.'

Carr nodded, closed the door behind him and crossed to the writing desk. He turned the chair in front of it round to face the bed, sat on it and looked at the other. Face deeply tanned, hair and moustache black, initial visual impression, in the poorly lit room, South American, but the voice placed him a long way north of there.

'I can offer you credit cards, an international driving licence and my . . .'

An impatient jerk of the gun silenced him.

'If you're Carr there's a visible identification mark on you. Show me under that lamp beside you and do it very, very slowly.'

Carr moved his right hand cautiously towards the light. The white scar on the back below the first and second fingers stood out clearly.

For a moment the American hesitated, then put the gun down on the table beside the bed.

'Okay, you're Carr.'

'I'm glad you agree,' Carr told him, then asked, 'Do you mind if we have a little more light in here?'

'Help yourself.'

Carr got up and walked slowly towards the switch beside the door. He was half-way there when, with no apparent premeditation, he catapulted himself sideways and scooped up the gun.

'It's your turn to tell me who you are,' he said, then watched with growing astonishment as the figure on the bed jerked its knees protectively upwards to cover its chest, the face above them registering something close to terror.

'Don't pull that trigger!' the American said. 'Don't touch it! Don't even think about it!'

Mildly Carr asked, 'What the hell's the matter with you?'

'That's a gas gun, friend. The kind the locals use to scare off muggers. Mostly they're designed to look like those old-fashioned fountain-pens, but some people prefer a replica of the real thing, like that one.'

'I see. And now you're going to tell me that tear gas makes you cry.'

'It's worse than that, old buddy. That thing's got a demonstration cartridge in it, same as the one the sales rep I bought it off used. It goes off with one hell of a bang and blows talc all over. I got so many funny looks from the guys I had to send my suit to the cleaners. The office still smells like a hooker's closet.'

Carr grinned, looked down at the gun in his hand and put it back on the table. There would, he decided, be no problem working with the American.

'Do you have a name?'

'Whitehead. I was notified that you might get in touch through your man Purvis. You just did and here I am. Identification in the left hand pocket of the jacket on the back of that chair.'

Ignoring the jacket, Carr said, 'I'm here to do an unpleasant job.'

'I know it and I have orders to help if you want. British Intelligence defectors aren't exactly our main concern, but we're more than a little interested in making life hard for the Commies in Central and South America.'

'What's your cover?'

'I run a one-man helicopter service out of Bucaramanga. Know where that is?'

Without answering the question Carr muttered, 'Helicopter, helicopter, helicopter,' thought for a moment, then asked one of his own.

'Where's Ratshelm operating nowadays?'

'Difficult to say, precisely. He has these groups spread all around and visits with each of them from time to time. Sometimes a visit means an attack in that area, sometimes it doesn't. Mainly he avoids the big towns, except for bank raids he doesn't take part in, and operates against things like pumping stations on the Andean pipeline, barge trains on the Magdalena River, mining settlements, coffee plantations, oil camps, anything isolated, anything to louse up the national economy.'

'Well, thanks for the "precisely",' Carr said. 'Even if we assume that anoxia rules out any chance of his camping nineteen thousand feet up La Horqueta Peak that still leaves us with not much under half a million square miles to worry about.'

'You know this country?'

Carr shook his head. 'Just been reading travel literature and talking to barmen. I've got one of those trick memories. Forget it and try to narrow the possibilities down a little, will you?'

'Sure,' Whitehead said. 'Until a month or two back he was concentrating on the Pacific west. There's a lot of platinum and gold mining over that way. When things got hot for him there he pulled his usual stunt and drew back into the mountains. There's so much Andes around for him to get lost in the army doesn't even bother looking. Waste of time if they did. The word now is that he's getting set for something in the Magdalena valley to the north of here.'

'Whose word?'

'DAS.'

'Colombian Security?'

'Right. They've infiltrated some of his groups.'

'Then let us put our trust in DAS,' Carr said and asked, 'What type's your chopper?'

'Little open-sided Bell three-seater.'

'Will you fly it for me?'

Whitehead turned the palms of his hands upwards in an almost Gallic gesture. 'Like I said, I have orders to help you. That makes you the boss.'

Carr completed his unfinished journey to the light switch by the door, flicked it down and walked back to the bed pulling the touring map of Colombia he had picked up in New York from his pocket. He unfolded it, pushed Whitehead's legs out of the way and spread it out on the rumpled cover.

'I'll be going in with Herrick,' he said, 'and I may need to be lifted out in a hurry. It's just possible that I'll have him with me, but leave that for the moment. For rendezvous purposes, the only geographical feature I can't very well miss, provided I know which side of it I'm on, is the Magdalena River itself. It practically bisects the country from north to south so I only have to travel east or west as the case may be until I fall into it. Now look . . .'

Twenty minutes later Whitehead said, 'Sure it's clear and sure I can handle it, but I think you're nuts.'

'You and Purvis should get together,' Carr told him. 'You have a lot in common.'

Whitehead's forefinger traced the meandering line of the Magdalena River shown on the map. It passed over the ten narrow oblongs Carr had drawn along the river's course from the west of Bogota to the port of Barranquilla on the Caribbean. They were labelled A to J and each was about fifty miles long. Each also contained a dot placed there by Whitehead himself to indicate where he could land near a location he hoped Carr would be able to recognize on the ground. Most were close to the outskirts of riverside villages or the junctions of tributaries and the main river.

He looked at Carr. 'You certain you can remember all these places?'

'I told you about my memory.'

'What happens if you can't tell me an area at all before you leave?'

'I'll hijack a llama and ride out,' Carr said.

When he left Whitehead, Carr went to look for Herrick and found him, as he had expected to do, drinking whisky in the deep gloom of the hotel's lower bar. He took the stool next to him and ordered scotch and soda. Apart from the barman they had the place to themselves.

Herrick drained his glass, signalled for it to be refilled, then told the barman to leave the bottle. Carr knew he was taking on ballast to hold himself down on the high plateau of nervousness he had inhabited for the past two days, that he could not sustain a more rarefied atmosphere of apprehension. Five minutes later he concluded that Herrick's ballast requirements were more than usually urgent this night and wondered why.

'We leave for Barrancabermeja on the seven-fifty Avianca flight in the morning,' Herrick said.

Sleazy river port on the Magdalena about 175 miles north of Bogota. Hybrid population shading from black to yellow. Occupations: pimping, mugging, political murder, irritable murder and occasional work on the Andean pipeline and oil barges. Distractions: rats and mosquitoes. Carr's memory of what he had learned presented him with the salient facts like information keyed on to an office computer screen.

'Where's Barrancabermeja?' he asked.

'Up north on the river.'

'And that's where we meet Ratshelm?'

'There, or thereabouts.' Herrick's speech was beginning to slur.

Carr finished his whisky and got up. 'It's gone midnight,' he said. 'I'm going to bed. You'd better do the same. There'll be some fast talking to do in the morning.'

'I'll stay here for a bit,' Herrick told him.

Carr glanced at the whisky bottle, shrugged and walked out of the bar.

Three minutes later he shut his bedroom door behind him, switched on the light and looked at the Doberman pinscher. Its body was sleek and muscular, shiny brown coat with black markings, eyes, yellow in the lamplight, fixed on Carr's throat.

'Nice doggy,' Carr said and the dog rumbled deep in its chest, its slim hindquarters tensed for a spring. Carr stood very still. Thirty inches at the shoulder, he thought, and about 95 pounds of useful killing machine.

'Nice doggy,' he said again and the vicious-looking head lowered fractionally and the jaws parted an inch. The rumbling sound increased in menace. The eyes never moved from the knot of his tie.

'All right,' Carr said, 'If you can't be civil let's play it your way,' and took one pace forward, dropping almost to his knees as the Doberman leapt. He heard the snap of teeth above his head as his hands clamped on the trailing fore-paws and jerked them outwards at right-angles to the body in an attitude of crucifixion. The dog screamed once and died. Carr stood looking down at its corpse wondering where Herrick had found the animal, then he lay down on the bed to wait.

It was nearly 1.00 a.m. when he was brought to his feet by a light tapping on the door. He opened it and watched for reaction on Herrick's face, but there was none. Alcohol had his nerves well under control.

'Yes?'

'I thought I had better brief you on Ratshelm.

Carr nodded, opened the door wider and Herrick said, 'My God! What's that?'

Carr closed the door. 'Well it isn't a horse. I rather think it's some sort of dog. Or it was. A fidgety, bad-tempered sort of dog. It wanted to bite me which is strange, because I always get on so well with animals and little children. Except for my niece, that is. She bit me once.'

'What did you do?'

'I bit her back and my sister crowned me with a flower vase. We haven't spoken since.'

'To the dog, man! It looks like a killer!'

'Oh. Haven't spoken to it since either,' Carr said. 'Not much point seeing it's dead.' He scratched a thumb-nail through the early morning stubble on his chin and added, 'I think I must be blown, Hendrix. Someone put that pooch in here. It hasn't got a key.'

'And you killed it just like that?'

Carr turned to him and smiled rather charmingly. 'No need to be afraid of dogs,' he said. 'What do you suppose our Commandos or Special Air Service blokes are trained to do when breaking into an enemy airfield or something and get jumped by a guard-dog? Offer it bits of steak?' He looked down at the body at his feet. 'They get their necks out of the blasted way and spreadeagle its forelegs, that's what they do. And they do it so fast it doesn't have time to make a sound. I was a bit slow tonight. This one yelped. Comes of drinking too much whisky with you.' He smiled at Herrick again and added, 'We mustn't make that mistake in future.'

Herrick stared at him woodenly and Carr asked, 'Will you help me to swing this thing out of the window? If we can throw it as far as the hotel gardens they'll think it was hit by a truck.'

Leaning out of the window, they could just discern the dark shape of the dog lying in the shrubbery near the roadside seven storeys below.

'Bad doggy!' Carr said.

Still leaning on the window ledge Carr turned his head and looked at Herrick. He was always suspicious of those who deliberately paraded their fallibility. It was such an obvious thing to do to lull others into a sense of false security. Could Herrick be credited even with such a minor subtlety? He doubted it. Herrick wanted him dead and twice he had failed to bring about that desirable state of affairs because that part of the brain controlling the clever hands few locks or safes could withstand, was not supported by an equal ability to assess the potential of human opposition.

Carr thought that Herrick had probably put in a plea to have him killed in Bogota, had it refused and tried himself when the long period of waiting to join Ratshelm had eroded his nerve. That Ratshelm would try to kill him, as part payment for Herrick's unique talents, when he was ready to do so, he had no doubts at all.

He looked down at the dog and toyed with the thought of sending Herrick after it. 'Man and dog fight in hotel bedroom. Both fall to death from seventh-floor window.' Fun for the newspapers. A commendation for the policeman who noticed that Herrick had no tooth-marks on him. No go.

'And as I'm blown,' Carr said, 'we'll skip the Avianca flight. Don't cancel the booking. We'll simply be listed as "no show".'

'Then what?'

'Then we drive down the mountain and hire a light plane from one of the airstrips at the bottom. I'm not going near El Dorado airport again while the natives stay hostile. Too many people to watch.'

'That makes sense,' Herrick said and the relief in his voice, the relief that he had no accusation to answer, came clearly to Carr's ears.

Carr moved away from the window, placed his case on the bed and the contents of the drawers beside it. He began to pack methodically.

'I'd like to know which particular bunch of natives has it in for me,' he said. 'I'd like to know why any of them has it in for me. I'm not known, except as a friend of yours.'

Herrick waited just long enough before he asked, 'Have you considered the possibility of its being Ratshelm's lot? They know about you from me. I can't think of anyone else here who has ever heard of you. Perhaps you shouldn't come to Barrancabermeja.'

Mentally Carr nodded his approval. Herrick was improving, offering him a way out, a way he did not dare allow him to take, but balancing the offer against his knowledge of Carr's dedication.

'I don't think that's the answer,' he said. 'From what you've told me, they wouldn't have botched the job. It'll be one of the smaller outfits trying to stop you getting to Ratshelm and maybe thinking of press-ganging you themselves. To do that, they first had to get rid of the body-guard. That's me. I could be wrong, but I think we should warn Ratshelm that there may have been a leak about you from this end.'

'We'll do that,' Herrick said. 'I'll go and pack and order a car.'

'And some protection,' Carr added softly when the door had closed behind Herrick.

There was only a night porter on duty in the foyer when he dropped a note to Whitehead in the mail box. It read, 'Areas D/E starting Thursday'. There was no signature and Thursday was two days away.

CHAPTER EIGHTEEN

Trelawney stood in the doorway of the Deputy Director's room, glanced round it, then looked at Rafferty seated behind the desk.

'Congratulations, Raff.'

'Yes, and you can get stuffed too, chum,' Rafferty said. 'Shut the door and sit down.'

'What on?'

Rafferty whispered, 'Oh hell,' half to himself and depressed a button on his desk-speaker.

'Yer, sir?'

'Liz, when I was last here, all of fifteen minutes ago, I had two visitors' chairs. Have the bailiffs been in?'

'I think Mr Fenner borrowed them for his meeting, sir,' the box said.

'Oh that's nice. In that case tell Georgina to stop giggling, get off your spare one and bring it in here.'

'Georgina isn't here, Mr Rafferty, so I couldn't really say if she's giggling or . . .'

'Then could you bring it in yourself? I know you're pushing twenty-six, but Mr Trelawney's older than that and if he doesn't sit down soon he may have one of his turns.'

The box snorted and a moment later a girl came into the room carrying a typist's chair. She smiled at Trelawney, scowled ferociously at Rafferty and went out again.

'Liz's crazy about me,' Rafferty said. 'Sit down, Al. How's your excessively alluring wife?'

Trelawney raised an eyebrow at him. 'Barry tell you?'

'Yes, it's essential for us Directors to know what you young people are about.' Rafferty grinned, then added, 'Thanks for the "best man" bit. I'd have liked to have been that. How is she anyway?'

'All right now, but she was pretty tired after Bangkok. We "young people" aren't as young as we were, Raff.'

Rafferty nodded. 'That's one of the reasons why I'm seeing you both today. I've asked Jane to come here at four this afternoon, so I'm getting you out of the way first. There has to be some advantage to seniority.'

Trelawney sat perched on the typist's chair. It was much too small for him but, his mind groping for a reason for Rafferty's mentioning a briefing for Jane, he didn't notice the discomfort. Neither of them was ever told that the other was to receive an assignment nor, until it was over, did they discuss it between them.

'You've never done a "hit" job, have you, Al?'

'What? Oh no, I haven't.'

'And I don't imagine you fancy the idea too much.'

'No, I don't.'

'Well,' Rafferty said, 'I'm afraid you're going to fancy it even less when I tell you that the target is Herrick.'

Trelawney's black eyebrows almost met above his nose as he frowned.

'So Herrick's been "turned".'

It wasn't a question, but Rafferty replied, 'Yes, if he was ever straight.'

Still frowning Trelawney asked, 'Why can't you use John Carr? It's more his line of country than mine.'

Wordlessly Rafferty handed the papers Martha had given him across the desk. For a moment Trelawney continued to look at him, then took them and began to read.

When he had finished he said in a toneless voice, 'I see. At the moment I'm only the back-up man. If Carr makes it I just come home. Right?'

'Right. *If* Carr makes it. I don't know how well you know him, but my reading of the man is that he cares so little about anything that he has a distinct edge over us lesser mortals when it comes to survival. Perhaps he'll even pull this off, although it's difficult to see how, but I don't have to tell you that "perhaps" isn't good enough, Al.'

Trelawney sat staring moodily in front of him, saying nothing.

'You have the right to refuse the mission,' Rafferty said.

'But you're asking me not to.'

'But I'm asking you not to. I could send Fenner or Clarges. I could bring Barton home and send him. I don't want to do any of these things because you're better than they are. That's not a compliment, it's a fact.'

'Oh great,' Trelawney said. 'If I fall round your neck will you put me in for a salary increase? Raff, it's pretty hard to stomach the . . .'

He stopped talking when Rafferty slammed a fist down on to the desk top and said with controlled violence, 'Please do not give me that crap about shooting a man down from cover. I'd probably sob and I like to keep that for Monday mornings. Let me remind you that before you had been operational in this organization for more than a few months you sat in cover and watched a whole bunch of Arabs blown to blazes in a mine-field you'd sown. I suppose that was all right because you hadn't met them socially. Well, this time you have met your target but, since you last saw him, Herrick has joined this really fun crowd who go into villages and slice pieces off the kids with their machetes until the parents remember that they'd always wanted to be guerrillas. Does that make it any easier for you?'

'Just get on with the briefing.'

Rafferty said, 'Jesus Christ!' then began moving files and loose papers about on his desk as though searching for something. He abandoned the hunt abruptly and looked at Trelawney.

'Al, I did not ask for this bloody job. In fact I refused it when it was offered to me, then agreed to do it on a very temporary basis. If this first briefing of mine, which I don't seem able to get off the ground, is anything to go by, refusing was the most sensible thing I ever did.' He sighed and added, 'For what it's worth, Herrick organized the killing of Michael Chandler in

Bucharest. I shouldn't really tell you that, sounds like I'm ordering a vendetta, but anything to produce a detectable degree of enthusiasm in your voice.'

Trelawney said, 'I'm sorry, Raff. Of course I'll do it. You caught me off balance. Herrick always strikes me as so damned helpless.'

'Are you absolutely sure? I'm not climbing into bed with any reluctant virgin. Not from this chair I'm not. If I can't score I don't start.'

'I'm sure.'

Rafferty's nod conveyed complete acceptance. 'Okay. Go to Caracas and stay there until you hear from the boss. He told me to set this thing up, but after you leave this room he's running it. You're an independent oil consultant by the name of Stephen Armitage drumming up business for yourself in Venezuela and Colombia. You can remember enough of the oil lingo to make the right noises, can't you?'

'Yes, I can.'

'Good. Here's all your documentation and assorted bits and pieces.'

Trelawney took the large buff envelope and said, 'Contacts?'

'None in Venezuela. Man called Purvis at the Bogota Embassy in Colombia. He's one of ours. Fair hair, blue eyes, five foot ten, medium build. He'll make himself known to you at the airport. I've sent him some hardware by diplomatic bag for you to choose from.'

Rafferty talked on for fifteen minutes and ended by saying, 'Shove the notes on the Ratshelm organization into the shredder before you leave. They're copies. Any questions?'

'No.'

'Very well. Now, about Jane, It's been . . .'

'Stop it right there, Raff,' Trelawney told him. 'We don't play it that way, she and I.'

'Why,' Rafferty asked amiably, 'don't you shut your face? Barry's decided to offer her a job as a Junior Mission Controller. No more field work. Bangkok was the last. But don't worry. She won't be allowed to run any mission of yours.'

He watched, amused, as Trelawney fought to keep a look of indescribable relief beneath the surface of his face, nodded dismissal at the resultant belligerent glare and smiled when the door closed behind him. It was nice to be given the chance of playing Santa Claus. Perfectly aware of the selfishness of the thought, he hoped Trelawney wouldn't spoil it all by getting himself killed.

In his own room Trelawney tipped the contents of the buff envelope on to his desk and was sorting through them when the telephone rang.

'Trelawney.'

'Have you been briefed by Mr Rafferty, Mr Trelawney?' Martha's voice.

'Yes, Martha. I've just left him.'

'Then would you please come and see the Director now?'

'Of course,' Trelawney said, scooped the documents into a drawer, locked it and walked along the passage to Barry's room. A few moments later he left it again, his expression thoughtful.

Paradoxically, Jane Trelawney's anonymity as an agent came from an appearance so stunning that it rarely occurred to anyone to connect her with such a role in life. On this evening she had surpassed herself.

Her husband closed the door of their apartment behind him and stood, eyebrows raised, staring at her across the big studio room, taking in the long-sleeved, high-necked white jersey dress, its virginal cover-up provocatively revealing, the lilac high-heeled boots fringed above the ankles.

'Well, look at you! Full war-paint and all. Don't tell me Barry's given you a man-trap assignment.'

She rested a hand on one out-thrust hip, drooped her lashes over long grey eyes and formed her lips into a moue, parodying a pin-up stance.

'Much more important than that,' she said. 'I've been made a Mission Controller which means that I shall control missions and men. Dozens of them. Men I mean.'

'You're kidding.'

'I am *not* kidding!'

He moved quickly towards her, smiling delightedly, then stopped in obedience to an imperiously raised hand.

'Unfortunately,' she went on, 'I am barred from controlling *your* activities at work, so I have decided to do so at home. You may kiss my hand and take me out to dinner. With my new salary I can afford to let you do that out of the house-keeping now.'

Trelawney laughed happily and swung her off the floor.

'I'm so very glad, my love.'

'I thought you might be. Stop ruining my lipstick.'

For long seconds he ignored the injunction until she drew her head back and said, 'You're a darling for being surprised.'

'What do you mean?'

'Raff told me he'd told you.'

'Blabbermouth.'

'You're going away, aren't you?' It was more statement than question.

'Did the bloody man tell you that as well?'

'No. I just knew.'

It was true, he thought. She almost always knew as she had when he had been ordered to Cologne and Malmo. He nodded and set her back on her feet.

'Where shall we go to dinner?'

'Nowhere, darling,' she said. 'The tarty effect's just for you.'

CHAPTER NINETEEN

The protection Carr had anticipated was introduced in a mixture of Spanish and broken English as the driver's two cousins. They lived at Mosquera, a village beyond the nearest airstrip, and would be grateful for a lift if this could be permitted.

'Okay,' said Herrick, Carr added 'Why not?' and the driver said 'Muy bien. Gracias.'

One of them got in the front beside the driver, the other between Carr and Herrick in the back. Carr settled himself down to sleep. He expected no trouble during the drive and the smell of the man sitting next to him was something he would be glad to be unaware of. When the car stopped beside the airstrip's small office building he awoke. Dawn was breaking hesitantly and his watch told him that he had slept for two and a half hours.

He got out of the car, walking away from it and the smell, leaving Herrick to bargain with the driver. Before he reached the building, the door opened and a man came out hitching up his trousers with some difficulty because of the rifle he was carrying. Eventually he had them settled above his hips to his satisfaction and took the rifle in both hands, looking past Carr at the group around the taxi.

'Good morning,' Carr said and the man continued to stare past him.

'*Habla Usted inglés?*' Carr asked, expending half his Spanish vocabulary and getting no more reaction than he had done before. Only when he raised his arms, made flapping motions with them and said 'Barrancabermeja?' did the eyes flick towards him and immediately away again.

Carr stood waiting, relaxed, until he heard doors slam, the engine start and the taxi move away, then he turned to see Herrick approaching.

The man with the rifle said, 'You armed?'

'No.'

'Take off your jacket, turn around and roll your pants up over your knees.'

Carr offered no resistance and Herrick followed his lead.

The man said, 'So all right, you're clean and I fly you to Barrancabermeja. I don't want no trouble with Ratshelm. You tell him I treated you fair. I just don't want my plane hijacked into his goddam army is all.'

He turned away and they followed him around the building to where an old single-engined 'Beaver' was parked.

'Who's Ratshelm?' Carr asked.

'Oh sure!' the American bush pilot said. 'I don't know him neither. Ask those three guys who brought you.'

Apart from the pilot's inaudible exchanges with the control tower at Barrancabermeja, nobody spoke again until they climbed down on to the shimmering tarmac of the airport. It was still early in the day, but Carr could feel the heat beating at his head and shoulders and clawing through the soles of his shoes.

'How much?' he asked.

The pilot squinted at him in the sun's glare. 'Nothin',' he said. 'And you tell that to Ratshelm too.'

Herrick watched while the pilot clambered back into the cabin of the plane, but Carr strolled away in the direction of the reception lounge, indifferent to the fear that Ratshelm apparently instilled in others, wondering what it was they felt and why they should feel it. After a few paces he abandoned the line of thought. It was no stranger to him but, outside his experience as it was, he had nothing on which to base a conclusion. Behind him he could hear Herrick's hurrying footsteps, but he didn't look round.

On the forecourt of the fly-blown airport building, the fourth taxi in line drew across and stopped beside them. There was no expostulation from the drivers of the three in front of it. Herrick spoke to the man at the wheel, received a reply which seemed to satisfy him and motioned Carr to get in. They drove towards the town.

Suddenly Carr said, 'Tell the driver to stop at the tobacconist up ahead there.'

'I have plenty of cigarettes,' Herrick replied. 'And anyway you should have . . .'

'Do it.' Carr had spoken quietly, but his tone brought the taxi to a stop outside the tobacconist. 'Thank God someone around here understands English,' he said, pushed past Herrick's legs and crossed the pavement to the shop. He returned holding a pack of cigarettes and got back into the car.

'I'd like to know where we're going,' he said. 'So would three men in a grey Buick parked a hundred yards back on the opposite side of the road and that character on a Honda fiddling with his saddle-bag one block in front. He passed you when I was in the shop.'

'We're being followed,' Herrick said.

Carr whispered, 'Oh Christ,' lay back in his seat and closed his eyes. 'Ratshelm's men or police, driver?' he asked and wondered how Herrick had managed to stay alive so long.

'*Policia*, señor. I know these men from two years since.'

'Okay,' Carr said. 'What do you want to do about it, *Hendrix*? You seem to have had yourself well advertised and the chances of the driver losing them in a town as small as this are nil.'

Herrick sat still, sweat gathering on his forehead and upper lip. Carr could feel it doing the same on his own. It was very hot in the stationary cab. He waited for Herrick to say something, but nothing came.

To the driver he said, 'Is there a cat house within twenty minutes' walk of our destination?'

The man turned and looked at him, puzzled.

'A cat house, señor?'

'Girls. A brothel.'

'*Ah! Si*, señor. Many, many.'

'Open at this time of day?'

'Open all day, all night, señor. Very good business.'

'Take us to one with a back entrance, not too close to where we're going.'

'All close, señor. Small town with many homes for the cats.'

'Just take us to one before you get a parking ticket,' Carr said.

The cab drew out into the light traffic and the motor-cycle took up station ahead of it. Leaning forward and angling his head to the left Carr could see the reflection of the Buick in the shop windows keeping two cars between itself and their taxi.

Without looking at him, he said to Herrick, 'If there's anything in your bag which shouldn't be there, take it out now and shove it down your shirt front. Both our bags stay here.'

'Why?' Herrick asked, his voice testy.

Carr looked at him. 'Because you don't take a week-end suitcase into a cat house. Not at our age you don't.'

Herrick grunted and said, 'There's nothing incriminating in mine.'

'Well,' Carr replied, 'that can't be bad.' Enquiringly he added, 'I take it you know where we're going and how to get there.'

'Yes,' said Herrick.

Carr passed some money over the driver's shoulder. 'When we get to the brothel you just wait. If nothing happens, wait for two hours, then go in and ask for us. If the police leave, or you think they've left, you still wait for two hours. If the police search the place, you go in after them. You want your fare. Understand?'

'*Si*, señor.'

'Right. If the police don't take them off you, you can keep the bags and what's in them. You won't be seeing us again. All right?'

'*Si*, señor. *Muchas gracias.*'

'And, my friend, for your own good, all you know about us is that we wanted cigarettes and girls, so you found them for us.'

'Cigarettes and girls is what I know. Not one goddam anything else of nothing.'

'Good for you,' Carr said.

The man at the reception desk got up when Carr and Herrick walked in. He was wearing a frilled white evening shirt, black tie, brown trousers and sandals. He smiled and his teeth matched his trousers.

'Good morning, misters. You want girls?'

Carr turned to close the door. 'No sex please,' he said. 'We're British.' He thought that was rather funny and grinned. The taxi had moved a car's length clear of the front entrance and the driver was settling himself down to sleep. The anonymous grey police Buick slid slowly by. He pushed the door to.

'What you say, mister?'

Carr turned. 'I said we'd have a drink and look at what you've got to offer.'

Another brown smile rewarded him. 'Is good. What you like?'

'Whisky, and I'll see the bottle first.'

They followed the man into a small passage bar and watched him reach for a bottle, begin to pour from it.

'I said I'd see the bottle first.'

The man looked at Carr, his expression pained.

'You no trust me?'

'Of course I trust you,' Carr said, 'but Ratshelm likes us to be careful. He dislikes wood alcohol, diseased girls and people with memories.'

In absurdly slow motion the bottle was replaced on the shelf and another, from under the bar, presented for Carr's inspection. The pained expression had gone, leaving none at all.

Carr took his drink and walked out of the far end of the bar. He located the stairs to the floor above and others leading down. He examined both levels then, satisfied, returned to the bar. Herrick was sitting, staring moodily at the whisky in his hand. The receptionist-barman was chewing his lip. Carr sat down and three girls walked into the bar in single file. It was too narrow for them to do it any other way. They cast sidelong glances at the men as they passed, trying to appear not to do so. All three were naked.

Swivelling on his bar stool Carr watched them go by. 'I'll take the black girl,' he said.

She heard and understood because she gave a little leap, turned and skipped towards him, laughing.

'And your friend?' There was strain in the man's voice.

'He doesn't like girls,' Carr said and felt rather than saw Herrick's baleful look. He took the girl's hand, jerked his head at Herrick and walked in the direction of the stairs. Herrick followed slowly, scowling, At the foot of the stairs, his arm around the black girl's naked waist, Carr told him what he had to do.

'I hope you know what you're doing,' Herrick said.

Carr slid his hand up to cover the girl's right breast. 'If you're putting in some heavy hoping,' he said, 'hope that they don't.'

Half-way up the stairs the girl said, 'Why does he have to stand by the kitchen door, honey? So he don't like girls, but what's with him an' doors? Ah thought ah knew it all, but doors! You're openin' up a whole new world for me.'

Softly he said, 'There are thousands of Colombian black girls, but you're not one. Where are you from?'

'Memphis, honey.'

He nodded. 'If you want to go back to Tennessee some day, you'd better start right and do exactly what I tell you to do this morning.'

Her body answered him with a rapid undulation more like a seismic shock wave than a shiver. She added to it by saying breathlessly, 'Anything you want, lover.'

At the top of the stairs he handed her bank notes. 'I don't know where you can put those,' he said, 'but we all have our problems.'

She thumbed through them and looked at him wide-eyed. 'That's a lot of currency, honey. Is this where ah get acquainted with doors?'

'Yes,' he said. 'That one.'

She followed the direction of his pointing finger and shook her head. 'That room's occupied. The one to the left is free. They're all the same.'

'Not to me they're not.' His voice hardened. 'And don't tell me things I know. It sounds like a massacre in there. Go in and join it. The man won't object. If the girl does, stuff some notes in her face. I'll be through fifteen seconds later.'

'Through?'

'Through and out of the window. Now move and it's been nice knowing you.'

He pushed her roughly away. She staggered, recovered her balance and looked back at him. 'It could have been good, honey,' she said, then opened the door and walked into the room.

For seven seconds Carr listened to voluble Spanish. At eight the words cut off and there were only noises. He counted steadily up to fifteen, opened the door, closed it silently behind him and crossed to the window in a running crouch with no more than a glance at the writhing figures on the bed.

He squatted on his heels on the window ledge watching the motor-cyclist directly below him speaking into a microphone, waited patiently until it was returned to its rest and jumped.

Herrick opened the back door to his knock, followed him up the steps of the service area to the street and stopped at the sight of the figure sprawled on the ground beside the toppled Honda.

'Is he dead?'

'No.'

'What happened?'

'They made a mistake. They should have covered the back alley with the car. You can't jump on a car roof with three men under it and expect to get away with it, and you can't jump on motor-cyclists in the main street without attracting attention. Now let's get the hell out of here. It's your play.'

'This way. I memorized the map.'

'Clever of you,' said Carr and Herrick scowled at him again, started to say something, changed his mind and walked off. Carr followed five yards behind him.

Herrick led the way to a grimy building near the port without faltering. Nobody followed them until the last fifty yards when two men in mechanics' overalls fell in behind.

'We have company,' Carr said.

Without turning his head, 'Ratshelm's men,' Herrick replied. 'I was warned that they staked the place out.'

For some reason it surprised Carr to find that the owner of the building was a woman. She was tall for a Spaniard and about sixty years of age. Addressing herself solely to Herrick she explained in fair English that she ran an apartment building for a certain type of customer, that he and Carr came into that category, that their apartment number was 7, that if the police called they would be told that number and that no interference or assistance would be forthcoming from the staff or the other guests.

Sententiously, she ended, 'The whole is greater than the sum of the parts you understand, but I can give you the means to protect yourselves if you need.'

'A bottle of whisky, please,' Carr said. She looked at him coldly, opened a cupboard and handed him the whisky without a word.

'Thanks,' he said, took the key marked 7 from its hook and walked up the stairs. Behind him he heard Herrick say, 'I think I'd prefer a gun.'

He was washing when Herrick came into the small apartment and went into the bedroom. Standing in the entrance to the shower cubicle drying himself, he watched the bedroom door speculatively.

Herrick appeared in the doorway. 'I think I'll turn in. I'm tired.'

'You do that thing,' said Carr. For a minute he continued to stand where he was thinking back over the past few days, wondering if he had missed some opportunity of killing Herrick without implicating himself. He didn't think he had.

CHAPTER TWENTY

The triple knock was anything but tentative and Carr wasn't surprised when it was followed by a voice saying, '*Policia!* Please be opening.'

'So much for romping about in knock-shops,' he said to himself and got slowly to his feet. That attempt at evasion had had little chance of success in a town as small as this, he knew, but it had been worth trying. When he reached the door he opened it wide because there was no merit in peering furtively through a crack.

'You will be Señor Carr?'

Carr looked thoughtfully at the handsome, immaculately dressed man standing in the doorway. 'I already am, and hope to continue to be so,' he said.

'Please?'

'Yes, I'm Carr. Who are you?'

'Is good,' the man said and held out a warrant card. Carr glanced at it, then asked, 'What can I do for you, Major Garcia?'

'Answer the questions I am asking, señor, and I shall be delightful '

'But if I don't you'll start throwing your weight around. Is that it?'

'You have my meaning with precision, señor.'

Carr stepped to one side. 'You'd better come in. I'd hate to see you work yourself into a lather. The climate's all wrong for that. May I offer you a drink?'

'A small piece of that whisky I am seeing there will be tasteful, señor.'

Gesturing towards a chair Carr walked towards the empty bookcase, took the whisky bottle from the top and poured a small measure into the only glass. He handed the drink to the plain-clothes man and said, 'Fire away.'

'Your health, señor.'

'Is excellent. Next question.'

The policeman smiled with gentle reproof before saying, 'Now is not the moment to twist language with me. My English speaking is not always so perfect as I wish. Sometimes there is a slide of the tongue. But you are to understand that I am here in seriousness with urgency and I expect this of you also, otherwise I shall throw the weights around with much lather.'

'You're overdoing it, Garcia,' Carr said.

'Please?'

'Knock it off, will you? You and your "seriousness with urgency".'

'Ha! You remember my each word.'

'I remember everything, Garcia, including a lecture you gave to an international audience of Treasury officials in Panama during 1973. The subject was illegal currency manipulation in the Americas and your English is as good as mine.'

Garcia said, 'Mmm. Comes of being educated at Harrow and Trinity, Dublin, I suppose. Oh well, I always was a lousy actor, but even *my* hick cop image works sometimes.' He paused before asking, 'So you're a Treasury man, are you?'

'Was,' Carr told him. 'I'm nothing now. Just spend my time travelling and seeing new places.'

'You pick strange travelling companions.'

Carr frowned. 'Do you mean Hendrix? What's strange about him? From what I've seen of this country it could, with respect, use as many agronomists as it can lay its hands on.'

'Agreed, Carr, agreed. But who told you he was an agronomist?'

'He did.'

'And you believed him?'

'Not at first.'

There was heightened interest in Garcia's voice when he said, 'Why not?'

'I like to check my facts before jumping to conclusions.'

'So?'

'So I looked the word up in a dictionary.'

'Very funny,' Garcia said and stared down into his whisky glass. Carr watched him impassively, wondering if Herrick was asleep or listening at the bedroom door.

Moving his gaze back to Carr, Garcia asked, 'Where's Hendrix now?'

'He said something about buying "field" equipment, whatever that entails. When I came out of the shower he wasn't here, so I suppose that's what he's doing.'

Garcia nodded, finished his whisky and began to talk almost meditatively. 'Barrancabermeja's a rotten town, Carr. Lawless, Communist-ridden, malarial and this so-called apartment building is nothing more than a transit camp for anti-government elements. We let it exist for the obvious reason that it helps us to know who is where. Take my advice and go to Cali, or Bucaramanga, or Medellin. Cartagena is worth a visit too. When you've done that, go home.'

'What about Hendrix?'

'We'll take care of him.'

It was a quiet statement of fact, spoken without emphasis, and Carr had no doubt that it was the voice of DAS. They could do it too. DAS had penetrated some of the guerrilla groups Whitehead had told him, so it was possible that they had foreknowledge of Ratshelm's latest valuable acquisition. The speed with which the police had been on to them after their arrival at Barrancabermeja airport that morning made the possibility a virtual certainty. For a moment he wondered why they had waited so long, then concluded that demonstrated intent would weigh more heavily with the courts than rumours of it.

'Why so pensive, Carr?'

'I'm puzzled,' Carr said. 'If Hendrix is into something illegal, as you seem to be implying, I'd have thought I'd be considered contaminated.'

'So would I and so you are,' Garcia told him. 'But we know about Hendrix and don't know about you.'

Carr experienced the merest ripple of irritation. If Garcia's acting was as bad as he claimed, his material was an affront to his audience. How long, he wondered, had it taken to obtain statements from the police motor-cyclist, the man and the black girl at the brothel? Five minutes? Ten? *'Oh, that's all right, Señor Carr. Policemen get assaulted all the time here. We don't give it a thought.'* So Herrick was to be pulled in and questioned about Ratshelm's present whereabouts while he himself was let loose on a long rein to see where he led them. *'Colonel Barry? This is Purvis in Bogota. Herrick has been put away for five years and Carr wants to know if he should wait until they let him out, ask Ratshelm to organize a jail break, or just come home.'* He stifled the grin that tugged at his mouth before it could form. It appeared that the time was approaching when he would be obliged to assault his second policeman of the day.

'There's nothing of much to know,' he said. 'Like some more whisky?'

'No thanks, Carr. But I *would* like you to lie face down on the floor with your arms stretched out in front of you.'

'Okay,' Carr said amiably and did so. The gun in the policeman's hand didn't seem to give him much option.

Garcia backed away from him to the bedroom door and reached out cautiously for the handle.

Of the nine shots Herrick fired through the door, three entered Garcia's stomach, one his chest and one grazed his neck. The last and the remaining four pock-marked the opposite wall. He died at once, flung on his back by the impact of the bullets, splinters of wood sticking to his clothes and face like so many blow-pipe darts.

Squatting on his haunches Carr watched the ruined door open and Herrick come into the room, a machine-pistol pointing at the body on the floor, a look of astonishment in his bald eyes. When he spoke the astonishment was in his voice too.

'I never killed anyone before!'

Garcia's automatic was under the end of the sofa. Carr noted the precise angle at which it was lying, butt almost directly towards him. Favourable. He shifted his balance fractionally, ears straining for any reaction to the sound of the gunshots. Nothing.

'I know,' he said. 'You try to arrange it by proxy.'

Do it now with Garcia's gun? Make it look as though the two of them had shot each other? The machine-pistol was dangling from Herrick's left hand. No problem. But they were closely connected in a number of people's minds, adjacent rooms at the Tequendama, joint aircraft bookings, shared taxis. Assault on one policeman, accessory to the murder of another. No dice.

'I watched him through the keyhole,' Herrick said.

'Crafty of you,' Carr told him. 'But, unless you've got any ideas on getting out of here, shut up and let me think.'

Herrick dragged his eyes from Garcia, turning them slowly without moving his head to look at Carr.

'I know a safe way out. The woman downstairs told me. It comes up in a garage two blocks away.' His eyes turned back to the dead man as though drawn there against his will.

'I like it. I really like it,' Carr said. 'So suppose you stop standing there admiring your handiwork and we go and find us a garage.'

For a moment longer Herrick remained motionless, then he nodded, propped the machine-pistol upright in an armchair and walked into the bedroom. Carr watched him push one of the two beds aside, work his fingers under the edge of the cheap carpeting and jerk. The carpet came clear of the floor with a sharp ripping sound and two or three tacks shot upwards to settle on the grimy bed-cover.

'Bring the guns, will you?' Herrick asked and began lifting boards from the floor. Carr hooked the machine-pistol into the crook of his arm, not touching it with his fingers, left Garcia's automatic where it was and moved silently to the door. With his ear pressed against it he thought he could hear faint sounds coming from the other side, but wasn't certain. He joined Herrick in the bedroom.

Kneeling by the opening Herrick looked up at him. 'Each apartment has an access point to the air-space beneath the floor leading to . . .'

'On your way,' Carr broke in. 'Save the commercial for later and try not to put your foot through the plaster.'

Straddled across two joists he followed Herrick's grunting progress into the darkness, watching the receding patch of light marking the position of the displaced floor boards. It dimmed, then vanished suddenly and the noise of hammering reverberated through the eighteen-inch cavity as the carpet was nailed back into place.

'Quick of them,' Carr said and continued his crab-like movements, wondering how the policeman's body would be removed from the building. He stopped at the pressure of Herrick's hand against his shoulder.

'It's downwards now,' Herrick whispered. 'There's a gap between this house and the next, but it's blocked front and back. Give me time to get to the bottom, then feel for the pitons driven into the brickwork.'

When Herrick's soft call came up to him he put a foot over the edge feeling for the first piton. He went down slowly in the darkness, finding foot-holds, locating his next hand-hold with the barrel of the machine-pistol before letting go of the one above. When he reached the bottom Herrick asked him what had taken him so long.

'Your blasted artillery,' Carr said.

'Give it to me!'

He held it out, still cradled across his forearm, in the direction of the voice and felt it taken from him.

'And the other one.'

'I only brought yours.'

He felt the barrel of the gun touch his side, then centre on his navel.

'I want the other one too, Carr.'

'Then you'd better go back and get it,' Carr said. 'If you want to be picked up with a murdered cop's gun on you, I don't.'

The barrel left his stomach and Herrick said testily, 'There should be a tunnel here somewhere.'

'There should,' Carr agreed. 'There are nearly always tunnels in this type of situation. Shall we try a little illumination and look?'

The only response was the flare of Herrick's lighter.

The tunnel was an old disused main sewer. It smelled of dust and the air tasted dead, but the flame of the lighter burned brightly. Carr followed so closely behind Herrick that he was stepping in his shadow.

In the garage Carr helped a very small man, half Indian he thought, push a large battered refrigerator over the hole in the floor through which Herrick and he had climbed. The man said, '*Gracias*,' and, with a glow of achievement, Carr plucked '*De nada*' from his memory banks, then looked about him. He looked at the closed, unpainted double doors, a greasy work-bench littered with rusty tools, an ancient Chevrolet taxi and a chipped enamelled metal sign bearing a red star with a green letter 'T' superimposed on it. At the bottom the legend read, '*Use lo mejor – Use TEXACO. TEXACO a sus ordenes.*' He wondered if 'use' was really a Spanish word or if the big oil company was as bad at the language as he. There seemed to be nothing else to look at so he looked at the small man and raised his eyebrows questioningly.

'You wait now,' the man said.

Ten minutes later, bright sunlight flooded the dirty space as the double doors were opened from the outside and another small half-breed came in.

'You go now,' the first said and pointed at the Chevrolet.

Herrick and Carr got in the back and the new arrival seated himself behind the wheel, his eyes barely level with the bottom of the windscreen. The starter groaned tiredly at the listless urging of a flat battery, but eventually the engine fired and the taxi jolted out on to the hot street. It turned towards the edge of the town and accelerated through the crowd of disinterested jay-walking peasants. The buildings fell behind it and the appalling condition of the road deteriorated further. Soon it was running on sand and the jungle began to close in. A mile further on the taxi slowed, stopped and the driver turned to peer at them over the back of his seat.

'Don't tell me,' Carr said. 'You walk now,' and got out on to the sand. It was red and soggy. He watched the taxi turn and start back towards Barrancabermeja then looked at Herrick.

'They'll have heard what happened back there,' Herrick said. 'Someone should be along soon.'

Carr nodded. 'Then I suggest we get away from this track. That someone might come from the wrong direction.'

Two of the armed men walked ahead, two behind, and Carr was impressed by them in an indifferent way. They had materialized out of the undergrowth less than ten seconds after he had first become aware of their approach and he had been amused by Herrick's start of surprise at their appearance. The frisking had been carefully done and Carr had watched with interest as Herrick's machine-pistol was wrapped in cloth, content that no prints of his own were on it, that the murder weapon should be Herrick's personal Sword of Damocles.

They had followed the narrow track for about two miles before it led them on to grassland. A truck was waiting for them there, backed into the edge of the rain forest. Gun barrels prodded them to their places. Herrick into the cab between the driver and one of the escorts, Carr into the open body at the back with the remaining three. For seventy minutes the vehicle lurched and skidded over the soggy uneven ground, never more than a few feet from the shelter of the trees, then it stopped and they were walking through jungle again.

The tent was so cleverly painted and concealed that Carr noticed it only seconds before he was pushed inside. Two of the men followed him in and stood, watching him impassively. He ignored them, concentrating on the squelch of retreating footsteps, trying to guage the direction being taken by Herrick and the other two. Minutes later he picked up the sounds again approaching from the same bearing, then Herrick ducked through the entrance, a carbine in his hands.

'Ratshelm wants to see you, Carr.' They were the first words spoken since the guerrillas had picked them up.

'It's all go,' Carr said.

Herrick spoke briefly in Spanish to the two men then turned back to Carr and gestured towards the aperture with the carbine.

Outside Carr spotted the larger tent at once. It was as beautifully camouflaged as the one he had just left, but he had known where to look for it. The knowledge was valueless, but acquiring it as much a life pattern as turning to Herrick and asking, 'Which way?'

CHAPTER TWENTY-ONE

There were eight men in the bigger tent, seven of them, dressed in ragged, drab *ruanas* and patched trousers, were seated on the ground, backs to the tent walls. All of them had weapons ranging from old British Lee-Enfield rifles to modern Czechoslovakian machine-pistols across their knees. They looked dirty, tough and efficient. Some wore the 'Che Guevara' moustaches Carr had forecast to Herrick. All seven were unshaven to varying degrees. Only their guns looked clean, oiled, very functional.

The eighth was sitting on a canvas stool behind a collapsible aluminium table. His narrow, clean-shaven face, neat white suit and shirt, sober blue tie and pince-nez gave him the look of an intellectual banker. No square head, no Heidelberg scars, no 'en brosse' haircut Carr noticed and was mildly disappointed. Perhaps that had been the war before.

'*Guten Tag, Herr Sturmbannfuhrer!*' he said, glanced round the tent and added, 'The Panzergrenadier-division "*Gotterdammerung*" seems to have shrunk a little. I thought you might welcome a new recruit.'

Washed-out blue eyes regarded him gravely through the old-fashioned spectacles.

'"*Gotterdammerung*".' Ratshelm seemed to taste the word, savouring it as though it were an unexpectedly good wine, 'The twilight of the gods. As a military unit a figment of your imagination and no doubt intended as a sneer, but I find it not inappropriate for the circumstances of those days.' He paused, then went on, 'But now, Señor Carr, you will tell me how you come to know of my one-time rank in the SS and my service as a Panzergrenadier.'

'Your Knight's Cross is sticking out of the front of your shirt,' Carr said.

'That too? You are remarkably well informed. And if I were wearing it you could deduce the rest from it?'

Carr smiled cynically. 'Perhaps not. Hendrix runs off at the mouth a lot. I must have heard it all from him.'

He supposed that, behind him, Herrick had been about to remonstrate because Ratshelm raised a hand before saying, 'You credit Señor Hendrix with greater knowledge than he possesses, Carr.'

'An easy error to fall into, *Herr Sturmbannfuhrer*.'

The German sighed, glanced down at the table in front of him, then up at Carr again. At both movements of his head the reflected light of the pressure lamp glinted from his glasses.

'If you insist on rank,' he said, 'the extent of my present command places me in the General Officer class and, I would have thought, in a position calling for a measure of respect. I do not relish groundless criticism of my officers, neither do I appreciate scathing references to the size of the assault groups I control. They are of the precise composition I have proved time and time again to be the optimum for mountain and jungle operations. We infiltrate, strike and vanish like smoke. Are you capable of comprehending that?'

Carr yawned. 'Brilliant in conception, startling in its simplicity. Clausewitz would have been overwhelmed.'

Ratshelm sighed again and, with no trace of anger in his voice, said, 'I really believe you're the most irritating man I've ever met.'

'You disappoint me,' Carr told him. 'You're supposed to beat the hell out of your varicose veins with a swagger-stick and call me an insolent British swine like they do in World War Two movies.'

As though he hadn't heard, Ratshelm asked, 'What is your interest in Colombian politics, Carr?'

'Fuck-all, Ratshelm.'

'Then you're a mercenary, perhaps?'

'No. I'm a refugee from the big bad world as you know perfectly well from Hendrix, but I shan't complain if you pay me the going rate for the job.'

'And what would you consider that to be?'

'During my probationary period I'd say five times whatever you pay this bunch of spastics.'

Ratshelm flicked his eyes to Carr's right and said, 'Pepito!'

Carr looked the same way, realized his mistake almost too late and reversed the movement of his head. Peripheral vision showed him the half-risen form of one of the guerrillas, and his instinct the blurring arc of a rifle swung by the muzzle. He had time only to drop his chin to his chest before the butt tore at his scalp just above the base of the skull.

He found himself on all fours, shaking his head from side to side, feeling loss of orientation and a crawling sensation as though blood was seeping between his hairs searching for the freer area of flow on the bare skin behind his ears.

Clarity of vision and hearing returned to him simultaneously. He was looking at Ratshelm's shoes and listening to his voice say, ' . . . unemployable in any capacity. Goodbye, Señor Carr. I'm afraid you chose the wrong monastery to seek sanctuary in.' Rapid Spanish followed.

Carr felt both his arms grasped from above, was pulled

upright, turned about and pushed through the tent opening. The big red disc of the sun, streaked and freckled by branches and foliage, was less than four diameters above the horizon. It occurred to him that it had been a long day and that he should have discussed overtime with Ratshelm.

Herrick said, 'I think you may have been a little hasty over that.'

'May I indeed? You wanted him killed and, after due consideration, I have had him killed. What an exceptionally boorish fellow.'

'I mean . . .'

'Never mind what you mean,' Ratshelm said. 'I wish to explain the coming operation to you. Can you read a map?'

'Yes.'

'Then look at this. We are here.' A well-manicured fingernail tapped the paper to indicate a pencilled cross. 'Here, one kilometre away, is an oil camp protected by an army guard and here, two kilometres to the south, the present drilling site. You passed quite close to it today. This is clear?'

'Perfectly.'

'Good. At one hour before dawn on Thursday, that is to say in approximately thirty-six hours, we shall eliminate the army guard at the camp. This consists of one lieutenant and eleven men. The camp will then be open to us and we shall take all American and European personnel prisoner for future ransom negotiations. By American I mean North American of course. The Colombians – well, let us say they have two choices.'

Ratshelm looked up at Herrick. 'I am sure you will agree that when dealing with new recruits, or prospective new recruits, an example is a great persuader.'

Angrily Herrick said, 'I came here under contract to do a job I'm highly qualified at. I don't need any veiled threats from you to encourage me to do it.'

'I'm so glad,' Ratshelm replied. 'And that brings me to your part in this affair. When all opposition has ceased you will be conducted to whichever of the two army trailers contains the safe and any strong-boxes. You will open these and remove all code books, operational orders, lists of radio frequencies and the like. You are to use your own initiative in this regard, bearing in mind that I do not wish to have my men encumbered with requisitions for new boots or similar trivia. I take it that your

Spanish is good enough to tell the difference.'

Herrick told him stiffly that it was.

'Excellent. I should, perhaps, warn you that the army has recently taken to wiring its lock mechanisms to explosive charges or the electricity supply, but I don't imagine that these primitive devices will cause you any concern.'

From just inside the tent flap Carr said, 'None whatsoever. He can open a booby-trapped chastity belt with a lump of ear wax.'

Only Herrick's head did not snap in Carr's direction. He stood looking down at the German and said, 'That's what I meant by "hasty", Ratshelm.'

Carr's hair was ruffled and his jacket had split from under the right arm-pit almost to the hem, but he appeared to be unmarked. For countable seconds the tableau remained static then, as though roused from a trance, one of the five remaining men raised his rifle and pointed it at Carr.

'I shouldn't if I were you, laddie,' Carr said. 'The General wouldn't like it.'

Ratshelm spoke one short sentence in Spanish and the rifle returned to its original position across the man's knees.

'See what I mean?' Carr asked.

'Where are my men, Carr?'

Carr waved a hand vaguely towards the back of the tent.

'Out there somewhere.'

'What happened to them?'

'We had a difference of opinion, so I persuaded them to lie down and think it over. It's the best way. Increases the flow of blood to the head.'

'I don't believe you.'

'Well, I can't swear to it,' Carr said. 'But I do remember reading in this copy of *Vogue* at the dentist that a few minutes flat on your back, preferably with the feet slightly raised, is worth . . .'

'Silence!'

For the first time there was an edge to Ratshelm's voice. Carr stopped talking and listened interestedly, but without understanding, while the five seated men were given their orders. Four of them got up and left, leaving only the one called Pepito.

His voice calm again, Ratshelm said to Carr, 'As you seem incapable of telling me, you will show me.'

Carr nodded. 'I'm glad you thought of that. Shall we go now?

It'll be pitch-black out there in a minute or two and I don't suppose you're any more anxious to use a flashlight than a gun.'

In the fading light they stood looking down at the two men. Both were flat on the ground, face upwards, their lower legs doubled back around the trunks of two small trees, their insteps jammed behind the calf of the opposing leg. They were conscious, but taking quick shallow breaths as though fighting pain.

'Carr?'

'Yes?'

'What is this?'

'Christ,' Carr said tiredly, 'you don't know much do you? "Grape-vine" it's called. It's a way of tying someone up when you forgot to bring the rope and stop prodding me in the back with that gun will you? I don't want to have to break your arm just when we're getting to know each other. Surely they warned you about *that* in the SS.'

Ratshelm didn't speak, but the pressure of the gun muzzle left Carr's spine.

'Thank you,' Carr said. 'Now, if you don't mind I'll let these two go. They're hurting pretty badly. The circulation in the legs is obstructed and they'll die if they're left there.'

Without waiting for a reply he knelt down, pulled both men into a sitting position and released their feet, then he began kneading and massaging the calves of one of them. The tropical night had come quickly, but there was light enough left for him to see Ratshelm kneeling beside him, copying his actions, working on the second man.

One of them began to moan, the sounds increasing in volume. Carr groped for, and found, a small fallen branch. He held it against the man's mouth and said, 'Bite! Bite on that. It helps. Oh for the love of Mike, stop horsing around. I know you don't speak much English but . . . Hell! Tell him for me, General, and do the same with yours. I don't want to have to lay them out again.'

After three minutes both men were sitting, flexing their legs experimentally, talking quietly to Ratshelm.

'So you did it alone, Carr.'

'Yes, you can call in your search party. There isn't anybody for them to find.'

'How did you do it?'

'Listen,' Carr said, 'they're only half-trained peasants. I expect the rest of your army is the same. That's why you need me. I had to do something because my horoscope says this isn't my week for getting killed, but if I'd decided to kill them that would have been a lot easier and this suit wouldn't have been ruined. My trouble is I'm too considerate.'

A heavy black-out curtain had been hung inside the flap of the bigger tent. Carr edged carefully round it and found himself looking at the muzzle of Pepito's rifle. It slanted towards the ground when Ratshelm appeared behind him. Sitting on the aluminium table Herrick stared moodily at them. He stood up and moved to the side of the tent when Ratshelm walked to the chair behind the desk and sat down.

Ratshelm looked at Carr in silence for a moment, then took off his pince-nez and cleaned them carefully with a spotless handkerchief. Carr waited patiently, apparently absorbed in contemplation of the red indentations left by the glasses on either side of Ratshelm's nose.

Suddenly the German said, 'You deliberately set out to provoke me into ordering your execution, Carr. There is no other logical explanation of your insufferable rudeness which, interestingly enough, has abated considerably since those instructed to do away with you failed in their task. I deduce three things from this. Firstly, you believed your life to be in jeopardy at my hands. Secondly, and in consequence, you wished to demonstrate your potential usefulness to me by neutralizing the men who were to have killed you. Thirdly, you were aware from the beginning that you would not be shot out of hand in this tent, a fate, I suggest, even you would have found difficult to avoid. The third point is supported by words and actions of yours revealing knowledge of the undesirability, under present circumstances, of the use of excessive noise and of showing naked lights.'

Ratshelm paused, replaced his glasses on his nose, then went on, 'I conclude from the foregoing that you are in possession of information, outside information, which could be dangerous to me and my cause. What have you to say?'

'I have to say,' Carr said, 'that that was a notable piece of stolid Germanic thinking. I also have to say that when you people learn to speak English you really do it. Yes, you really do. I haven't listened to anything like that since my old headmaster felt it necessary to . . .'

'Carr!'

'All right, all right. For starters, if you'll pardon the expression, I don't have any outside information, except for a potted biography on you I asked London for when my old pal Hendrix let slip who he was joining. I told you he runs off at the mouth. But if you can take it in basic English I'll make you free of the brilliance of my thought processes.'

Ratshelm turned to look at a white-faced Herrick then back to Carr and asked, 'Why did you contact your people in London?'

'To check on your credibility. I didn't want to get involved with some nut who thought he was the reincarnation of Simon Bolivar with a red star on his hat. After the Colombian authorities and, I imagine, the CIA, London knows as much about you as anyone in the West outside Cuba, so having no Colombian or CIA chums over here I did the next best thing.'

'I see. Go on.'

Carr crossed to the table and sat on a corner of it, looking down at Ratshelm.

'Relax,' he said. 'If I wished you any harm you'd have bought it out there in the woods. Why would I try anything in here with Pepito pointing that cannon of his at my back?'

Slowly Ratshelm removed his right hand from under the lapel of his jacket and let it sink to his thigh. Carr nodded his approval then began to talk rapidly.

'Yes, I provoked you and, if it's any satisfaction to you, I found you a difficult man to unbalance. Yes, I believed my life to be in danger at your hands because Hendrix loused up his own attempt on it in Bogota and I guessed he would hand the job on to you. Yes, I thought an example of what I can do would improve my chances of employment. Yes, I was aware that there would be no shooting because there were no silenced guns around, including yours. Your suit's too sharp to accommodate the extra length.'

While he had been talking, three of the men from the search party had come into the tent and settled down, as before, backs to its walls. A fourth followed and stood, looking around as though deciding where to sit. He was very big.

'As you missed all the action,' Carr said, 'would you like me to pull some pieces off Junior there? I'd hate you to feel deprived.'

'No, thank you,' Ratshelm replied. 'You've made your point in that direction. I'd much prefer to hear your explanation of the necessity for our – er, I believe "maintaining a low profile" is the modern idiom.'

'Oh, that. Well, on the way here we left the truck about two miles before it seemed necessary, because the edge of the grassland ran almost parallel to the track we subsequently followed. We were also cautioned by sign language to remain silent and every time I opened my mouth to pick my teeth someone shoved a gun barrel up my nose.' He paused, then asked, 'Are you sure you wouldn't like me to have a go at Junior? I think he was the one that did it.'

'Get on with your story, Carr.'

'Pity,' Carr said, shrugged, then went on, 'These tents have probably the best camouflage jobs I've seen. You'd miss them at ten yards if you didn't know they were there. Add that to no sign of fire, no smell of fire, people eating cold mush out of cans and it all spelt "advanced base". No, General. No way were you going to shoot me and keep this place secret.'

'You're a very observant man, Carr.'

'Yes, I am. I can hear quite well too. There's an army diesel-generator running not so far off, almost due north of here.'

Ratshelm's voice was very soft when he said, 'I think you have just made a bad mistake, Carr. You did say "army", did you not?'

Carr frowned, then nodded. 'You're partly right. I did say "army", but I don't make mistakes. I may have arrived surprisingly at an unjustifiable conclusion, in which case go ahead and surprise me.'

'Explain yourself.'

'Jesus Christ!' Carr said. 'It's pretty bloody obvious, isn't it? If you take your ear-trumpet outside and listen really hard you may be able to detect the sound of a diesel. I don't think it's a London bus, because Route 29a doesn't run this far and it's been parked in the same place too long anyway. So I assume it's a generator. Now the rest is only hearsay, but when I clawed my way out of the grave and back here you and Hendrix were talking about knocking off an army post. Forgive me if I'm wrong in thinking that the generator provides their power.'

His tone of quiet menace had gone when Ratshelm spoke again.

'You have the job you were seeking, Señor Carr.'

'Thank you, General,' Carr said. 'Could I have some food too? It's been twenty-four hours.'

Sunlight seeped lethargically past the unlaced flap of the smaller tent as though exhausted by its passage through the tangled undergrowth. When it touched Carr's face he awoke, sat up, looked at the dozing figure of his latest companion and wondered again if he was supposed to be under guard. He found it difficult to believe that he was. Each man had been replaced by another at exactly two-hourly intervals throughout the night, but as the new arrival had invariably settled down to sleep or to smoke marijuana the routine appeared to have more to do with outside sentry duty than watching him. For all that, he thought, it was odd that they slept sitting up, guns across their knees, as though afraid of becoming too comfortable, too deeply asleep.

A mental picture formed of Mexicans in similar positions sleeping in the shade of their big hats. Perhaps it was just an ethnic trait. Grinning briefly he pushed the puzzle out of his mind. He wasn't going anywhere yet, but when he did go he knew that he had ninety minutes at the outside to get there and back again which wasn't very much.

That problem went the same way as the first. Worry about it when the time comes he told himself and lay back on the ground scratching behind his knees where the insect repellant he had been given had let him down worst.

There were six new faces in the crowded bigger tent. They, Carr calculated, allowing for sentries not present, made a minimum of twenty men and were, presumably, what Ratshelm had been waiting for. Studying them carefully, trying to assess their capabilities from faces, shoulders, hands, told him a little, but he knew that he would have to watch them in motion before making anything approaching a worthwhile judgement. There was the rest of the day to do that in. Elbows on knees he rested his chin on his cupped hands letting Ratshelm's careful Spanish flow past him unheeded. He was thinking about a pretty woman with red hair he had picked up in a Mayfair bar. Melinda? No, Melissa . . .

'Señor Carr?'

'Yes, General?'

'Ah, I'm glad you're still with us. I will now repeat what I have said in English for your benefit and it will do these people no harm to listen. Most of them have some knowledge of the language. Now, in view of your remarkable qualities it will be your privilege to lead the frontal attack on the army contingent of one officer and eleven men.'

'Fantastic, man. Fantastic,' Carr murmured.

'What did you say?'

'Nothing.'

'Your section will be seven strong and you, personally, will be armed with a machine-pistol. Your . . .'

'No I won't,' Carr said. 'I'll be armed with a bolt-action Lee-Enfield, or an automatic rifle set to single shot. As there are only twelve of them they aren't exactly going to counter-attack in droves and if I see a piece of soldier sticking out from cover I want to hit him, not defoliate the undergrowth.'

'You're a marksman too, Carr?'

'I'm a marksman too, General.'

Ratshelm nodded.

'So be it,' he said, then continued his briefing.

CHAPTER TWENTY-TWO

The smell of marijuana was heavy in the smaller tent and Carr watched the guerrilla's head sag forward, jerk momentarily upright, then sink again until his heavy jowls spread on his chest like the half-inflated inner tube of a bicycle tyre. From the first inhalation of tobacco and cannabis smoke, the transition through mild excitation and giggling to sleep had taken three-quarters of an hour. By Carr's schedule that was fifteen minutes too long, but he still waited another five before moving silently to the tent wall opposite the access flap.

On the outside of the tent, pegs driven into the ground through eyelets set at intervals in the heavy canvas formed an effective seal against the escape of light from the pressure lamp. Earlier Carr had loosened six of them and they came away easily when he forced his forearms between earth and wall and prised upwards. He glanced once more at the sleeping man, slid out through the gap he had made and pressed the pegs back into their holes. Waiting for his eyes to adjust to the darkness he crawled to the end of the tent and peered round. It took more than a minute to distinguish the outline of the sentry he had expected to be there, shoulders propped against a tree, the slightly paler blob of the face turning periodically in his direction.

'Ratshelm, you are a distrustful old bastard,' Carr said to himself, turned and inched his way into the tangled vegetation, moving as close to due south as it would let him and his senses could judge. The few stars visible above couldn't help him. *Polaris*, or the constellation of *Ursa Major*, if it was above the horizon at this hour, could have done, but this close to the equator he knew he would need a mountain top to see them from. He hadn't got a mountain top, or the time to climb one, so he kept the distant sound of the army generator at his back, a sound so faint now that it was little more than a vibration on the still air. When he thought he was in danger of losing it altogether he began pushing sticks into the soil, the first two aligned with the sound, subsequent ones with the two that he had placed last. In the darkness they couldn't be far apart and his progress was slow. Twice he had to work his way round impenetrable clumps of vegetation. He made only right-angle turns doing that in an effort to preserve his line.

Seventeen minutes and a third of a mile from the guerrilla encampment Carr stumbled on to the track. He tore off his shirt, thrust it into a bush and ran.

The drilling site wasn't floodlit as it would have been with the rig in operation, but there were some lights and he saw them from a quarter of a mile away. A minute later he thought he could hear the clink of metal on metal above the sound of his own dragging breaths. He slowed his pace and turned off the track into vegetation which looked sparse enough to allow him to remain upright.

Just short of the edge of the area of bare, flattened soil he stopped. Only a few feet of the bottom of the big rig and the platform on which it stood were illuminated. The rest, except for the red aircraft warning light at its very top, swallowed in darkness. Somewhere a small portable generator rumbled quietly. Four men were working on some heavy machinery near the base of the rig and beyond them an obvious Anglo-Saxon was sitting smoking on a huge, yellow-painted earth-moving machine. Staying in shadow Carr moved quickly round the circular site until he was behind him.

Carr said, 'Don't look round. If you can hear me distinctly scratch your left ear.'

The man scratched his left ear, then went on smoking placidly.

'Listen very carefully,' Carr told him. 'I don't have much time and neither do you. There are guerrillas camped less than a mile south of your accommodation compound led by a man called Hans Ratshelm. Numbers are twenty plus. Arms are light automatic weapons, rifles, hand guns and fragmentation grenades. One hour before dawn this morning they intend to knock off your army protection and hold your lot to ransom.

'The attack will come in three waves. Frontal from the west, flank from the south, then another from the south, not the north. I understand that's meant to be subtle. Your wired compound covers the east. I suggest you call in a lot more army than you've got and, without wishing to teach the lieutenant his job, the choppers should land well out of earshot to the north. Persuade him to keep his radio traffic down to a minimum too. They may be monitoring it. If you've got all that scratch your ear again.'

The man flicked the stub of his cigarette away and slid off the seat of the outsize bulldozer. Without hurry he walked to the edge of the lighted expanse, moved on into deep shadow and began to urinate against a tree ten yards from Carr.

'My ear don't need scratching right now,' he said. 'Come where I can see you, feller.'

Carr did as he was told.

'Sound like a Limey to me.'

Carr nodded impatiently. 'You got it in one. Which will you take? The colour television, the deep freeze, or the five shares in Consolidated Edison?'

'A funny Limey too. What are you? "On Her Majesty's Secret Service" or something?'

'I'm the Fuller Brush man. Now why don't you go and tell the boss what I've just told you? You've only got about three hours to get those troops moved in.'

'Because I'm the Field Superintendent. That makes me the closest thing to a boss between here and Tulsa, Oklahoma.'

'Congratulations,' Carr said. 'So go tell the lieutenant.'

'I might do that thing. Ratshelm has quite a reputation in this country, but I'd like you to tell me something first.'

Carr stood, saying nothing, while the American took a cigarette from his shirt pocket and lit it.

'How come you didn't go north and explain all this to the army yourself? It's half the distance from where you say these people are, so where's the percentage in heading the wrong way to what might have been a deserted drilling location? And how in hell did you know it was here anyway? We haven't spudded-in yet because the draw-works are jammed. There's been no noise and you didn't see these little lights through any mile of jungle.' He hesitated for a second, then went on, 'Well, maybe you did from the track, or you saw the airplane hazard light, but . . .'

Harshly Carr said, 'Why don't you do yourself a favour, shut up and listen to me? I didn't see anything from Ratshelm's camp. It's too deep in cover for that. I noticed the top of your rig from the back of a truck after his boys picked me up near Barrancabermeja and drove along the edge of the grasslands. I noticed it because I'm paid to notice things.

'The chances of this site being deserted were minimal. You don't leave expensive equipment standing around unattended for peasants to cart away and oil companies like a non-functioning rig the way Pam-Am likes 747s sitting empty on the ground, so somebody had to be here working on it. They pay me to know things too. Finally, I didn't go north because Ratshelm has perimeter guards posted between himself and his target and I didn't want to fall over one of them in the dark. Now will you get on your sodding mule, or whatever you use, and make like Paul Revere?'

The American's teeth flashed whitely. 'Sure. You better come along too. The access road we built to move the rig in is just over there. We'll be talking to Lieutenant Descola in less than five minutes.'

Carr shook his head. 'I have a little over a quarter of an hour to get back into my tent before they change guards. If that happens with me missing, Ratshelm will attack at once. Wouldn't you?'

He turned and jogged into the darkness, raising a hand in ackowledgement as a voice called, 'Luck, whoever you are.'

Once on the track he had followed with Herrick and their

escort almost two days earlier and run back down only a few minutes ago he lengthened his stride. From near the drilling site he saw the lights of some vehicle move away. It was travelling in a northerly direction as was he, but on a diverging course and was quickly lost to view. It seemed to take a long time after that to reach the marker he had made of his shirt. He put it on, turned left off the track and followed his line of sticks, pulling them out of the ground as he went.

When Carr crawled back under the tent wall the guerrilla awoke and lurched swayingly to his feet, swinging the muzzle of his gun towards him. He looked confused and frightened.

'Where you go?'

'Make pee-pee,' Carr told him.

'You goddam lie. I take you to leader. He ask you hard!'

'You do that and he'll cut your fat throat for letting me out of your sight,' Carr said and drew a finger across his own neck in demonstration.

The man scowled in concentration, trying to extract meaning from the strange foreign words, then his expression relaxed and he said, 'You goddam right. We stay here, huh?'

'We stay here,' Carr agreed and lay down by the gap he had made, trying to work the external pegs back into the ground. He managed them all but the last.

Lying on his stomach, chin propped on forearms, Carr stared across the seventy-yard stretch of ground separating the jungle edge from the two army trailers. They appeared as featureless dark oblongs visible mainly because of their background of dimly-seen, white-painted oilmen's huts standing in regular lines like some unenterprising building development. He looked at the faintly luminous dial of his watch, slid his rifle further forward and took the grenade from his pocket. The grenade was the signal and there were two minutes to go.

He wondered how frequently the army had to bulldoze the open expanse to keep their killing-ground clear of cover then, because the answer could be of no possible interest to him, he stopped doing it. The slightest breath of air touched his cheek, the first wind he had felt since leaving Bogota. It carried some scent he couldn't identify. Not immediately important. Disregard.

One minute. Pull pin from grenade, holding lever down with

fingers of right hand.

The zephyr on his face again and, he had it now, the smell of burning vegetation. Farmers clearing their land of the rampaging rain-forest growth by fire. Sometimes, he had been told, the miles of damply smouldering river-country produced enough smoke to close El Dorado International Airport, nearly nine thousand feet above.

Ten seconds. Five. Four.

Carr grasped the rifle in his left hand, stood up and threw the grenade. Where it landed he had no idea, until it exploded with a flash and a not very impressive bang far short of the trailers and any sentry who might have been patrolling near them. He moved forward, not hurrying, and sensed rather than saw the three men to his left, four to his right, running ahead of him. Not knowing what to expect, but expecting something, he hurled himself to the ground the moment the floodlights on and around the army trailers smashed the darkness back against the wall of jungle behind him.

Lying motionless, he watched dispassionately as a storm of machine-gun bullets cut down the sprinting guerrillas. Many of the bullets passed close to him, splitting the air like the cracking of whips. He didn't blink. The concentrated firing lasted for twenty seconds before switching suddenly towards the south. 'Overkill,' Carr said and squirmed backwards into cover. When he reached it, severed twigs and small branches were still making their pattering way from limb to limb of the larger trees towards the ground. The shooting stopped abruptly.

It was difficult to be sure with the tang of cordite on the air, but he thought that the smell of burning vegetation was stronger than it had been. He looked back towards the brilliantly lighted area beyond the trees to see if smoke was visible there. It was not, but soldiers, twenty or thirty of them, were fanning out from the trailers, moving cautiously across the open ground, stopping to prod the bodies lying there with their guns. Carr shrugged and moved on, unconcerned about the approaching troops. They would have more sense than to pursue trained woodsmen into the jungle at night. Not, he thought, that there would be many to pursue. *Teniente* Descola had done his job well enough to be *Capitan* Descola by evening.

To reach the guerrilla camp site took him fifty minutes, partly in silent motion, mostly in watching patches of shadow until he was satisfied that they had not moved and would not do so. By the time he had skirted the camp to approach it from the opposite direction the loom of the floodlights in the northern sky was fading at the advance of day. Near the tents he crawled behind a tangled screen of some vine-like growth, lianas he supposed they were, hanging from the branches of a tree and lay watching, listening.

Then he *saw* the smoke. It was moving slowly in isolated drifts about three feet above the ground like ectoplasm undecided whether or not to materialize. He frowned, thinking that if it thickened it could make things difficult for Whitehead in his helicopter. Around him the night sounds of the jungle, the rustlings and sudden scrabbling noises, increased with the coming of the sun, the night people alarmed by the smell of fire. In front of him a long black shape undulated gracefully across an open space and was gone. Jaguar, Carr told himself. Somewhere he had read that occasional litters held one of that hue.

Still he waited, the daylight strengthening enough to turn blacks and greys into colours, but nobody came and there was no sound from either tent. They *had* to come, those few of them that were still alive. This was to have been the gathering point for the victorious guerrillas, their expatriate prisoners and the Colombian 'volunteers'. This still had to be the escape route for the survivors. Their transport, three heavy trucks, including the one he had ridden in, was parked close by. At the briefing Ratshelm had said that the trucks would be brought quietly along the trail from the direction of Barrancabermeja immediately after dark on the previous evening when the demand for electricity in the army trailers and the oil company accommodation compound would be at its height, the generators at their noisiest. They had been. He had heard them and now that it was light he could see parts of all three showing through the piled branches and foliage which camouflaged them.

Quite suddenly it was much more difficult to see them, much more difficult to see anything as a denser drift of smoke enveloped him like an earth-bound cloud. Carr muttered softly, irritably to himself. It was going to be much more difficult to finish what the army had begun unless the visibility improved.

The smoke thinned, then drifted slowly away and Carr reassessed the situation. He was expecting Ratshelm and

Herrick at least. Ratshelm could not conceivably have allowed himself to face the dangers of a night raid, nor permitted his virtually irreplaceable new specialist to be exposed to them. Of the two, he had decided to kill Ratshelm first because he was the more formidable and Herrick would never react with sufficient speed to save himself from the second bullet. If there were more of them – well, it rather depended on how many more, so disregard.

Guaranteed good visibility, he had chosen his cover well. Lianas almost entirely around the tree and a variable but adequate field of fire in most directions. But now there was no guarantee of good visibility with the forest burning not so far away. For a few seconds he considered the possibility that Ratshelm was waiting for the smoke to thicken significantly before making his approach and the further one that the fire, on this occasion, had been started at his order. Pointless speculation, so again disregard.

What he was quite unable to disregard was the fact that any number of men might now be able to reach the transport without his seeing them, let alone shooting at them and that the only place from which he could prevent that was under one of the trucks. With eighteen wheels blocking his line of vision, interrupting his field of fire? Not very satisfactory, but what else?

'Get with it,' Carr said to himself and moved, crouching, towards the trucks. There was adequate low cover but, for once, a large patch of clear sky. He wasn't interested in the sky until, a third of the distance covered, the first jet slammed low overhead and he froze. A second followed, then a third. At that altitude and speed he knew that only movement could betray his presence to them, so he stayed where he was in case there were more to come.

Far off the three reappeared above the trees in a near-vertical climbing turn and the 'H' configuration of the first two told him that they were old British 'Vampires'. The third looked like an early Mark of American 'Sabre' and he wondered which museum the Colombians had found them in. But, antiques or not, the thunder of their passing, like the concussion of a heavy naval gun, made him feel as though his head had been driven down between his shoulders. He shook it ruefully in an attempt to clear his senses.

It was then that Herrick said, 'Drop the rifle, Carr, and walk five paces forward.'

Carr remained where he was, propped on one knee, the rifle in his left hand resting on the ground, his eyes fixed on the jets. They had completed their turn and appeared to be suspended nose down in echelon, pointing straight at him.

'Thank God!' he said, 'I thought you'd bought it.'

'Drop the rifle, Carr, and walk!'

There was no sound from the planes yet, but they were growing in size. Carr wondered who was with Herrick. Not Ratshelm certainly, or Herrick wouldn't be giving the orders.

'Unless you want to end up on the wrong end of three salvos of rockets I suggest both of us keep very still until the fly-boys bugger off,' he said and heard a grunt which he took to be acquiescence. No translation into Spanish. Interesting but not conclusive. There were always hand signals.

A growing banshee howl, three separate thunder-claps and the fighters had gone, trailing the smell of burnt kerosene. Carr made the natural movement of turning to watch them. There was only Herrick.

'For the last time,' Herrick said, 'drop it and back off!' The machine-pistol in his hands didn't look particularly steady, but Carr thought it didn't need to be at a range of eight yards. He let go of the rifle, stood up and took three paces backwards.

'You bastard!' The tremor of Herrick's hands was reflected in his voice.

Carr nodded. 'I believe that to be substantially correct. I distinctly recall having a regular succession of daddies.'

Furiously Herrick said, 'Someone sold us out to the army. It was you, Carr. It had to be you!'

'Tell me something I don't know.'

'Why, Carr? For God's sake, why?'

'Because it's boring being told what I do know.'

'Why did you do it, Carr?'

'Oh, hell.' Carr said. 'I have the same trouble with Foster He's another who keeps telling me who I am.'

'Why?' It was little more than a soft exhalation.

'I don't know. You'll have to ask Foster.'

Herrick's mouth whitened and his gun inched forward.

'Don't pull that trigger,' Carr said.

It was as though Herrick allowed himself a moment to expand

physically before saying, 'Well now, that's better, but you surprise me. I never thought of you as a bad loser. How does it feel?'

Carr shrugged. 'I've no idea. I always win.'

'Then why plead?'

'I'm not pleading, you stupid oaf. You're in the same spot Ratshelm was. Bang away with that thing and you'll have half the Colombian army here in three minutes. Probably less. They're feeling a little jumpy this morning. And, while we're at it, stop saying "Why, Carr?" like a bloody parrot. You damn well know why.'

'I don't understand you.'

'All right,' Carr said quietly. 'Let's cool it and I'll paint the picture for you. But first we'd better get off this clearing. Those jets may be back.'

Herrick frowned and Carr added, 'It's okay. You keep pointing your gun at me and I walk anywhere you say as long as it's concealed from the offensive gaze of people we haven't been introduced to.'

Sitting under a spreading bush facing Herrick and his gun, Carr asked, 'Where's Ratshelm now?'

'Gone. I don't know where. He took the jeep.'

It was the first Carr had known of the existence of a jeep. He nodded and said, 'Good.'

'What's good about it?'

'I only had one magnetic "bleeper". It seemed likely he'd use the jeep as a life-boat if there was a foul-up, so I stuck it on that rather than on one of the trucks. How did you get it to the southern assault take-off position without attracting attention? Push it?'

'Yes, but what was the point of . . . ?'

'I'll tell you in a minute. How many men got away with Ratshelm?'

'Four or five. I think that was all there were left,' Herrick said, then added defensively, 'I'd had to take cover, you see, and when I . . . when I realized they were pulling out I ran after them shouting but, well, they just kept on going, so I came back here. Perhaps they didn't see me.'

The smoke wasn't yet dense, but it was everywhere, the isolated drifts joining to make a continuous translucent veil. Carr could see Herrick with his gun resting across one thigh clearly enough, but the undergrowth a few feet beyond and to either side of him was hazy and appeared to have no depth. He could, he knew, be in it and invisible before Herrick could act. Then what? By the time he had located the rifle he would have as little chance of finding the frightened man again as an angry Ratshelm had had before dawn in the blackness beyond the reach of the army floodlights.

'No, I don't suppose they saw you,' he said, ' but that's my cnaritable side talking. The other side thinks Ratshelm was in too much of a bloody panic to care. Do you really want to work for a man like that?'

Herrick started to say something, but Carr talked on. 'Look at his track record since we arrived. His men let me ride around in the back of an open track so I can get a good view of the scenery all the way to his boy scout camp in the woods. Then he tries to have me killed and louses that up. Next . . .'

'I tried to . . .' Herrick said, then snapped his mouth shut.

'Warn him? Thoughtful of you. But he was too stupid to listen, was he? You needn't answer that. Let's just chalk up another strike against him. So next he shuts me up in that little tent somewhere over there in the smoke and sends in a series of pot-heads to keep me company. Dead crafty that, because the real guard is outside watching the tent flap. It's rather bad luck for about fifteen of his men that he didn't put another sentry round the back. Are you still with me?'

'Yes, I'm still with you. I've had quite a bit of experience listening to you cataloguing your own brilliance, but I don't know what the hell you think you're leading up to.'

'I'm leading up to a take-over bid,' Carr said. 'You and I couldn't do it any worse than Ratshelm. Which would you rather do? Be told to lead a suicidal frontal assault on your first job like me, be left standing at the altar like you, or run the show?'

'So it's Carr the military expert now. Obviously there's no end to your accomplishments.'

Carr moved his shoulders impatiently. 'At least I know enough to have taken out those trailers with a bazooka, or done it with two men. One to nobble the sentry, the other to place explosive charges under them. Whooping in like a bunch of Zulus is out of date.'

'Ratshelm was waiting for them, but they didn't come.'

'Zulus?'

'No, damn you. Charges and bazookas.'

'Well,' Carr said, 'that seems to place his logistics on a par with his logic. Do you want to have a go, or would you prefer to wander around Colombia until you're picked up on a charge of murdering Major Garcia?'

Herrick was silent for so long that Carr let his mind drift to the next stage, how best to make the rendezvous with Whitehead if Whitehead could make it himself and if Herrick fell in with his absurd plan. Take one of the trucks obviously. The smoke made the jungle as treacherous for the army as the darkness would have done and he didn't think *Teniente* Descola would be looking for a posthumous captaincy, so there was little chance of running into a patrol. They'd follow the track past the drilling site to the grasslands and turn west towards the Magdalena River, walking the last bit if they had to. Whitehead, assuming that he could land at all, would do it first at the Area D location, wait five minutes, then come on to Area E which should make the time about . . .

'Okay,' Herrick said. 'What do you have in mind?'

'A helicopter. I arranged for it to land not so far from here at about 12.15 each day as soon as you told me our approximate destination. It's equipped to track the "bleeper" on Ratshelm's jeep.'

'You think of everything, don't you, Carr?'

Carr was glad that it hadn't occurred to Herrick to ask what he proposed to do when they caught up with Ratshelm, because he had neither the means nor the slightest desire to do so. He was also vaguely sorry that he had been unable to kill Herrick without involving Whitehead, but the machine-pistol still pointing at him put that out of the question.

'I try to,' he said. 'That's why I always win.'

CHAPTER TWENTY-THREE

One moment there was nothing but smoke, smoke so nearly opaque that Carr found it hard to distinguish the bulk of Herrick standing within three yards of his left shoulder, smoke and the omnipresent hiss of the invisible fire. The next, the greyness assumed forms, whorls and convolutions which shuddered and trembled before they flattened to hug the blackened turf like an early morning summer mist.

Carr could see Herrick clearly now and the rhythmic beat of rotors and the staccato rattle of an engine reached his ears above the sound of the fire. They seemed to be coming from directly above his head and he began to walk towards the perimeter of the area of greater visibility, not hurrying.

'Stand still, Carr. You're as likely to walk into it as away from it.'

Carr ignored him and walked on until the smoke began to thicken about him again, then he turned. The helicopter appeared quite suddenly, about fifty feet up and twenty yards away. Nose down, it was pointing almost directly between the two men and drifting slowly to its right. It looked impossibly fragile, a perspex bubble floating in a nothingness of grey. When it turned broadside on, the skids, the engine block and the arc of the tail-spinner guard gave it some substance, but the frail trellis-work of the main spar added little. Carr thought of it as an ephemeron, too delicate to survive the coming night.

It bounced gently once on landing, the engine note died, the rotors slowed, sagging tiredly, then the smoke closed in again. Carr became conscious of the cold clamminess of his shirt in the ninety degree heat. He supposed the down draught had cooled him and began to walk slowly in the direction of the machine.

Herrick loomed up beside him and said, 'That man's bloody good. Back in Bogota I heard someone saying that Colombians came down out of the trees and got straight into aircraft. That's why they can fly anything anywhere, but don't have any roads.' He laughed snickeringly and added, 'I believe it. How he got that thing down in this visibility I'll never know.'

Carr didn't reply and Herrick asked, 'What is he?'

'Ex-police pilot. Got booted out on suspicion of running a protection racket amongst the small shopkeepers in Cartagena.'

Herrick snickered again. '*La policia esta al servicio de los ciudadanos* – that is if the citizen happens to be one of the "four hundred".'

Ghost-like in the murk the helicopter appeared in front of them. Herrick stooped under the still gently revolving rotors and began to climb through the doorless oval opening in the perspex cabin.

The pilot said, 'Wait please' looked first at Herrick then at Carr and added, 'Señor Carr in the middle I think. This man big like me. Better him at side to balance chopper. Very light machine.'

Herrick nodded, stepped back to the ground and Carr got in. Herrick clambered after him and the pilot passed the single safety strap across all their knees, leaning across to clip it in position by Herricks' right thigh. The starter motor whined and the engine fired at once, the rotor arms increasing the speed of their whip-lash circular course.

The helicopter seemed to stretch upwards as though trying to attain its full height, hesitated, then the skids left the ground and it slewed on its axis to face the direction from which it had approached. A moment later it was racing forward blindly in the smoke, nose down again but climbing.

At 200 feet it broke into brilliant sunlight and Carr looked down at the motionless pall of greyness stretching along the Magdalena valley. For the most part the blanket of smoke was flat but, here and there, stalagmites of vapour pointed skywards. He supposed the fire was burning more fiercely below them. There was nothing else to see except the outline of the Andes hazy with distance.

Raising his voice to make himself heard above the clatter of the engine behind their heads he said, 'Stay on north for ten minutes, Lopez, then start a box search for a vehicle transmitting on this frequency.'

The pilot took the tattered piece of paper Carr gave him, glanced at it, nodded and put it in his pocket. The helicopter thrashed on and up until the altimeter read 4200 feet. Ahead a cloud bank seemed to have formed. It drifted closer. Carr watched it, frowning, then heard Herrick say, 'What do you propose to do when we catch up with them? I seem to be the only one with a gun.'

'Napalm,' Carr replied shortly, then tapping the pilot on the shoulder, 'Do we *have* to fly as high as this? You frightened of cloud or something?'

The pilot angled his head back and sideways, mouth to Carr, eyes to his front. 'It is best that we do, señor. That cloud is smoke and that smoke is very full of mountain.'

'Christ! Smoke at this height. Bloody peasants!' Carr said and gripped the safety strap with his right hand.

Shrugging impassively the pilot made some adjustment on the control panel, then turned his head to look at Carr. His expression was one of disinterested dislike.

'You know some way more quick, more cheap, to clear many million hectares rain forest and jungle for the next planting of the crops, bloody peasants like to hear from you, señor.'

Carr grunted and leaned back, but his grip on the strap remained firm.

'Scared, Carr?' It was Herrick on his right. Carr glanced at him. He was lolling back, relaxed, his gun cradled on his knees.

'I hate heights.' His teeth snapped shut on the statement and Herrick nodded indifferently, then shouted more loudly than the conditions warranted, 'Dig long enough and you'll find the soft spot.'

Carr allowed his eyes to slide downwards to where, in places, it was possible to make out parts of the ridge jutting through the smoke like a long archipelago in a sea of skimmed milk, the nearest island almost directly below them. The safety strap slackened fractionally to his left, but an imperceptible movement of his wrist maintained its tension between Herrick and himself. With his free hand he groped behind the pilot's back for the anchor he had asked for and twisted the rope's end he found there twice around his palm. For perhaps five seconds he listened to the sound of the wind through the oval entry port snapping the material of Herrick's shirt sleeve like rifle shots, then the helicopter went into a violent starboard bank. Carr took his right hand from the safety strap and hurled himself sideways.

Half in and half out of the cabin, the rope burning his skin, he watched Herrick windmilling down towards the smoking mountain. 'If you want a soft spot I'd start digging about now,' he shouted, but the slipstream took the words and threw them away.

When the machine levelled he drew himself inboard, groped for the trailing safety strap and passed it back to the pilot.

The pilot said, 'Have got,' secured it, untied the length of rope and dropped it into space. Herrick's gun had become wedged under the instrument panel. Carr freed it with his foot and kicked it after the rope. 'Okay, Whitehead,' he said. 'Let's get on to Bucaramanga. I'll bring you up to date as we go.'

While Carr talked the helicopter clattered on towards the plateau on which the town lay. Peaks appeared ahead, lifting high above the carpet of smoke. Soon they were amongst them, and the green, rock-splattered slopes of the foot-hills slid by on either side. A half-completed ribbon of road twisted below like a contour line, until it ended at nowhere in particular as though the cartographer had been called away with the map unfinished.

When Carr stopped talking Whitehead said, 'When you decide to do something the hard way you sure don't fool around.'

'If I'd noticed an easy way I'd have taken it,' Carr told him.

'Yeah, I guess you would at that. But are you telling me that he was nutty enough to believe that take-over crap?'

'No. I'm telling you he thought *I* was. I'm not renowned for my modesty or lack of self-confidence. All he believed was that with you and this chopper I could locate Ratshelm. When we'd done that he'd have forced you to land at gunpoint, shot us both and rejoined the old team. Jubilation at return of prodigal son bearing gift of one helicopter. With all that and me finally off his back he really must have thought he had it made.'

The CIA man nodded. 'Figures,' he said, then looked at Carr and grinned. 'But napalm, for crissake!'

Carr grinned back at him. 'I know. I'd been worrying all morning about what to say when he asked me how we were going to take Ratshelm. Couldn't very well have him playing gun-ships with that little machine-pistol. Fortunately, by the time he got around to asking he only had thirty seconds left to think about the answer.'

CHAPTER TWENTY-FOUR

Capitan Caycedo's English was very good indeed. Carr thought that if he had any accent at all it was a hint of American and hoped that he was not as efficient as he looked and sounded.

He was saying, 'I greatly appreciate your offer, Señor Whitehead and, believe me, I would accept it if I didn't consider the chances to be nil.'

Whitehead said, 'I rate them higher than that. There aren't many places I can't put a chopper down and I think you ought to let me try, Captain. I feel it was my fault in a way.'

Carr shifted uncomfortably in his chair. 'If it was anyone's fault,' he said, 'it was mine. I should have gone down the rope to him, but I get vertigo just sitting in those things let alone climbing out of them.'

'You have a winch?' the Captain asked.

Whitehead shook his head. 'Only a static line.'

Caycedo nodded. 'I see no reason for either of you to hold himself responsible for the accident. Hendrix lost his footing and chose a remarkably dangerous place to do it from.' He looked at Carr. 'You are certain it *was* Hendrix, señor?'

'Absolutely. I was almost close enough to touch him, but what I don't understand is what he thought he was trying to do up there. Those fires aren't dangerous really. Most of the place is too damp to do more than smoulder. Anyway, there's that oil camp within a day's walk of where he was or, if he was afraid of getting lost, he only had to make for the river and follow the Andean pipeline to one of its pumping stations.' He paused, then added, 'Sorry, Captain. You know all that better than I. I'm just curious and was thinking aloud.'

'I know it as *well* as you, señor. No better. You are very knowledgeable for a stranger.'

'Not really. It's simply that I remember what I read and what I see on maps.'

Caycedo settled himself back in his chair and crossed his arms on his chest, his brown eyes regarding Carr friendlily. After a moment he said, 'I'm sure you do. As to what he was doing, I think he was hitch-hiking.'

Carr grinned. 'Of course, Captain. Silly of me not to have thought of that myself. In my younger days I was a great one for hitch-hiking from mountain tops.'

Caycedo smiled faintly. 'Señor Carr, Señor Whitehead picked you up from a clearing near the river bank, did he not?'

'That's right.'

'A clearing, you have told me, only a few miles from the oil company's drilling camp.'

'Yes.'

'The oil company flies helicopters or light fixed-wing aircraft between the camp and Bucaramanga at least twice a day. The route passes right over that ridge. He had an excellent chance of being picked up by the first or reported by the second. You followed an almost identical route and saw him.'

Whitehead said, 'And dropped him. I don't know how. He only had to get the sling round himself and we could have brought him here like that even if we couldn't get him aboard.'

He took a cigarette from a pack on the table, lifted it to his mouth and put it down again unlit.

'Captain,' he said, 'I'm as puzzled as Carr. You say he was hitch-hiking and you weren't kidding. So all right. Could you give us some idea why? If he could climb that hill he was in good shape and could have walked out like Carr said. It just doesn't figure him standing up there like that waiting for a sky hook. Not on a day like today. Surely he'd guess that the oil company planes would be grounded.'

Caycedo leaned forward and flicked his lighter into flame.

'You flew yours, señor.'

Whitehead picked up his cigarette, drew on the proffered flame and nodded his thanks.

'Yes, but I'm a charter pilot, not an oil company. If they don't fly, about the worst that can happen is a few of their boys miss their trick at some cat house. If I don't, I'm breaking a contract and forfeiting money which is something I can't afford to do.'

'You would risk your life for money by flying into the smoke areas on a day as bad as this, Señor Whitehead?'

The pilot shook his head. 'No risk involved. I couldn't have found the oil camp, but finding Carr was easy. I flew west from here until I hit the Magdalena River somewhere south of Puerto Wilches. It's easy to tell when you are over a big chunk of water like that when the countryside is burning. The thermal currents are different. Then I came down almost to water level and followed the river bank to the place Carr and I had chosen as a rendezvous where the Rio Sagamoso joins the Magdalena.'

He chewed reflectively at a thumb-nail and added, 'Only problem was the engine over-heating at that altitude. Suppose I'll have to strip it down.'

'You make it sound easy, señor.'

'It's not so hard.'

Caycedo nodded and switched his gaze back to Carr.

'What I would like to know from you, señor, is what your business was in the Magdalena valley. It is a long way from being one of our greatest tourist attractions.'

'Not for me it isn't,' Carr told him. 'I find it fascinating. Granted your mountains are scenically superior and I enjoy looking at them, but only from a respectful distance. As I mentioned before, I suffer from vertigo.'

'So you did.'

'Originally, my intention was simply to visit Bogota, Bucaramanga, Cali, Medellin and the north coast ports. Cartagena anyway. Then on the plane from Miami I was talking to Hendrix and he told me about his agricultural survey of the hot country. He was an – what do you call it?'

'Agronomist?'

'That's the word. So I thought it might be an idea to stop acting like a tourist and get right off the beaten track if Hendrix would take me. He said he would be glad of the company.'

Carr hesitated, then added, 'But to answer your question, I didn't have any business in the Magdalena valley at all. I hope I wasn't breaking the law in any way.'

Caycedo shook his head. 'None that I'm aware of and even if you had been in view of the considerable service you rendered the army and the oil camp . . .' He shrugged his shoulders. 'It was extremely fortunate that you overheard that conversation and we are in your debt for acting on it as you did. So, no doubt, is the oil company. Their people would have been held to ransom. An increasingly popular pastime in a number of countries as you know.'

'Yes,' said Carr.

'You are still looking puzzled, señor.'

'No, Captain. The expression on my face is one of dawning comprehension. I've just worked out what Hendrix was doing on top of that hill.'

'Yes?'

'He was on the run. When I disappeared, he was immediately suspect as the man who had introduced me into the group. He was running away from his own people. Probably he thought he stood a better chance hitching a ride than escaping from guerrillas experienced in tracking on the ground. Their own ground.'

'We are of the same mind, señor.'

Caycedo got to his feet and said, 'I'm afraid I must ask you two gentlemen to stay here for the inquest. That shouldn't delay you too long. With the information provided by you the ground search party should have located the body and brought it in by tomorrow evening at the latest. The inquest will be held the following day.'

Carr and Whitehead stood up as Caycedo said something in Spanish to the sergeant. Carr had forgotten about the sergeant. He glanced round in time to see him rise from his chair, salute and walk out of the room with his shorthand book.

As the door closed behind him, Caycedo spoke again.

'Thank you, Señor Carr, for what you have done, and you, Señor Whitehead, for your courageous offer to attempt a rescue.'

He held out his hand.

Whitehead took it and said, 'I still think I ought to try. There's just a chance he might still be alive.'

Caycedo raised one eyebrow. 'Is there? You were flying the machine so you ought to know what altitude Señor Carr pushed him out at.'

A red and yellow bus was caught in a jam of traffic just outside the police station, its ancient engine vibrating wildly making the blue tassels on its window curtains dance and tremble. The driver's view through the windscreen seemed to be largely obscured by a figurine of the Madonna. Carr regarded it gravely, watching the haze of heat shimmering above the bonnet.

He said, 'If that was meant to be a joke, Captain Caycedo, it was in worse taste than the colour scheme of that bus.' He turned his head away from the window and looked at the policeman.

The policeman looked back at him and Carr received an impression of the mild brown eyes glowing momentarily like dim coals.

'An off colour joke, eh, señor? Perhaps you will agree with me that the important thing from your point of view is that it is off the record. I would recommend to you and your friend here that it is kept that way.'

Without emphasis Carr said, 'I don't know what the hell you're drivelling about.'

Caycedo sighed and the sound carried mild irritation with it.

'Listen to me, you two. Hendrix fell over a cliff during an attempted helicopter pick-up. The tragedy is recorded in the sergeant's notes and will soon constitute part of an official report. The coroner will return a verdict of accidental death and that, as far as you are concerned, will be the end of the matter.' He sighed again. 'Nobody will mourn his passing, least of all me but, if you will permit me a cliché, we prefer to make our own laundry arrangements without unsolicited alien assistance.'

Irritably, Carr said, 'Apart from an abortive attempt to join a group of crazy revolutionaries, what is Hendrix supposed to have done that makes you so damned pleased that he's dead?'

Caycedo looked at him levelly. 'In the few short days Hendrix unfortunately spent in this country he made my wife's sister a widow. Her name is Garcia. Her husband, Major Miguel Garcia, was a very fine man and a senior officer of DAS, which, as you know, is our security organization. He was also my immediate superior and my friend.'

'Oh,' said Carr.

'That is all you have to say, señor?'

'There isn't much I can say, Captain. I'm sorry about your brother-in-law? Empty words. I've never heard of the man until now, so how can I be sorry about him?' Carr paused, raised his eyebrows high and went on, 'Having known you for an hour, perhaps I could reasonably say that I am indeed sorry that this tragedy has been brought to your family by one of my countrymen.'

His eyebrows sank slowly down, then he said, 'But one of the family having just accused me of murder doesn't make me feel like throwing my arms round his neck.'

Caycedo fingered his moustache, nodded and said, 'Reasonable. I won't quarrel with that. The cold logic of the Englishman is, once again, altogether too much for the emotional Latin, but I was fond of the emotional Latin who was coldly slaughtered by Hendrix in Barrancabermeja. Now, if I could tie you in with that killing as well, Señor Carr . . . but I can't. The results of my investigations indicate that, although you were in the vicinity at the time, you were not necessarily implicated. At least, it was not you who was given a gun.'

'That killing as well, I think you said, Captain. Let me tell you something . . .' Carr stopped talking at the sight of Caycedo covering his ears with his hands, then watched him uncover them again.

'No, Señor Carr. Let me tell *you* something. Quite unofficially and entirely personally I am grateful to you and that, according

149

to our code of ethics, which you may find strange, places me in your debt. The debt is one of honour almost overriding my sense of duty as a policeman. The fact that the murderer has been brought to – as I can't say justice let us say book, places me in the happy position of being able to repay the debt by not harassing you without troubling my conscience unduly.'

Carr said, 'I'm sorry to disappoint your tape recorder or, if you don't run to one, the sergeant with his ear glued to the keyhole, but I still don't know what you're talking about. Colombian law isn't one of my things, but in most places slanderous statements are actionable and my witness is standing right here beside me.'

'We have finished acting out our little scene for the sergeant, señor, and there are no tape recorders, no bugs.'

'Great,' said Carr. 'Then if your charge sheet is so bloody empty, why not book Whitehead here for eating meat on Friday. I saw him do it. You'd be on safer ground than throwing accusations of murder at a total stranger.'

Caycedo sighed for the third time and walked to a filing cabinet at the side of the room. He opened one of the drawers, took out a docket and dropped it on to the table in front of Carr.

'Not really a total stranger, Señor Carr. Go on. Read it if you want to. There's nothing in it you don't already know, except perhaps the comments of your superiors. You'll find them rather complimentary, that is if you consider approval of your particular attributes a compliment.'

Carr picked it up, glanced quickly through the first five pages, riffled the rest with his thumb like a pack of cards and slid the file across the table to Caycedo.

He said, 'Page one. For "bullet" read "meat skewer" scar – right hand. Page four. For "Prenzlau" read "Neustrelitz". Page four again. For "February 1956" read "March 1956". Can't vouch for anything after page five. You bought it I suppose. I'd be very interested to know from whom?'

Expecting no answer, Carr turned his head and stared moodily out of the window. The multi-coloured bus had gone. He was puzzled, wondering why Herrick should have parted with his life insurance policy so cheaply. The doctored file would have commanded a higher price in many places other than Colombian Security. Here, its use had been as a lever. He concluded that Herrick hadn't sold it to DAS. To do so would simply have drawn attention to himself so that meant that DAS had found it.

'We didn't buy it, señor. We opened Hendrix's safe deposit box in Bogota after he had killed Major Garcia and there it was. Odd, isn't it? I brought it with me from Bogota last night after you had so properly reported the accident to the police here. Why, do you imagine, he had it?'

Still watching the passing traffic, Carr forced a frown of concentration on to his face. He lit a cigarette with slow movements.

'I imagine that Hendrix must have been a foreign agent, foreign to your government and mine I mean. How he got hold of that file I have no idea, but I also imagine that he saw it as giving him some hold over me. He must have had plans for me in the guerrilla movement. That could account for his getting into conversation with me on the plane.'

'When did you leave England, Señor Carr?'

'Ten days, a fortnight ago.'

'Then the file must have been stolen during that time.'

'Why?'

'Because, surely, your people would have told you that it was missing.'

'Oh, I see what you mean. No, they wouldn't have done that. I retired last year.'

'I see,' said Caycedo and pushed the file towards Carr. 'You had better return their property to them, had you not? It might assist them in any enquiry they may wish to hold on their internal security. I don't suppose such documents are normally on sale on the open market.'

'That's good of you, Captain. I expect you want me to leave the country at once. With my record, I can hardly blame you.'

'Leave the country, yes. At once, no. The same goes for Señor Whitehead. You, Señor Whitehead, will remain in Bucaramanga. You will be given reasonable time to dispose of your machine as you wish and wind up your business affairs. When you leave this office you will go to your apartment and, except at the inquest, have no further contact with Señor Carr.

'Señor Carr, you will remain in your hotel, then return to Bogota on the first available flight after the inquest. There, your movements will not be restricted, except to Bucaramanga. Be prepared to stay in Colombia for a minumum of ten days. After that you will receive notification that you may leave, which you will do immediately. I imagine it is unnecessary for me to tell either of you not to try to come back.'

'Why the delay, Captain?'

'Because, dear Señor Carr, the news of the murder of Major Garcia has not yet been released. That will come out at the inquest, as will Hendrix's part in it. Your connection with Hendrix and your action in allerting the military detachment at the drilling camp will also become public knowledge as, of course, will your unsuccessful rescue attempt.

'For some days you will be an object of curiosity, even something of a hero. Were you to leave at once, the press would note the fact and people, important people, might wonder. They might even arrive at the right conclusion. Why let them do that when in a few days they will have forgotten all about you and you can leave unnoticed? For reasons, some of which you know of, I would prefer that you left unnoticed, Señor Carr.'

'Still harping on the theme that I killed Hendrix? For heaven's sake don't let's start all that again.'

Caycedo nodded placidly. 'I agree with you. Let us not do that. I might be unable to prove the charge, but it might take me two years to demonstrate my incompetence and I'm sure that you have more interesting things to do than wait that long in a cell down the passage for the small satisfaction of laughing at me.'

'See you at the inquest,' said Carr.

CHAPTER TWENTY-FIVE

The plane lumbered along the runway at Bucaramanga airport and lifted in a climbing turn towards Bogota. It steadied on a southerly course and continued to climb slowly as it would do throughout the duration of its flight to land several thousand feet higher than it had taken off.

Carr had seen Caycedo amongst the crowd in the small arrival and departure area but, apart from exchange glances, there had been no communication between them and that had suited Carr very well. Over the past seventy-two hours he had had more than enough of officialdom. The double inquest on Garcia and Herrick plus the enquiry into the abortive guerrilla attack on the army post had taken up fourteen hours of the previous day.

For part of that time he had retold his prepared story sentence by sentence, pausing after each one to allow the interpreter to keep pace with him, but for by far the longer period he had simply sat, barely conscious of the seemingly endless proceedings going on around him in a language he didn't understand, Occasional questions put to him had come as a welcome relief.

Towards the end he had listened to complimentary speeches by the coroner and a senior army officer, wryly amused that London would know the outcome of the mission long before he could tell them of it through Purvis at the Embassy. The still swiftly moving pencils in the press box guaranteed that.

Carr looked through the window at the smoke cloud below the plane. It seemed thinner than it had from Whitehead's helicopter and in places he could see the reflection of sun on water. Not the Magdalena, they were too far to the east for that, but some of the scores of smaller rivers which served it. Somewhere over there Herrick had died and Carr's mind turned fleetingly to the man's personal file, the only remaining point of interest connected with the distorted broken body the search party had brought in. Had he done the sensible thing and destroyed it, or had Caycedo read that too? Either way it made no difference now, he decided, and turned away from the uninteresting view.

Next to him a nun was sitting, head bent, telling her beads. She reminded him of the sight of Garcia's widow at the inquest, head also bent, a handkerchief held to her eyes under heavy black veiling. He fastened his safety belt and angled his seat back, preparing to sleep, wondering idly and for no particular reason if Lippmann had left a widow. The illusion of the small grey-coated figure rushing backwards in the early morning light towards the motor-cycle came to him again. He remembered the turn of the head, the change of expression on the face from faint curiosity to suspicion, from suspicion to terror. The decision to jump had formed there too, but so slowly, too slowly for the message from the brain to reach the knees. People were funny he thought, like rabbits caught in the headlights of a car and Barry's file had described the man as so damned good! Perhaps, behind a desk, he had been.

The place had been called Zwickau, but the names of the two Czechoslovak operatives in the van who had finished the job for him were not on record in his mind. They would not have told him their real ones so he had not bothered to imprint them there.

Some woman had seen it, but it hadn't mattered. She hadn't wanted to know, but even if she had stayed long enough to look, her description of a man wearing crash-helmet and goggles would have been useless.

Foster had planned that one well, as he planned most things well provided that he could take them at his own pace. He could rise to the occasion too as that last briefing had shown. Carr smiled at the memory of it. Foster feeding him all the right lines to ensure that their animosity was clearly recorded on tape for Barry's benefit. Once or twice he had felt that Foster was overacting, but the tremor in his voice could be explained as anger at a subordinate's impertinence.

Or had he been nervous? Drowsily Carr considered the possibility, then filed it mentally for future reference. He hadn't seen enough of him over recent weeks to form a judgement and the evidence of Foster's ruthlessness pointed the other way. It had been his decision that Ludwig Keller should be betrayed and returned to a British prison for the good of the cell, his decision that the elimination of Herrick should proceed for the same reason.

Carr approved, just as Prague had done and, therefore, presumably Moscow. If a colleague was of greater value imprisoned or dead, so be it. He knew little of Keller or his worth, but balance one 'breaking and entering' man against someone of Lippmann's calibre and Herrick fell from the tilting scales just as he had fallen from the helicopter.

That was something Carr, who had no politics, liked about the Eastern bloc. No false sympathy, no creeping about, checking and double-checking, then half-acting like the British, no hysterical flailing of arms like the Americans. Just a shot, actual or metaphorical, in the back of the neck. Two other things he liked were being paid twice and hedging his bets. He guessed that Herrick had also been motivated by the last two points, but of what made Foster tick he had no idea.

Carr yawned. They'd need help now that Herrick was gone.

Perhaps that London University lecturer . . .

The gentle double jolt as the aircraft landed at Bogota woke him. He glanced sideways in time to see the nun abandon her beads and cross herself.

CHAPTER TWENTY-SIX

'Mr Carr's mission appears to have been successful, Colonel.'

Barry looked at his secretary speculatively. 'What do you mean by "appears", Martha? Has it or hasn't it?'

'That depends on how much faith you are prepared to place in newspaper reports, although in this instance their sheer volume argues that it has.' She gave the smallest of smiles and added, 'Yes, of course it's been successful. Here's the gist of the press coverage sent from Bogota by Mr Purvis. I'm afraid there's rather a lot of it.'

He made no move to take the sheets of paper she held out to him.

'Is he under arrest?'

'Far from it. Two of the leading articles recommend that he be given a medal.'

'A *what*? Oh, never mind. Sit down, my dear,' Barry said. When she had done so he took the pages from her and began to read.

She watched the clever eyes scanning back and forth across the paper. Sometimes the shaggy grey eyebrows lifted a millimetre, then settled again. Once or twice the wayward beard twitched. None of the movements gave any indication of his reactions to what he was learning. Not that she expected them to. She had known him too long for that. It was just comforting to look at him, to thank him for being there without his knowing that she was doing so and not to want to tidy him up as she was aware other women did. It was comforting too to love him without desire and to know that she was loved in the same way in return.

Years ago he had proposed marriage and had done so at more or less annual intervals ever since. Always she had refused, not because she thought the proposals were born of pity, but because she had hoped and still hoped he would find some pretty thing to lie with him. She hoped that very hard indeed for, in that way, she was incapable of helping him.

'Well I'll be damned,' Barry said and fanned the five pages of the message out on the desk top as though they were a poker hand an opponent had demanded to see. He stared at them for several seconds then, as if anxious to dispel any lingering doubts, repeated his forecast.

'Any instructions, Colonel?'

'Yes. Got your book with you?'

She opened it on her lap and nodded to him.

'Right,' he said. 'Take this down for Purvis in Bogota, will you?'

CHAPTER TWENTY-SEVEN

Carr stood by the news stand in the Tequendama Hotel looking down at the cover of an English language magazine called *Rugged Men*. It depicted a naked brunette chained to a post while she awaited the application of a Swastika-shaped branding iron by a bosomy blonde half in and half out of an exiguous Gestapo uniform. The faces of the women wore expressions of mild concern and glee respectively. There were no men, rugged or otherwise, in evidence. He groaned, ran his eyes over the rest of the rack and groaned again. Everything else seemed to be in Spanish, including the newspapers which carried his own over exposed and virtually unrecognizable photograph on their front pages.

Bored, he turned towards the jewellery counter. Emeralds and gold and more emeralds. Emeralds everywhere. Gold formed into strange angular ornaments after the Inca culture.

He stood for a moment, absorbed, trying to remember something he had read in a travel pamphlet they had given him at Miami. Something about the tribes that had given rise to the legend of El Dorado by gilding each new chieftain, then bathing him in a sacred lake. Their name eluded him momentarily and he frowned. It was unlike him to forget anything he had read.

Chibchas! A faint smile replaced the frown and he walked

slowly back into the foyer, the smile fading in its turn as he tried to think what he was going to do with himself in Bogota for the next ten days. The hotel didn't seem to have much to offer. He sat down in an armchair and lit a cigarette, watching the movement of people to and from the reception desk.

Discounting the small page boys, they fell into four distinct groups. The obvious North Americans, the obvious British, the obvious Latin Americans and the obvious oilmen who somehow contrived to conceal any trace of national origin beneath checkered shirts and khaki slacks tucked into leather boots.

Carr yawned and stuck the butt of his cigarette into the white sand of the big ash-tray beside his chair. He thought of going to the bar downstairs at the back of the hotel where he had drunk with Herrick, decided it was too dark down there, probably deserted and not worth the effort. There was another, he remembered, beside the main doors, equally dark, but nearer and probably occupied. Turning his head in that direction his eyes caught a flash of brilliant colour through the glass main doors which almost certainly came from the red *ruana* of an Avianca air hostess.

Someone in New York had told him he should fly down by the Colombian national airline. 'Five-hour direct flight. No hanging about at Miami like some of the others,' the man had said. 'And brother, their hostesses! Talk about dishes!'

He might have done it too if he hadn't learned that Herrick was joining the Braniff flight at Miami and remembered saying, 'No. If I can't fly British I fly American. They started the whole thing at Kitty Hawk in nineteen-o-whenever. They should know the score.'

The girl came in through the swing doors with a swirl of near-scarlet cloak and climbed the half-dozen steps to the foyer. Carr watched her indifferently, unexpectantly, then suddenly went very still. He was, he concluded, looking at a dish and thought what a fatuous way that was to describe a miracle.

She had the drooped eyelashes, indrawn cheeks and faint smile of the beautiful woman who is well aware that everyone is staring at her and is pleased about it. Her legs and the way she moved them were a study in insolent perfection. Her hat, her ridiculous uniform hat, perching on top of shiningly black hair as though she had put it there for a joke and only succeeded in making it look like a coronet . . .

Carr stopped itemizing abruptly. She was standing by the reception desk, drawing off her white gloves, blue eyes, wide open now, staring directly at him. He fought down the impulse to glance behind him to see who else she might be looking at and returned her gaze steadily, realizing with near amazement that he was nervous. He thought of getting up, but the stillness which had come upon him held him motionless. Then she smiled quickly, turned away from him and held her hand out to the desk clerk for her key.

'*Novecientos setenta, por favor.*'

Her voice carried clearly to Carr, then she had turned to her left and was walking towards the bank of lifts, the key swinging by its tag from her fingers. She hadn't looked at him again.

He continued to sit where he was, thinking he hadn't seen so delectable a woman since that infuriatingly distant bitch of Trelawney's and contemplating his enforced sojourn in Bogota, or at least part of it, with a degree of enthusiasm as great as his earlier mood of lethargy and depression. Certain that she could not have recognized him from his newspaper photograph he wondered for a moment if she had noticed him somewhere before, perhaps at the airport, and had been trying to place him. Possible. He knew he was attractive to most women and it could simply be a matter of a face briefly glimpsed nudging at her memory. Nothing more.

'Balls!' he said, and an American sitting near him asked, 'You say something?'

'Yes, I said "balls",' Carr told him, got out of his chair and walked towards the main doors. Before he reached them he turned left, picked up a house phone and asked for Room 970. He knew enough Spanish to have understood that.

He got to his feet when she came through the bar doorway and watched smiling, as she peered around her, trying to adjust her eyes to the gloom. When he raised a hand she saw him, inclined her head and moved in the direction of his table.

She was wearing a jet black ciré trouser suit unrelieved by any jewellery or colour, except for the shifting reflection of the dim bar lights on the material and the high gloss of her belt and shoes. The deep collar of her jacket was turned up, enclosing her hair, blending with it so that it was difficult to see where one black ended and the other began.

Within three feet of him she stopped, stance erect, chin slightly raised, unsmiling, her arms hanging loosely. It annoyed him a little to find that she was taller than he.

Carr said, 'You're very beautiful.'

'Yes.'

'Something from another world.'

'Yes.'

For only the second time in his life he felt the pricking of nervousness, that unfamiliar sensation he had had to identify when first she had looked at him three hours before in the foyer. It wasn't unpleasant, but the strangeness of it confused him a little.

She moved her head fractionally, enquiringly but without interest, waiting. The collar and hair seemed to become one, giving her a hooded appearance.

'Like the Dark Angel,' he said.

She made no reply and his voice roughened when he said, 'I want you.'

'I want you too. That's why I picked you up.'

A frown pressed fleetingly on his eyebrows and was gone.

'You're very direct.'

'Pot calling kettle,' she said. 'Are we going to stand like this all evening, or may I sit down?'

He held a chair for her. 'What's your name!'

'Cecilia.'

'Cecilia what?'

'It isn't important. Women who pick up men don't need surnames.'

'I shall call you Cecilia Ruana. You looked wonderful in that red uniform cloak of yours. Kind of devilish. So you do in black for that matter.'

She looked at him coolly.

'We've already established my desirability,' she said. 'Shall we talk about something else now? What I would like to drink, for example, and where you are going to take me to dinner.'

Her regard was moving slowly across the other occupants of the bar when she added, 'Or can't you wait that long?'

The contrast of the jet black hair and black-fringed deeply blue eyes was startling in its impact. She really is shatteringly exotic he thought. Some Irish-Spanish cross probably and conceited as hell.

'For a "femme fatale" you don't run true to form at all,' he said. 'You're much too aggressive. The correct procedure is languid charm and reliance on your irresistible allure. I don't know why I'm putting up with you.' To his annoyance there was a trace of tension in his voice.

Her eyes met his and, unexpectedly, she smiled.

'Perhaps because you rather like the idea of becoming one of my fatalities,' she said.

He relaxed. 'Okay, you win, Cecilia Ibarra. What would you like to drink?'

'So you got my name from the desk clerk.'

'Of course.'

'I would like a martini, please.'

Carr snapped his fingers at a passing waiter.

It was easier after that. She laughed at his expression when his mucous membranes recoiled from the touch of paraffin in the local gin and told him the second sip was better. He watched as she talked, wondering whether she was more striking animated or in repose and deciding that it was impossible to tell. Either way she was superb, although he was glad that she had stopped trying to be tough.

The second sip wasn't so bad and he ordered more.

'You haven't told me *your* name yet.'

'It's John Carr.'

Glass touching her lips she seemed to freeze, then she put it carefully down on the table and said, 'Oh my God!' as though it were one word.

'What's the matter?'

'You're the man in all the papers. How very embarrassing.'

'Yes,' Carr said. 'It is, isn't it?'

'I meant for me.'

'Oh? Why?'

'It doesn't matter. Do you want to tell me all about it, or shall we talk about something else?'

'Something else, please.'

'That's nice,' she said.

She knew just the place for them to dine, but it was too far to walk. Their taxi, like the bus in Bucaramanga, was heavily ornamented and had a figurine of the Madonna above the dashboard. It swooped and soared through the improbable over-underpass system outside the hotel solely, Carr decided, to please the driver because suddenly they were back on the main artery from which they had started. He was sure, or nearly sure, of that and confirmed it a moment later by the tawdry, flickering light of a violet neon advertising display which lit up a street sign on the corner of a building. *Av el Libertador* it read.

They travelled south for several blocks, turned left, left again, then right and he thought he caught the sign '*Calle 17*' on a garden wall, but the street lighting was too poor for him to be certain. The taxi turned several times after that and he knew he was lost. It worried him a little. He liked always to know where he was.

The driver finally stopped the cab at the gate of an ordinary house. The lamp above the front door and a dim glow from behind ground-floor curtained windows seemed to be the only illumination in the entire street. The place looked like no restaurant he had ever seen and he glanced at the girl speculatively, the bomb inside him beginning to tick.

'Here we are,' she said.

Carr got out of the taxi and she was out of the other side, standing in the roadway, before he could offer her his hand. It occurred to him that he had not yet touched her and that it might be too late now. He paid the driver, watching her out of the corner of his eye, but she did nothing except walk round to stand waiting on the crumbling pavement. As the taxi drove away he followed her along the path to the front door, flexing his fingers, totally alert and conscious of a slight shortage of breath. Most visitors to Bogota were afflicted by that he knew, but this was something more, something he had experienced right down to sea-level whenever what he thought of as a situation was developing. Except that he felt sorry about the girl he wasn't unhappy.

The door swung inwards at the touch of her outstretched hand and they walked in, Carr very close behind her. It was a restaurant, a really rather attractive restaurant and nothing more.

He looked around him at the scattering of small tables, silver and crystal glinting in the soft lighting, white linen and flat bowls of sub-tropical flowers. At each end of the room long low open fires flickered at him. Two couples and one group of three people were already dining.

Feeling foolish he almost laughed aloud, stopped himself and listened while the ticking of his own personal bomb faded into silence.

'I hope you like lobster,' she said. 'This is one of the best places in the world for it.'

'Funny place to find lobster. Nearly nine thousand feet up and hundreds of miles from the sea.'

'It comes in from the coast by air with all sorts of other fish every morning. The plane carries passengers on the return trip. The smell is so awful they're nearly always sick.' She smiled at him with her eyes, her first friendly smile.

He smiled back at her and picked up the wine list, shrugged at the Spanish and handed it across the table.

'Can't read it. You choose.'

Without looking at it, 'Chilean Riesling,' she said.

Two hours later Carr discovered that he was happy, positively happy. It had taken him a little time to identify that sensation too.

He rode with her in the lift to the ninth floor of the hotel and found that he was holding her hand as they walked along the corridor to her room.

At the door she said, 'That *was* a nice evening, John. Thank you so much. Sleep well.' She touched his cheek lightly with her finger-tips.

Puzzled, he said, 'I thought you wanted me.'

Lashes like twin black fans dropped momentarily, lifted again. She started to say something, half smiled and then let herself into her room. Carr stood looking at the closed door for several seconds, then turned and walked to the lifts.

His telephone rang at 7.30.

'Carr,' he said.

'Good morning, darling. Did you sleep well?'

'No I did not. I was thinking about you all night.'

'So I should hope. Come and have some breakfast.'

'I'd better shave.'

'Yes, you *had* better. Ten minutes.'

He replaced the receiver, said, 'Well, I don't know,' and walked into the bathroom.

Cecilia wheeled the breakfast trolley into the corridor, transferred the 'Please do not disturb' sign from the inner to the outer handle and pulled the door shut after her as she came back into the room. She slid the bolt home.

Staring unblinkingly at Carr she said, 'I'm sorry about last night, darling. It was your telling me who you are and me convinced that you must think I was one of those awful women who have to drag the nearest celebrity into bed. Then by the end of the evening I knew I'd started to fall for you. It seemed to make a difference.'

The zip of her long, pale blue house coat hissed from throat to ankle.

'You're very beautiful – everywhere.'

'Yes,' she said and held out her hand to him.

Cecilia said, 'Let's go camping.'

Muffled sounds came from Carr.

'What?' she asked.

Carr reached behind his neck for her interlaced fingers, drew them apart and raised his head.

'Your inability to hear other than through your ears and the restrictions you are placing on my powers of speech are hindering communication between us,' he said.

'Never mind. You don't have to talk, just listen. I've got it all worked out.' She pulled his face down between her breasts again. 'I was going to spend my leave in New York, but I'd rather take it here with you now. Would you like that?'

He moved his head affirmatively.

'We'll hire a Land-Rover and a tent and things and drive to a part of the *llanos* I know. It's beautiful. Nothing but grass and sky as far as you can see and the nearest people a thousand miles away.'

He lifted his head an inch from its prison.

'What'll we do?'

'We'll think of something,' she said.

'Cecilia.'

His voice sounded serious to her ears and she slid her hands from the back of his head to his cheeks, cupping them. Then she tilted his head back so that they were looking at each other.

'Yes, darling?'

He looked at her for a long time, then said, 'I'm a sucker for beautiful women. Crazy about them. Always have been. But now I . . .'

'But now you what?'

'Now I . . . Oh, nothing. Tell you later.'

He let his head sink down on to her again, wondering what had happened to him.

CHAPTER TWENTY-EIGHT

'Do you speak English?' asked Carr.

The girl in the Avianca uniform seated behind the booking desk smiled at him.

'Of course, señor. We are obliged to.'

Carr smiled back at her. 'Silly question. Can you tell me where I can find Cecilla Ibarra?'

Her face stiffened and then relaxed until it was merely prim.

'I am not permitted to discuss our air hostesses, señor, or any members of the staff.'

'I wasn't asking you to discuss her. Just tell me where she is.'

'I am sorry, señor. It is not permitted.'

'But you do know her.'

She tossed her head irritably, jealously, Carr thought.

'Who doesn't?' The omission of the honorific was pointed and Carr accepted it for what it was, The conversation was over.

'Thanks anyway,' he said and walked out of the El Dorado terminal.

Thirty minutes later he paid off the taxi driver at the street intersection he had indicated on his tourist's map, watched until the cab disappeared round a corner, then walked nine blocks to the British Embassy and asked for Purvis.

'Got a message for you upstairs,' Purvis said. 'I couldn't find you at the hotel this morning, but it isn't urgent anyway. It says, "Confirmation successful outcome noted. Return immediately on expiry movement restriction imposed by local authorities." Do you want a copy?'

Carr smiled. 'Fulsome bastards, aren't they? No, I don't want a copy, but send this, will you?'

'Glad to,' Purvis told him, read the message Carr had printed on hotel stationery, then muttered, 'Jesus.'

'Jesus what?'

'Christ. Who else? Some people have all the luck.'

'Just send it. I'm not interested in your vicarious kicks.'

Purvis looked at him calmly. 'I've already said I would. I'll also bring you the reply. H.E. doesn't want to know about you, so it'd be better if you stayed away from here if possible.'

'I'll do that. I'm not all that gone on knowing about the Ambassador,' Carr said and walked out of the small interview room.

Over dinner Carr said, 'I've got the Land-Rover and the tent.'

'And I've got the provisions and the cooking equipment. Did you remember the sleeping bag?'

'First thing I thought of.'

'Your mind, my sweet, runs on a single, circular track with no branch lines.'

'Now who's calling kettles black?' Carr asked her then, without waiting for a reply, 'How do you manage to speak English so perfectly?'

'By opening and shutting my mouth, darling.'

'Come off it.'

She grinned at him. 'I'm only Colombian by marriage.'

'Oh,' he said. 'Where's Señor Ibarra?'

'In New Mexico.'

'I see.'

'In an urn. The police said he was doing ninety-five when the tyre burst.'

'I'm sorry.'

'No you're not,' Cecilia said, 'and neither am I.'

'The computer run on the girl is negative, Colonel.'

Barry moved his head up and down slowly. 'Nothing remotely resembling her?'

'Not really. There is an Israeli agent who might be able to stand in for her in a film, but she's two inches shorter.'

'Who? The Israeli?'

'Yes.'

'High heels?'

'No,' Martha said. 'It doesn't work. Mr Carr is a very accurate observer, he's also extremely height conscious because he's rather short and, knowing him, he's probably had more than her shoes off her by now anyway.'

'Mmm. Very well, my dear. Tell Purvis, will you?'

'Yes, Colonel . . . Colonel?'

'Mmm?'

'Are you feeling all right?'

'Me? Yes, I'm fine. A little tired perhaps.'

She continued to look at him gravely for a moment, then turned and limped back to her room.

Carr was not turned away from Cecilia's room that night. At three in the morning he was lying on his back listening to the faint night sounds of the city and her soft breathing beside him. Occasionally the reflected beams of some passing vehicle moved slowly across the ceiling like the luminous sweep hand of a huge watch.

'When shall we leave?'

'Well, hello,' Carr said. 'I thought you were fast asleep.'

'No. Let's go after breakfast.'

'Not on your life. After lunch will be quite soon enough. I've got to get some sleep some time.'

'Have you indeed?' she said and slid on to him like an eel.

At dawn he left her and returned to his own room. An hour and a half later the telephone woke him.

'Purvis. I'm in the hotel. May I come up?'

'You do that,' Carr told him, replaced the receiver and swung his legs over the side of the bed. He sat there rubbing the sleep out of his eyes with the heels of his hands, then went into the bathroom and brushed his teeth. When the knock came on the door he opened it two inches, recognized Purvis and let him in.

'Answer to your signal,' Purvis said and held out a piece of paper.

'Thank you.'

Carr looked at the brief message then nodded at Purvis. 'You'd better drift. I don't expect I'll need to bother you any more. Thanks for your help.'

'Pleasure,' Purvis said and left.

When the door closed behind him Carr looked at the message again. It read, 'No female answering your description known'. He smiled, flushed the paper down the lavatory, then telephoned room service.

After he had eaten and dressed he went down to the little

jewellery store in the foyer and bought a ring with a single large emerald set in it. Certainly it could be exchanged if it didn't fit, the girl told him. Back in his room he hid the ring inside a pair of rolled up socks. The still novel feeling of happiness had strengthened in him.

CHAPTER TWENTY-NINE

An hour after they had begun the winding drop from the Bogota plateau, the climate had turned from northern European to sub-tropical. Carr eased the Land-Rover round another tight bend in the mountain road. He wasn't hurrying. There was nothing to hurry for.

'How many's that?' he asked.

'I don't know. I lost count after thirty.'

He nodded as though question and answer had some special significance for him.

A car, which had been following them for some minutes, came into sight across a ravine a hundred yards wide travelling in the opposite direction to them. It was difficult to see how it could be on the same road.

'It's difficult to see how that car can be on the same road,' he said.

'Yes. Very difficult.'

Carr whistled a few bars of something unidentifiable through his teeth, then said, 'I was told there was an orchid farm somewhere around here. Orchids growing in the trees, would you believe? Might be worth looking at.'

'Orchids often grow on trees. They're parasites, like mistletoe and we've already passed the farm. It was on the left about half a mile back.'

'Oh,' said Carr.

He drove on in silence for several minutes, concentrating on the bends, not speaking, until he heard a soft burbling beside him above the sound of the engine. He glanced at his companion. She was looking at him through fanned fingers, palm covering her mouth, laughing at him.

'What's funny?'

'Johnny Carr's funny,' she said. 'Johnny is shy of the lovely lady and is trying to make conversation. He's doing it very, very badly.'

'Sure,' he said. He felt both hurt and foolish, and both sensations were utterly foreign to him. If anybody had ever laughed at him before he couldn't remember when, or if it had mattered. Now it mattered.

Without looking at her, he said, 'This won't come as any surprise to you, but it's one hell of a surprise to me. I love you. I'm not just in love with you. There wouldn't be any surprise in that. I love you – the whole bit – and that's something that's never happened to me with anyone in my life.' With near violence he added, 'I'm not equipped to deal with the situation.'

He felt her fingers touch the nape of his neck.

'Is that what you wanted to say in bed the other morning?'

'Obviously.'

'That's nice,' she said.

When he looked at her again he saw that she was watching him with no hint of amusement left on her face. He experienced a surge of wild elation and that was totally foreign to him too. 'That's nice' she had said and now her hand was resting on his thigh. It was enough for the moment. He drove on down the mountainside smiling faintly, not pressing the matter any further. After a little he began talking easily to her.

It was nearly six when they reached level ground and the daylight was fading, but it was hot. Somewhere in the mid-nineties Carr thought, and that made a forty degree rise in less than three hours.

A car appeared on the road ahead moving fast towards them. It flicked by on the start of its long climb to Bogata.

Cecilia said, 'You're fond of statistics. How many cars an hour have we seen since we left the plateau?'

'Not more than two,' Carr told her. 'Why?'

'Good,' she said. 'That gives me thirty minutes.'

She unbuttoned her shirt, took it off and folded it tidily on her lap. From the waist up she was naked except, incongruously, for a curl-brimmed stetson on her head. Carr thought she looked like an adult version of a *Playboy* centre fold and far too erotic for that magazine to print. He said nothing.

Almost immediately a car came into sight at the far end of a mile-long stretch of straight road. He waited tensely for her to cover herself as it swept closer and felt his shoulder muscles tighten when he realized that she had no intention of doing so. The car was less than a hundred yards away when he snatched the shirt and held it against her breasts knowing that he had added embarrassment to his newly acquired catalogue of forms of consciousness.

Suddenly angry, he only grunted when she said, 'You're not much of a statistician.' The anger was with himself as much as her and it deepened when he felt rather than saw her sidelong glance of amusement. Too many novel sensations were touching him and, as he had told her earlier, he was not equipped to deal with the situation. He didn't like that.

'Put your shirt on,' he said and was a little surprised to hear her say, 'Very well, sir,' and to see her do it.

It was several minutes before either spoke again, then, 'I'm quite surprised, darling, I thought you were the type who could escort a nude woman round Canterbury Cathedral without turning a hair.'

Curtly, 'You're special,' he told her. 'I thought I had made that clear.'

'You did, darling. I'm sorry.'

The hand lay on his thigh again and he smiled.

'John?'

'Mmm?'

'Do you realize that you have never told me what you do?'

'That's because I don't do anything. Nothing regular anyway. Sometimes I accept commissions from people who want jobs done somewhere, provided the somewhere is where I happen to be going.' As he spoke, the decision formed in his mind that he was going to retire. He had served his two masters long and precariously enough. Now there was a reason for living.

'Jet set and fancy free,' she said. 'I suppose that's how you got four bullet wounds and five other assorted scars on your body. Such a perfect body too. Like a pocket Hercules. You must accept odd commissions from strange people.'

'Oh, that. That was working for that woman.'

'What woman, for heaven's sake?'

'You know,' he said. 'The one with the big town house at the end of the Mall and all those places in the country. Name escapes me but she's often in the papers. She hands out commissions by the thousand.'

'Oh, you idiot!' She sounded pleased. 'What were you?'

'Royal Marine Commando. Major. No need to stand up when I come in, but mocking references to my lack of inches will be treated as insubordination and dealt with summarily.'

'I shall enjoy that. Who shot at you?'

'North Koreans, or maybe they were Chinese. I didn't stop to ask.'

'I see, but that was rather a long time ago. There's quite a new one through the side of your stomach. Who did that?'

'An Irishman with an over developed sense of fun,' he said. 'That's what finished it for me. Medical Board and out. Ten thousand Asiatics all have a go and then one bloody "Mick" does it in Belfast. Comic really.'

'Poor sweet. Do you mind having been invalided very much?'

'Not now that I've met you.'

'Then that's all right,' she said. 'Let's camp before it's pitch dark. I'll put on a starched skirt and change your dressings.'

CHAPTER THIRTY

They stood looking at the tangle of canvas, tent poles and guy-ropes lying in the headlight beams. Carr had a mallet in one hand and a clutch of pegs in the other. 'It's time they invented aluminium frames in this country,' he said.

'Oh, they have. You just didn't bother to ask.'

'Silence, woman. We have work to do.'

Cecilia had a finger clenched between her teeth. She remove it.

'Tigers and leopards,' she said.

'I thought they were Asia and Africa.'

'Panthers, pumas, cougars. Perhaps you can tell the difference between them, but I don't see how that helps us.'

He looked at her in mock exasperation. 'It was your idea to go camping. It's a bit late to start listing the more inimical forms of fauna.'

'It was my idea to start out after breakfast. We would have been safe in the uplands by now. But you had to go all hoggish and sleep until lunch time, so here we are stuck in the *tierra caliente* with huge Brahmin cows, bulls too, cheetahs, piranhas, anacondas probably and ten to one there are . . .'

She stopped talking when he put his arms around her and stood for a long time, fingers kneading the back of his neck, lips moving against his mouth.

When they drew apart, ' . . . mountain lions,' she said.

'They're supposed to be in the mountains.'

'Yes, I suppose they are, but I think I'd rather sleep in the back of the Land-Rover anyway.'

'Good idea,' Carr said. 'That'll fool 'em. Only rhinos dare tackle Land-Rovers.'

He lifted suitcases and boxes from the vehicle, folded the tent into the shape of a mattress and arranged it on the metal floor with the sleeping bag on top of it. Then he tied the mosquito net to the supports for the canvas roof.

Four hours later Carr was still awake staring at the moon and, every so often, at the long contours of the sleeping figure beside him. The moon had painted it silver with black bars of shadow, bars which flexed gently as she breathed. Desire rose in him again, but he stamped it down. There was something to be done before morning and, although he labelled it habit, he knew he would have to do it.

It was another ten minutes before he moved, sliding like a snake from the makeshift bed on to the truck floor, inching the mosquito netting from under his body and the tent canvas which anchored it, then replacing it again when he was clear. No creak came from the chassis or springs as he lowered himself to the ground and no sound marked his opening of the cases she had packed. His movements were smooth, economical, professional.

There was a surprising amount of lingerie with no design or purpose other than seduction. Strange creations to take into the wilderness, he thought, even if she had had need of them which she indubitably did not. There was more practical clothing and two pairs of workmanlike shoes. Two wigs made him smile and he decided to ask her to wear them for him until he remembered that he was not supposed to know that they were there.

A make-up case held his attention for several minutes while he sniffed at the contents of each container. Her sponge bag was already unpacked, lying on the Land-Rover's bonnet. He went through that too. The cooking equipment box was the most difficult to deal with, but he moved each potentially sound-making object with infinite care, then did the same with the stores.

Tracing every inch of the underside of the Land-Rover with his finger-tips took the longest time of all. When he had finished he cleaned his hands carefully, removing oil stains with grass, soil and friction, then went back to bed the way he had come.

'I suppose I should look at the engine,' he said when Cecilia was cooking breakfast.

She smiled up at him. 'I wish you would. I don't understand engines.'

Carr lifted the bonnet. When he was called to breakfast he was greasy and very happy. There had been only engine and the normal ancillary equipment inside. Habit died hard, but it was dead now.

They reached the grasslands that evening, turned off the highway and drove until, as she had described it, there was nothing but grass and sky as far as they could see and the nearest people were a thousand miles away. Then they put up the tent.

Carr changed his mind about the lingerie as he watched her moving towards him in the dusk and a billowing negligee which would have been red if the material had had sufficient substance to support the colour.

'Astonishing,' Carr said.

'What's astonishing, darling?'

'The innumerable colour combinations in the world.'

She turned on to her side and looked at him. 'For a profound remark that leaves a lot to be desired,' she said.

They were lying on a blanket in the late afternoon sunshine, the high grass around them bringing their horizon to within a few feet. Neither was wearing clothes.

He waved a languid arm in a half circle. 'How many colours can you see from here?' Then not waiting for an answer to his question, 'Four. Grass green, sky blue, cloud white and canvas, sort of pale brown.'

'What about me? What colour am I?'

'Shut up,' he said. 'I'm purposely not looking at you and don't interrupt when I'm expounding. Take grass green, for example. It doesn't exist. I've just counted eleven different shades and even they keep changing when the wind blows. That cloud isn't only white. It's got pink and grey and a little purple in it too. As for the sky and the canvas, they both have four different . . '

She kissed him lightly on the mouth and he turned his head and looked at her, grinning.

'When did these great truths strike you, Johnny?'

'After a period of exposure to you and about the same time that I found I didn't mind being called Johnny. By you that is. Nobody else ever called me that twice. I've discovered a lot of things since I met you.'

'What sort of things, apart from the colours of grass?'

'Oh, little things like life being worth living. Would you believe me if I told you that I literally didn't give a damn before? Probably not. I find it hard enough to believe it myself, but it's true for all that.'

Her index finger touched the small puckered depressions where bullets had entered his body and traced the irregular white marks of scars.

'It's not hard for me to believe, Johnny.'

He reached for her then, but she stopped him with the flat of her hand against his chest.

'Not now, darling. It's time for me to pack if we're to make any distance before dark. You stay here for a bit longer.'

She got to her feet and began walking away from him.

'Cecilia.'

Waist deep in grass she turned and looked at him enquiringly.

'Will you marry me?'

For a long moment she stood unmoving, what little expression her face showed difficult for him to read.

'Have you thought about it seriously, Johnny, or is it all this?'

Her hands moved as if to cup her breasts, but stopped before they reached them.

'I've thought about it, Cecilia. I've thought about it probably more seriously than anything I've ever thought of. In fact delete "probably". I'm more serious than I've ever been about anything.'

She nodded, an abrupt non-committal movement of the head, and said judicially, 'You've been babbling an awful lot of trite nonsense recently. I think you're a little off balance.' Then suddenly smiling she added, 'Ask me again when you've sobered up,' and Carr knew it was going to be all right.

CHAPTER THIRTY-ONE

'Put 'em over there and sit down, Julian.'

Havelock-Templeton arranged the armful of folders he had been carrying into two equal stacks on the table Barry had indicated, then sat down in an armchair near the desk. 'You've got a strong team,' he said.

Barry knocked dottle noisily from his pipe on the edge of a metal waste-basket. Some of it fell inside and the rest scattered over the carpet. One small, still glowing ember melded its redness with the green of the man-made fibre in a tiny wisp of smoke leaving a dark brown spot on the pile. He looked at it absently for a moment then turned his shaggy head towards the younger man.

'Yes, the quality's good. Very good. I only wish I could say the same for the quantity. You've just carried in the two top floors of this building, that's the entire executive, plus all the operational staff. It's the old money problem of course. Never mind. You're here now and much sooner than I expected. Thank you for coming.'

'Thank you for asking me, sir.'

'You used to call me Charles.'

'I wasn't working for you then.'

'Please yourself, but don't expect me to return the compliment by calling you Havelock-Templeton. Life's too short.'

Havelock-Templeton smiled but didn't speak and Barry began to attack the inside of the bowl of his pipe with a paperclip. When he had achieved a small cone of dislodged combustion products on his desk he looked up and asked, 'How old would you say I was, Julian?'

'Sixty-three, or thereabouts.'

'Well, I'm glad you don't waste time on flattery. In fact I shall be fifty-nine next week and I've promised myself that I won't stay here a day after sixty. That gives you one year.'

'To do what, sir?'

'To convince our masters that you are capable of running the Department. That's really what you were picked for. Acting as my number two should provide you with the opportunity of doing so. How do you feel about it?'

It was thirty seconds before the reply came.

'Would "frightened" be a satisfactory answer to that question?'

'Eminently,' Barry told him. 'If you were not, I would be. Now listen to me.' He filled his pipe with rapid automatic finger movements, fumbled for matches and lit it. 'You're inheriting a damaged house, Julian, so it's right that it should be re-built to your design. I'll give you whatever guidance I can and I'll retain the power to veto anything I have reason to know to be ill-advised, but basically, it's got to be your show.'

Barry drew on his pipe, but it had gone out and he lit it again carefully before asking, 'Mind if I give you a bit of advice?'

'Only if you ask me before giving it, sir.'

'Fair enough. Then it's this. Don't waste any time selecting a deputy of your own. He'll need the best part of a year's exposure to the powers that be before they'll so much as consider a nomination. I know it's quite a problem to have dropped on to your plate almost before you've started to be a deputy yourself but think about it, will you?'

There was another long silence before Havelock-Templeton said, 'I could give you a short list now.'

'Oh?'

'Look at it this way, sir. You've brought me in from outside the Department so, if I do succeed you, the last thing I shall want to do is bring in any more strangers, for two obvious reasons. First, there'd be justifiable accusations of empire building and morale would go down like a rock. Second, there are some pretty able people in that lot.' He gestured with a thumb towards the two piles of dockets on the table behind him.

'I agree with both your points,' Barry said. 'Who's on your short list?'

'Geddes, Resident Agent, but I've a feeling he's out because he's spent most of his life as a "Resident" abroad and doesn't know enough about this place. Carew, Senior Mission Controller, although he may be a bit old. Then there's Trelawney, Field Operative. I'd like your guidance on him.' He paused, looked slightly startled, then went on, 'My God! Listen to me! I'm just thinking off the top of my head, sir. I'd like your guidance on all of them.'

Barry nodded and said, 'Keep going.'

'Next, Carr, Field Operative. I don't imagine I shall like him very much from what you've told me, but he must be a strong contender. Finally, of course, there's Rafferty who's already had some experience as Deputy Director. He'd be ideal, but the alacrity with which he surrendered his room to me makes me think he wouldn't appreciate the offer of its return.'

'I suppose the red roses and the "Get Well" card on your desk came from him.'

'Yes,' Havelock-Templeton said and watched curiously as Barry got up and walked to the window, then turned to face the room as soon as he reached it. When Barry spoke his voice was toneless.

'I agree with you about Geddes and Carew for the reasons you have stated. Either could do the job at a pinch, but it would be best to look elsewhere first. Trelawney you should most certainly consider, but I would recommend to you that you work on Rafferty. He'll fight you all the way, but he must be taken off field duties soon. He's not young any more and he's slowing down. The old Rafferty would never have allowed himself to be knifed by a single assailant in Deauville or anywhere else. I know I made light of it at the time I told you, but . . . He's too good to waste, Julian.'

'Indeed he is. I'll have a go at him and . . . oh, you didn't make any comment on Carr.'

Barry walked back to his desk and stood looking down at the last message from Purvis in Bogota. It read 'Locked-on. Trelawney's move'. Then he lowered himself tiredly into his chair and said, 'Carr won't be back. Or, rather, if he does come back I shall be a very surprised man indeed. You see, Julian, he was the third. Foster the planner, Herrick the breaking and entering man and gadgets expert, Carr the action man. It was Carr who killed Lippmann. At least he knocked him down with a motor-cycle so that the van could run over him.'

'How did you find that out?'

'We have a man serving in the East German Criminal Police Central Records Office. The householders on the street where Lippmann was killed were questioned. Some woman had seen the whole thing. She said that the motor-cyclist had very wide shoulders, quite out of proportion to his height, and a white scar which looked like a bullet wound on the back of his right hand.

As far as I know, not wearing gloves that day was about the only mistake Carr ever made. You'll recall that he never put a foot wrong when I tested him out with that bogus Ludwig Keller escape. They must have decided that the continuance of their cell took precedence over Keller or perhaps they were so instructed.'

Barry stopped talking, apparently lost in thought, and the sound of traffic seeped into the room as though intent on filling the vacuum created by the silence of the two men. It was Havelock-Templeton who spoke first.

'There are one or two things I don't understand about that business, sir.'

'What? Oh, are there? Well, fire away.'

'I'd have thought that total secrecy was essential in a cleansing operation of such importance.'

'You'd have thought that, would you? Are you being sarcastic?'

'I'm suggesting, sir, that an advertisement in the *New York Times* could hardly be more public than asking for FBI and CIA co-operation.'

'Oh, I see,' Barry said. 'You must be a bit muddled about who was being cleansed, as you put it. We asked the US authorities for assistance in tracking down Herrick. Just Herrick, a safe-breaker who had been "turned", not potential Philby-style headline makers like Foster and Carr. We often help each other out over minor domestic problems.'

Havelock-Templeton frowned. 'So you had no real interest in what became of Herrick.'

'None at all, my dear chap, once he had set himself up abroad as a target. Foster and Carr were the people who had to have him dead, not I. The rest followed automatically I'm thankful to say. Disposing of somebody quietly in this country, particularly somebody like Carr who has to be accounted for in official circles, is really very complicated.'

Barry looked at Purvis's signal again, initialled it and put it in his 'out' basket. The movements seemed to change the direction of Havelock-Templeton's thoughts.

'What made the three of them turn Communist, sir?'

'I don't think they turned anything, Julian. I believe that Herrick and Carr never were and Foster always was.'

'Yes?'

'Yes. Herrick was a craftsman in a fairly specialized field and I doubt if he cared who employed him as long as they paid top rates. Carr? The same in a way, but – well, I've told you about him. Callous and probably genuinely without fear. I know that usually goes hand in hand with stupidity, but not in his case. I think, and this is hindsight talking of course, that he was . . .'

Hindsight appeared unwilling to speak on Barry's behalf. He scowled then shook his head and said, 'It's taken me a long time, but I've taught myself to stop whenever I find I'm about to use a word starting with "psycho". Hate catch-all expressions. Not appropriate in this case anyway. Let's just say that Carr's appetite for positive action was too large to be satisfied from one source.'

'All right. And Foster?'

'Remember our talk about Communists in Parliament? The people who don't stand as Communists?'

'Yes, I do.'

'Similar.'

Barry drew a folder towards him, spun it through 180 degrees and pushed it across the desk.

'Read that when you've got time. Perfect example of bending over backwards too far being no improvement on falling flat on your face.

'It's all there, Julian. An eighteen-year-old's panegyrics on Churchill as the only man to recognize the Red Menace. Excellent school essay. Similar stuff at Oxford. Churchill again. Why the allies should have skipped Italy as he wanted and struck northwards through the Balkans. Creditable Army service. Volunteered for Korea, but went sick before he could be sent there. Stood as a Conservative candidate on a rearmament ticket. Lost, but increased the share of the vote. There's a lot of it. Over seventy true blue pointers to his antipathy to Communism, but it doesn't notice much dotted throughout his record. It was only when we extracted the pertinent bits and lumped them together in the light of what we'd discovered that it occurred to us that he must have been one of the most solidly dug in "sleepers" they had. All the way from school to the office next to mine where they activated him. Not bad, eh?'

'No, I suppose not. But all that preparation and effort with really so little to show for it when there could have been so much. You know, with the valuable knowledge he must have carried in his head, I simply don't understand why he didn't make a run for the "certain" when he knew he was blown instead of killing himself.'

'Odd, isn't it? Strain probably. Couldn't stand the thought of being picked up by Special Branch at the airport or wherever.'

Havelock-Templeton nodded, stood up and said, 'Thanks for the run-down, sir. I've kept you long enough.' He picked up the folder on Foster, walked towards the door, but turned before he reached it.

'I forgot to ask. Who's taking care of Carr?'

'Trelawney,' Barry said.

CHAPTER THIRTY-TWO

More content than he had ever been, than he had thought it possible to be, and happy in the knowledge that the end of this interlude marked only the beginning of a pattern, Carr stretched luxuriously, then moved his naked shoulders against the coarse blanket material, enjoying the roughness and the faint movement of the flattened grass beneath it.

It was so tall, the grass, except where their weight on the blanket had flattened it, that he could see nothing but a section of pale blue sky and part of the Land-Rover's canvas top. The sound of Cecilia loading something, probably the little tent they had brought with them, into the vehicle, came to him faintly.

'Hey!' he called. 'That's my job.' There was no reply and no more sounds except the breeze sighing in the grass. He rolled on to his stomach, reaching for his shorts.

With them in his hand he stood up, stooped to put them on and saw his left knee-cap burst outwards in a splatter of gristle and flying droplets of blood. Even as he hurled himself sideways into cover he thought how strange it was that he should be preoccupied, at this of all times, with the phenomenon of his vision having recorded the event before his nervous system registered the impact of the bullet. Whether or not he had heard the shot he was unsure and the trembling of his shocked body made it hard to concentrate, difficult to decide if it was of any importance.

He lay on one hip, panting shallowly, steadying himself, trying to believe that a rifle had cut him down from a distance, that the bullet had reached him before the sound, that there was still a chance because the gunman had a lot of ground to cover before he could fire again, but it was no use. There was nowhere, no vantage point for a rifleman in all the flat desolation of the plateau. He knew where the shot had come from.

He crabbed his way deeper into the grass, seeking more secure cover and knowing there was none with the long stems flagging his every move. Because it was the only thing to do, the only thing that offered any hope at all, he turned and began to drag himself in the direction of where he thought the Land-Rover was standing. He could no longer see it with the grass close about him, but there might be something there he could use as a weapon.

The anaesthetic of shock was leaving his smashed knee now, to be replaced by pain expanding like a balloon, and he began to curse quietly to himself. From behind him Cecilia said, 'I shouldn't waste my strength if I were you. You have nearly forty miles to crawl. You won't make one of them, but I know you'll want to try when I've gone.' Her voice was calmly conversational in tone.

Carr rolled slowly from his side until his shoulders were flat on the grass again and looked up at her tall figure sunlit from head to knee, the rest in shadow. A long-barrelled Mauser hung loosely from her hand and he was reminded bitterly of the key to her hotel room dangling from its tag the day he had first seen her in the foyer.

She had pulled on her riding boots to follow him through the grass, but hadn't bothered to dress, and Carr stared her up and down, forcing insolence into his look. It wasn't easy because for the first time in his life he knew that he was afraid, afraid to die because he was afraid of losing what he thought he had won.

'Very kinky,' he said. 'You should dress like that more often.'

There was no doubt about his hearing the second shot, a sharp flat crack lost immediately in the vast emptiness of the savanna. Again there was no instant pain, but his right leg jerked convulsively and he guessed that the femur was broken. His mouth had gone dry and he tried to work saliva into it. There was no saliva.

'May I have something to drink?'

'No. You had better get used to going without. It'll be much worse in an hour or two.'

'You're a bloody poor advertisement for an airline hostess.'

'I'm nothing to do with any airline. It wasn't difficult to borrow a uniform and pay some people at El Dorado airport to vouch for me when you checked as I knew you would.'

Carr's mind windmilled, flailing for some contact point which would enable him to reason, but there were too many possibilities. So – it was his job to sift possibilities, probabilities, anything, but knowing that and doing anything about it now were very different things. The shocks had been too sudden, the worst of them psychological and his brain refused to settle.

The direct approach then. 'Who are you, Cecilia?'

'I, John Carr, am the widow of Major Miguel Garcia. Until a few days ago, when you and that pig Hendrix killed him, I was his wife.'

Pain welled up from both his legs with an all-enveloping intensity. It combined with the relief which swept over him and made his head swim to an extent close to black-out. Desperately he fought down both and, when his vision cleared, experienced a second wave of thankfulness. She was still there, and it wasn't Ratshelm, it wasn't Prague or Moscow. It wasn't even DAS, or London. It was a mistake.

His voice husky, he said, 'Thank God you told me. I saw you at the inquest on Hendrix, although I didn't realize it was you under your veiling. You were overwrought, crying all the time. You can't have understood what was said. The police, your own brother-in-law, stated that Hendrix killed your husband. It wasn't anything to do with me at all.'

He got no reaction. The beautiful face remained impassive, the perfect body, painted reddish gold by the setting sun, held the pose of a relaxed statue like some Inca goddess. Wrong civilization he remembered dully, but that was how he felt she looked. Elemental, he thought, but the boots and the gun destroyed the illusion.

'It's no use, John Carr. I know you planned it together and I know you carried it out together. It would have been pleasant to have made Hendrix suffer, but now you'll do it for both of you.'

'Listen. Listen to me,' Carr said. He felt ridiculous and childishly vulnerable lying naked, flat on his back with this figure of implacable, misdirected vengeance standing over him.

Painfully he worked his body until he had it supported on his elbows. The sweat on his lips tasted salty and he felt a wave of nausea at the sight of his ruined legs with flies and insects already feeding on congealing blood.

'You've got to listen to me!'

'Say it, whatever it is. It will make no difference.'

'I killed Hendrix! I avenged your husband!' He hesitated, then added, 'The police don't know that, so that puts me completely in your hands.'

Disinterestedly she said, 'It's not uncommon to kill a murder accomplice and you are already in my hands.'

'For Christ's sake!' he shouted. 'I've never so much as seen your husband in my life!'

She moved then, stooping and peering into the grass to one side. He saw that she was holding one empty cartridge case. Finding the other took her nearly two minutes. His eyes never left her.

The brass cylinders clinked together as she pointed with them.

'You crawl that way. A jackal against the vultures. Look. There's one up there already. They have an amazing instinct.'

When he looked down from the black dot suspended lazily on an air current, she had turned and was walking away from him. After a few paces the grass hid her from his sight. Minutes went by before the Land-Rover engine burst into life somewhere off to his right. He supposed she had been dressing. The sound receded and was gone, leaving only the whisper of the wind.

Carr became aware that his upper arms were trembling with the strain of propping his body in its half-raised position. Groaning, he lowered his back on to the grass and lay staring at the sky, fighting the panic urging him to scream. The effort left him calmer, but breathless and sweating heavily. What price his innate indifference now? He knew what had happened. For the first time in his life he had been taught to care, not just to love or desire, but to care.

She had been very clever, he thought, introducing him to the idea of there being an obtainable state of stability in the world. And he had grasped at the idea, life's nearest offering to a guarantee, as he had been meant to do, only to have it snatched away as soon as it had taken root in his mind. Yes, she had been very clever. She had made him care for her and for a state of mind, so that he had been obliged to care for himself to support the two conditions. The final irony was that he still did care. That was insupportable and he decided to end it quickly, not to die slowly like some mongrel in a ditch, its hindquarters crushed by a passing car.

How? He knew how to swallow his tongue if he had to, but the thought of choking to death revolted him. He had no death pill, nor even his watch. With the spike on the buckle of that, or a broken splinter of the perspex glass, he would have been able to gouge his way into a wrist artery. It scratched her she had said on that first morning when they had made love after breakfast and, since then, he had always taken it off.

For a moment he thought of dragging himself to the place where they had moved gently against each other in the sunshine before his new-found world crashed in ruins, but the illusion grew in him that that had been in some different stream of time. He considered the possibility gravely then trod it under for the hallucination it was, muttering to himself in a blend of irritation and despair. The present was two smashed legs which followed directly from a cordite-tainted past and the future was death by exhaustion if the vultures waited that long, unless he did something about it.

The black dot was still hanging there, almost motionless against the blue, no closer, no further away.

There was no point, he decided, in moving anywhere. Even if he could find the camp site there would be nothing there. Her careful search for the cartridge case told him that. Well – he still had his teeth.

The pain, as he tore at the inside of his left wrist, was bad and although partly clouded by the agony in his legs, it was still enough to force him to rest before he had achieved more than a mess of capillary blood on his wrist and mouth. He wiped the blood away with a handful of grass, not knowing why he had bothered to do it.

It was then that he heard the car engine.

The canvas top of the Land-Rover loomed into sight above the grass like some prehistoric leviathan. The vehicle changed direction slightly and came to rest beside him.

She was dressed now, as he had guessed, immaculate in white shirt, jodhpurs and boots, the brim of her stetson low over her eyes protecting them from the last rays of the sun. She stopped the engine.

The hope that lurched inside him died at the sight of the gun. The circle of the muzzle and the green reflection of the Land-Rover's paintwork on the foresight reminded him of the engagement ring waiting for her at the hotel. Emeralds are unlucky he told himself, but they were all they seemed to have in this bloody country.

It was finished, but a tendril of professional curiosity stirred in his brain.

'Where did you hide that thing?'

'In your bag until after you had searched everywhere else,' she said. 'With some other odds and ends.'

He nodded and saw the heavy automatic back in her hand.

Cecilia recovered the spent cartridge case from behind the driving seat, started the engine and turned the Land-Rover in the direction from which she had come. Without looking again at Carr's dead body she drove slowly away, the grass parting before the radiator like the bow wave of a ship.

CHAPTER THIRTY-THREE

Just before noon Cecilia stopped the Land-Rover ten yards from the edge of the shallow canyon, climbed out, took her suitcase from the passenger seat and put it on the ground. Everything else she and Carr had brought with them was hidden by the vehicle's canvas cover criss-crossed with rope holding it securely to the metal floor. With one hand she depressed the clutch pedal, pulled the gear lever into bottom with the other and jumped back. The Land-Rover jerked into motion and she watched it dive in a graceful arc to the water twenty feet below. It struck the surface radiator first and sank immediately.

For a few moments large bubbles buoyed its position, then there was nothing to see but the smooth brown river sliding towards the Amazon six hundred miles away. She turned and began to walk towards the north, the suitcase bumping against her leg at every step.

It was much hotter here than on the high *llanos* far behind her.

This was true *llanos* country, featureless as the other had been except for isolated low-lying mesas, patches of scrub and an occasional palm. The grass was brown, short, brittle beneath her feet and the insects were troublesome. To get them out of her mind she let her thoughts turn towards Carr.

In her cold way she had, she supposed, grown faintly fond of him. Nothing else explained her sudden impulse to return and make his end a little easier. That, she knew, was as unlike her as the pleasure she had obtained from making him think that he was dying for the wrong reason was typical. Her shoulders moved in an almost imperceptible shrug of dismissal. It had gone as she had meant it to go. First his conversion, then his sacrifice on the altar of his new-found philosophy.

There didn't seem to be much more to Carr to think about and her mind searched like an indecisive early-warning radar scanner before steadying on a fragment of remembered conversation.

'I suppose you *do* realize that we're only playing a hunch.'

'A reasonable supposition considering that it's *my* hunch,' she had replied.

'Female intuition?'

'Observation. It's a sexless faculty. As I keep telling you, he's a bundle of nerves.'

'And if that is shown to have an innocent cause?'

'I'll have lost my virtue again and you'll know who we aren't looking for.'

The next morning she had been given her way and a man called Foster for whom she felt nothing but contempt entered into the last three weeks of his life.

He had been such a fool. In addition to his failure at his self-appointed task, who but a fool would have allowed himself to be mesmerized by that pouting mother figure of a secretary of his, with her insufferable conceits, her saccharine bursts of compassionate understanding and coy attempts to control his smoking? Cecilia loathed her as heartily as she had despised Foster.

Foster had asked the irritating bitch to marry him and, because of the pressures he was under, gone to pieces at her refusal.

The hours before dawn on that last morning were clear on her mind. Foster rather drunk and hurt, pouring out his troubles to her. Foster drunk and maudlin. Foster very drunk and amorous. After a time too drunk to taste anything else in the neat whisky.

Finally, 'Here. You had better drink this.'

Some of the cloudy liquid had run down his chin, but he had swallowed most of it.

'Tashe foul.'

'It'll sober you up.'

'Shleep now,' he had said and nuzzled his face against her.

'Not here. In the next room with me.'

She had half carried the lurching figure to the kitchen, lowered it to the floor and gone to the bedroom. When she returned with a pillow and a bolster he was already asleep.

A critical look at the scene had satisfied her. The whisky bottle on its side under the sink where some unevenness in the floor had encouraged it to roll, the two glasses with their respective dregs of whisky and barbiturate standing rather tidily side by side on the composition tiles, the fork with grains still between its tines and the empty pill bottle on the draining board.

She had looked once more at Foster, feeling only distaste for the pale, sweating face resting on the pillow in the oven with air bubbling in and out between the slack lips. Then she had turned on the gas.

With the door closed behind her, she had drawn the bolster into position with two loops of string, blocking the narrow gap at the bottom where the carpet ended and the tiles began, and pulled the strings away.

'I hope the police don't give your secretary too bad a time over this, Mr Foster,' she had said.

The heat was pressing down on her now, its weight seemingly as real as that of her suitcase which she changed from one hand to the other with increasing frequency. She hoped she hadn't badly underestimated the distance she had to cover, then shook her head irritably knowing perfectly well that she had not. Nevertheless, it was a relief when she saw flashes of sunlight reflected from the glass or chrome of moving traffic.

She sat down cross-legged on the seared grass with the case flat on the ground in front of her. Momentarily her fingers hovered over the catches, then snapped them open and lifted the lid. Gazing intently at herself in a travelling mirror she hid her black hair under a brown wig and the knowledge that later she would have to bleach and dye the hair itself depressed her. Liquid from a small bottle deprived her teeth of their brilliance and contact lenses turned her irises from blue to brown. The two toothless dental plates nestling in cotton wool looked pinkly obscene with their mouth-distorting semi-circular hoops of plastic protruding from them and she stared at them with disgust before reaching for them and pressing them into her upper and lower jaws. They made her mouth feel unnaturally full and she thought she had better practise saying something before she had to talk to whatever driver she flagged down.

The woman only Barry and she knew to be the Department's executioner looked at her from the small square of glass. She frowned at the reflection and the reflection frowned back.

'I detest your stupid face, Fiona Langley,' she said. The lisping was faint, but it was there and she repeated the words until it had gone.

For a long moment she studied her image, striving to conjure back the delicately perfect outline of the lips, the graceful concavities below the cheekbones, the startling contrast of blue eyes and raven hair, but they defied her and, not for the first time, she wondered if it was worth it. It would be pleasant, she mused, to live less of her life as a caricature of herself when the original was so *very* satisfactory.

But, as she always did, she won the struggle with her vanity and began to rearrange the disturbed contents of the case. She had no real intention of discarding the shock weapon which had served Barry so well for the past five years and enabled her to do what she liked best. Not for her the sniper's rifle, or the crudity of the assassin's grenade. The stalk was everything. For that reason she was also prepared to live with the revulsion for her that Barry could never completely conceal. But that did not stop her resenting it, or wondering at a code of ethics which, it seemed, had allowed him to order her to kill on seven occasions, but to become progressively more disgusted by her successes. It was not, she thought, as though she revealed to him the gratification they brought her, or much of the means she employed to attain them.

The insects had found her again and that, and a glance at her watch, told her that it was time to move on. Tomorrow the police captain called Caycedo, who had sold her Carr on account, would be waiting for her in Barbados. A debt was outstanding and she was always scrupulous about paying what was due.

Settling the big black glasses on her nose with one hand she closed the case with the other, picked it up and walked towards the traffic sparkling in the sun three miles away.

EPILOGUE

'Excellent. They really splash it around, don't they? A whole page for one visit. What does *Llegada* mean?'

Trelawney stopped reading and looked at Barry examining his 'Armitage' passport.

'"Admitted" I suppose, sir. If you turn over there's another one covered in rubber stamps with *Salida* on them. I know that means "exit".'

'So there is,' Barry said.

Trelawney finished reading the seventh and last typed sheet, put it down in front of him and looked at Barry.

'I might have written this myself, sir.'

'I took considerable pains to make it appear that you did. Will you please sign it?'

Trelawney made no move to do so, his gaze shifting to the window beyond Barry's shoulder.

Almost to himself he said, 'So this is what I was really doing when I thought I was in Gibraltar.'

Barry grunted impatiently before saying, 'You have my absolute assurance that what I'm asking you to do is in the best interests of the Department and, consequently, this country. Is that clear?'

'Your assurance is, sir, and I accept it, but the rest is pretty foggy. I assume that I'm being used to shield somebody else.'

'Don't assume anything, Trelawney, and don't so much as think about it again after you leave this room.'

'Ha, ha,' Trelawney said.

For a moment Barry pulled at his beard, then nodded ponderously. 'Yes, that was a particularly stupid instruction. Let's put it like this. The existence of a deception plan is to be known only to you and me. All right?'

The door of the adjoining room was standing ajar and Trelawney gestured towards it with his head.

'Martha is out, and not by chance,' Barry told him

'I see, sir, but I think I must insist that I be allowed to tell Jane. She has a remarkable instinct as you know and I don't think she believed a word of my Gibraltar cover-story. If, as I suspect, you are going to tell me to leak this fabrication inside the Department, she isn't going to believe that either.'

There was a scarcely discernible pause before Barry nodded again. 'Agreed. I do want you to do that and that wife of yours would see right through you.'

Trelawney took a pen from his pocket, scrawled his signature on the last page of the fictitious mission report, pushed the papers across the desk and watched Barry write 'Highly commendable. Minister to see' on the top page.

'Oh my God! Is *that* necessary?'

'"Essential" is the word, Trelawney,' Barry replied and put the report in his 'out' basket.

'May I ask one question, sir?'

'No,' Barry said. 'You may not, but I'll tell you this much. I prefer to deal in certainties rather than send my field agents on suicide missions.'

It had been a long time since Trelawney had permitted himself the luxury of anger, but sitting, elbows on desk, in his own room he was close to it now. The almost forgotten tingling sensation, like tiny electrical discharges at the nerve-ends, was back in his shoulders, arms and hands. He didn't like being used and he wanted to hit someone or something. When Rafferty came through the doorway he looked at him coldly.

'Hello, Al. Nice to have you back,' Rafferty said.

Trelawney didn't reply and Rafferty went on, 'I just came in to say that, knowing how you felt about it, I'm glad you didn't have to kill Herrick after all.'

'So am I,' Trelawney told him. 'Having to kill John Carr was enough.'

Ross Macdonald

'Classify him how you will, he is one of the best American novelists now operating . . . all he does is to keep on getting better.' *New York Times Book Review*. 'Ross Macdonald must be ranked high among American thriller-writers. His evocations of scenes and people are as sharp as those of Raymond Chandler.' *Times Literary Supplement*. 'Lew Archer is, by a long chalk, the best private eye in the business.' *Sunday Times*

THE CHILL 80p
THE INSTANT ENEMY £1.00
THE WAY SOME PEOPLE DIE £1.00
THE WYCHERLY WOMAN £1.00
THE ZEBRA-STRIPED HEARSE £1.00

Fontana Paperbacks

Helen MacInnes

Born in Scotland, Helen MacInnes has lived in the United States since 1937. Her first book, *Above Suspicion*, was an immediate success and launched her on a spectacular writing career that has made her an international favourite.

'She is the queen of spy-writers.' *Sunday Express*

'She can hang up her cloak and dagger right there with Eric Ambler and Graham Greene.' *Newsweek*

FRIENDS AND LOVERS £1.50
AGENT IN PLACE £1.50
THE SNARE OF THE HUNTER £1.50
HORIZON £1.25
ABOVE SUSPICION £1.25
MESSAGE FROM MALAGA £1.50
REST AND BE THANKFUL £1.50
PRELUDE TO TERROR £1.50
NORTH FROM ROME £1.35
THE HIDDEN TARGET £1.75
I AND MY TRUE LOVE £1.50
THE VENETIAN AFFAIR £1.75

FONTANA PAPERBACKS

Fontana Paperbacks

Fontana is a leading paperback publisher of fiction and non-fiction, with authors ranging from Alistair MacLean, Agatha Christie and Desmond Bagley to Solzhenitsyn and Pasternak, from Gerald Durrell and Joy Adamson to the famous Modern Masters series.

In addition to a wide-ranging collection of internationally popular writers of fiction, Fontana also has an outstanding reputation for history, natural history, military history, psychology, psychiatry, politics, economics, religion and the social sciences.

All Fontana books are available at your bookshop or newsagent; or can be ordered direct. Just fill in the form and list the titles you want.

FONTANA BOOKS, Cash Sales Department, G.P.O. Box 29, Douglas, Isle of Man, British Isles. Please send purchase price, plus 8p per book. Customers outside the U.K. send purchase price, plus 10p per book. Cheque, postal or money order. No currency.

NAME (Block letters)

ADDRESS
